THE
DEATH MASK
MURDERS

THE
DEATH MASK
MURDERS

a reggie da costa mystery

laraine stephens

LEVEL BEST BOOKS

Historia
ESTABLISHED 2019

For my darling Bob

MURDER IN ARARAT
WOMAN'S BODY FOUND IN DAM
Sensational discovery

By GARFIELD FLYNN

Mystery surrounds the finding of the body of a young woman in a dam, three miles out of Ararat, late Monday afternoon. The body was recovered by Detective Lonigan and two constables after they had dragged the water for three hours. The dead woman had gone missing from her home six days earlier, according to her husband. She has been identified as Mrs Alexandra James, a twenty-seven-year-old former psychiatric nurse. She was the mother of a seven-year-old boy, and was expecting a second child.

Bizarre twist

The police were inclined to pronounce the death as an accidental drowning, but the evidence of relatives and the findings of the coroner point to more insidious forces at work. It appears that the victim was strangled and her body disposed of in the dam sometime on Tuesday. In a bizarre twist, the victim's head had been shaved.

The deceased's husband and a farmhand were taken in for questioning but were released shortly after.

[*The Ararat Advertiser* June 5, 1917]

i

Chapter One

I t all began with a storm.

Emma Hart sat on the pier at Brighton Beach, her legs dangling over the edge, her canvas bag lying next to her. Each day, weather permitting, she came to the same spot. There she would take pleasure in the moods of the sea and sky and sketch the scene, gaining relief from her duties as companion to her great-aunt.

It was invigorating being out in the open. She loved the feel of the wind blowing through her hair and ruffling her blouse. She would watch as the clouds scudded across the sky, while seagulls circled above her. This would be as close as she would ever get to being free of cares and woes. Clive was dead and life for her was different now.

It had been two months since she had left her hometown of Donald, in country Victoria. Two months of adjusting to the big city, with its noise and hectic lifestyle. Two months of adjusting to the whims of demanding and opinionated Aunt Florence.

Emma turned her attention to the view. The outlook today was very different from normal. The bay was choppy and steel-grey close to the beach; the air thick and sultry. Even the seagulls appeared listless, as they bobbed up and down on the waves. In the two months she had lived in Brighton, Emma had never encountered Port Phillip Bay looking like this.

On a new sheet of cartridge paper in her sketchpad, she wrote the date and title of the picture she was about to draw: 'February 2, 1918: Brighton: A storm is brewing.'

Emma looked up and studied the seascape intently. It was overcast, the sun hidden, the sea dark and sullen. A low horizontal band of charcoal grey cloud hung above a wall of velvety sky, the colour of slate. Occasional flashes of lightning underlined the turbulence of the coming storm. She tried to recreate the mood, her pencil dancing across the paper, shading and highlighting the cloud formations above the leaden colour of the water. The sun broke through, creating a vivid contrast with the stormy skies, dark and grim. How magnificent, she thought. She put her head down and endeavoured to capture the scene, drawing freehand, occasionally rubbing out an errant line and attempting to convey the ambiance of the seascape before it changed again.

Emma was distracted by the squawking of seagulls as they rose into the air, lifting off as one, heading inland. That's strange, she thought, watching them as they flew away. With the birds gone, she became aware of the moaning of the wind. Emma looked towards the south-west and noted the advance of the storm. It was gathering pace and heading in her direction, about five miles off the coastline. The band of clouds was rapidly changing shape and thickening; as black as pitch at their base. Three water spouts descended from the mass and were sucked back up again. Emma looked at her watch. It was half-past four.

A fisherman tapped her on the shoulder. 'That's a bad storm coming. You better get home fast, before it hits.' He turned to go. 'What the devil is that?'

She looked in the direction he was pointing and watched fascinated as the tide ran out at a great pace, leaving the seabed uncovered. Almost immediately the waves surged in again, beyond where they had been before. Just as quickly the water ran back, restoring the shoreline to its normal level.

'Go! Run!' yelled the man. He took off at a gallop, leaving his fishing gear behind.

A sense of urgency gripped Emma as she grasped the magnitude of the storm. It was so much closer now. She gathered her drawing materials together and got to her feet. With her bag clutched close to her chest and her straw hat held in position using the other hand, Emma took off after the fisherman, who was almost out of sight. Running past departing beachgoers and those who had just dismounted from the train at Brighton Beach station, she headed towards her great-aunt's home in Seymour Grove, about half a mile away.

The air felt sticky and intense, full of moisture. As if on cue, large raindrops announced the imminent arrival of the gale. The sky grew dark, blacking out the last of the sun. The wind dropped, an ominous calm before the storm.

Emma stopped and looked back towards the sea, awestruck by the sight that met her eyes. The clouds, jet black and crackling with electric energy, had transformed into a beast, bearing down on Brighton Beach. Great waves were breaking over The Esplanade, foam and spray rising up into the dark mass of the sky.

Then all at once the tempest burst, sweeping inland from the sea with irresistible force. The wind tore Emma's hat from her grasp. The rain came, ugly driving rain that drenched her skirt and blouse. Water dripped from her thick blonde hair onto her face and down her neck.

This was no ordinary storm. The wind came up, screaming like a banshee. Emma gazed in wonder as the sea surged over the end of Penney's Baths. A huge crash rent the air, above the wail of the wind. The dressing rooms disintegrated along with 100 feet of hoarding, its wreckage lifted up and dropped on the sands below the baths. The chimney of the Ozone tea rooms crashed through the roof. The rear wall detached itself from the building, and then smashed through the windows of the railway refreshment rooms opposite. People were running in all directions, crying out in fear. A bandstand on the roof garden to the side of the building lifted up into the air. It crashed into the railway reserve. An electric pole snapped off like a matchstick, its wires sparking before they were strewn haphazardly across the footpath. It was bedlam but it was just the beginning.

The wind tore around Emma, driving her along as if she were as inconsequential as a grain of sand upon the beach. Enthralled by its brute force and potency, she was blind to the storm's danger. She turned and faced the tempest, spreading her arms out to embrace the elements. For so long she had felt buttoned-up, drawn into herself, hidden away in her bedroom in Donald. It was exhilarating surrendering herself to the wind and rain. She screamed out in delight, giving vent to feelings that she had suppressed for so long. Her hair whipped around her head; her skirt billowed and twisted around her legs.

But the thrill was short-lived. The violence and destructive force of the storm struck fear into her as the gravity of her situation became clear. To her left was the railway station. Slate tiles, dislodged from the roof of the new signal box, became missiles carried by the howling wind. The standard supporting the overhead railway gear twisted at the base and fell across the tracks. Advertising hoardings and fencing flew through the air, landing haphazardly hundreds of yards away. A ten-foot beam hurtled past, missing her by inches. It smashed the South Road railway gates to smithereens.

Emma turned away from the sea and pushed against the wind, making little headway as she approached the train line. She crossed the tracks and entered South Road. To her right were the remnants of the bowling green and croquet club. Both pavilions had collapsed, people spilling from the wreckage. She watched in horror as the iron roof of the cricket ground's grandstand lifted off, borne by the winds. Trees were ripped out of the ground, their roots exposed. The storm was gaining in fury.

The light failed. Heavy clouds, thick with menace, descended, obstructing the weak sun. Emma put her arms out, as if she were blind, trying to find her way past the hazards that blocked her path. She fell hard, tripping over a branch. She dragged herself to her feet and was pelted by airborne debris. Tears, mixed with the rain, drenched her face. Her senses were besieged by the sound and fury of the storm, made worse by her imagination. The smash of breaking glass; the clatter of bricks as chimneys crashed; the high-pitched whine of the wind. Her muscles ached as she fought against the gale that whipped around her. She cried out in agony as bursts of hail pounded her bare legs and arms and struck her face. It was as if the storm were a wild beast that would not be satiated, tearing into her, attacking her.

A break in the cloud and midnight became twilight. Emma looked up and shrieked. Washing, torn from clotheslines, danced through the air, disembodied, like wraiths cavorting in the wind.

Just up ahead, a random beam of sunlight illuminated the figure of a man.

He was standing in the road not fifteen yards away. He was facing towards her, almost as if he were waiting for her. As she drew nearer, she saw that his hands were pressed against his ears. He was staring up into the blackened sky as the thunder rumbled and the lightning flashed overhead.

Just as quickly, the light died and darkness descended again. He was gone.

Emma sank to her knees, her strength ebbing away. She wrapped her arms around her head to protect herself, but it was no use. She was pelted by the rain, which felt like icy needles pricking her face. Any attempt to resist was ineffectual. Her clothes stuck to her, filthy from the mud and slush surrounding her. She floundered in the darkness, unseen, hope gone.

A strong blast of wind barrelled in from the sea. The trees bent and groaned, pitted against the gale. Lightning lit up the sky as the thunder boomed right above her. There was a mighty crack. Emma looked up in horror as a huge pine tree was hit by a jagged bolt of lightning. Sparks flew and the trunk split near its base, falling forward towards her as if in slow motion. She was right in its path. She tried to get up but it was too late. The last thing that she would remember was the whack of something hard striking the back of her head and the pungent odour of pine needles.

* * *

Emma awoke. The sound of the storm was muffled. She must be inside, she thought, but where she did not know. At first, she kept her eyes shut, trying to block out the throbbing from the gash on the back of her head. As her awareness grew, her senses were heightened. She moved her hand and could feel velvet beneath her. Her fingers felt for the edge of the chair. She was sitting on a chaise longue, with her feet up and her back supported by a cushion. She sniffed and registered the musty smell of mildew and decay. Thunder rumbled in the distance, growing closer. It sounded like cannon on the battlefield.

Slowly her eyes grew accustomed to the darkness. She could make out the vague outline of furniture, swathed in dust covers. The odd flash of lightning penetrated the gap in the curtains and briefly illuminated a large

5

portrait hanging above the mantelpiece. Thunder rumbled, closer now.

There was a creak from a chair on the other side of the room. She was not alone. Someone was sitting in the deep shadows. She could feel his eyes upon her. She held her breath, waiting for him to reveal his presence. Lightning flashed again and this time she saw him. It was the man whom she had seen in South Road.

The floorboards creaked as he crossed the room. She could hear him breathing as he leaned over her. Emma shrank back into the cushion.

Her voice was feeble. 'Who are you?'

'I'm Max. What's your name?'

'Emma.'

'Let me look at that cut of yours. I won't hurt you.'

He grasped her shoulder gently and drew her forward. She winced in pain as he tentatively touched the cut on the back of her head.

'It's stopped bleeding. Heads always bleed the worst.'

The lightning flashed outside. Emma had a quick impression of fair hair and green eyes, and then the darkness returned. She touched the back of her head. Dried blood had formed a matted, tangled mass in her hair.

Emma lay back against the cushion. 'Where are we?'

'The Crabtree mansion.'

'Do you live here?'

'No, but I know it.'

'What happened to me?'

'The tree fell. You were trapped by one of the branches. I found a fence post and levered it off you. Then I brought you here.'

The rain changed direction. It started to hail, striking the windows. Thunder rumbled and lightning split the sky. Emma could hear the bushes slapping the side of the house as the wind moaned and whined outside. She shivered. A chill was stealing into her bones, partly from her drenched clothing, but more so because the house felt oppressive and bleak. As soon as the storm passed, she would ask this man to take her home.

'Do you live around here?' asked Emma.

'North Brighton.'

'I'm in Seymour Grove. Do you know it?'

'I've heard of it.'

'Thank you for helping me.'

'Not at all.'

He stood and walked away then returned with a bowl of water and a towel.

'I'll clean you up a bit. Hold still.'

'That's not necessary. I'm alright.'

'Don't be silly.'

Emma lay rigid as he wiped the dirt from her face.

'How's that?'

A massive thunderclap was quickly followed by a blinding flash of lightning as the house was struck. The bowl of water slipped from Max's hands. There was a deafening crash overhead. The roof ripped open. Slate tiles shattered on the wooden floorboards, the plaster ceiling giving way. A flood of filthy rain and hail poured in. The chimney collapsed, fragments of brick and mortar scudding across the floor. The portrait above the mantelpiece tilted forward and fell, disappearing beneath the rubble.

Max stood transfixed; the towel grasped in his hand. Another crack of thunder exploded overhead and lightning illuminated the entire room.

Emma cried out. Max turned towards her, his face taut, his eyes wide open and unseeing.

'Help me,' she whispered.

He stood motionless, his arms hanging limply at his sides.

'What's the matter with you?'

She stood up too quickly, then crumpled to the ground in a dead faint.

* * *

When Emma regained consciousness, she found herself in the kitchen, propped up against the wall.

Max was sitting next to her. 'Take some deep breaths and put your head between your knees,' he said. She did as she was told.

'My head is thumping,' she moaned.

Max went into the pantry. He pulled on the latch of a trapdoor built into the floorboards, setting it back on its hinges.

Another bolt of lightning struck, illuminating the interior through the gash in the roof. Another gust of wild wind buffeted the house.

Max went deathly pale. He licked his lips nervously. 'We'll go down into the cellar until the storm passes over.'

Emma glanced away. 'Do we have to?'

'Better than here.'

She slumped against the wall, trying to quell her doubts. 'I'd rather stay here, if you don't mind.'

'I won't hurt you, I promise,' he said.

He lifted her off the ground effortlessly. She put her arms around his neck as he negotiated the primitive steps that led down into the cellar. Once they reached the bottom, he placed her gently on the last step and moved away from her.

The lightning flashed through the kitchen window, illuminating part of the cellar. It revealed a small table, upon which sat a paraffin lamp and a tin of matches. Max lifted the glass and lit the wick. Light flooded the room. He came back and kneeled in front of her. His face was long, she noticed, with a square jaw and eyes, an unusual shade of green. Sandy-coloured hair, tousled and still damp from the rain, fell to just below his ears. She thought he looked tired.

'Are you alright?' she asked.

He nodded then moved away and sat on a chair.

Emma took in her surroundings. The cellar was large, about ten feet wide and twenty feet long, with earthen floors and reinforced walls. In the middle was another table. On it was a vial of oil, an enamel basin, and a pitcher of water, with shaving implements stacked neatly alongside them. A second chair was positioned against the wall. Three hooks had been nailed into the timber-lined wall, from which hung clean white towels and a leather strop. Max got up and draped the towels around Emma's shoulders.

'You look cold. We'll leave when the storm dies down.'

'Thank you. What is this place?'

'I have no idea,' replied Max, sitting down. He shifted in his chair. 'I'm sorry about before.'

'What do you mean?'

He looked away. 'The War. The storm brought it back.'

'I'm not sure I understand.'

'Don't worry. It's nothing.'

'The War is to blame for a lot of bad things. We lose those we love.'

'We lose ourselves,' he whispered.

The silence stretched between them. She studied him, unable to fathom his mood. He had withdrawn into himself and seemed to be almost unaware of her.

'What's behind that curtain?' she said, trying to elicit a response from him. She pointed at a piece of cloth at the end of the room that had been rigged up to conceal a set of shelves, part of which was showing.

'No idea. Don't worry about it.'

Emma got slowly to her feet, leaning on the wall to keep her balance.

'You shouldn't do that.'

'I want to see.'

She made her way tentatively to the back of the cellar until she stood in front of the makeshift curtain. She pulled back the cloth and cried out in shock. Whatever she'd been expecting, it was not this.

Catching the light from the lantern, three white faces stared back at her, their eyes closed in eternal sleep.

She reached out and touched one of them on the cheek, then pulled her hand back as if she'd been stung. 'They're cold. What are they?'

Max came up behind her and looked at them over her shoulder.

'Death masks. I saw them once at Kreitmayer's Waxworks Museum.' His voice was flat and unemotional.

'What are death masks?'

'Plaster casts of dead people.'

'That's awful.' She screwed up her face and backed away, but she couldn't take her eyes from them. 'Why are they here? It makes no sense.' She looked at Max, expecting him to answer her question.

'Not a lot makes sense. Come away.'

'They're all women, did you notice?'

Max was silent.

'Why are they bald? Is that normal?'

'I don't know.'

'That woman on the right, her eyes are half-open. Is this what she was like when she died? I feel like she's looking at me.'

'You're imagining things. They're probably very old and some past owner stored them here.'

'You think they're old? But the towel? The water bowl? How can that be?'

'I don't know. Forget about them.'

She sat on the step again. 'Should we tell the police?'

'No!'

The word hung in the air between them.

Emma stared at Max. 'Why not?'

'There's nothing to tell.'

Max sat on the chair again; his eyes closed. Emma rested herself against the wall, unnerved yet with eyes drawn to the masks of the three women. From time to time she glanced at her companion but he sat very still, registering nothing. She shivered involuntarily. The cold was eating into her bones and her head was throbbing.

Max looked up. 'The storm's over. We should go.'

Emma took one last look at the death masks and shook her head in disbelief.

'I don't understand this.'

'Forget them. They're none of your business.'

Max extinguished the lantern. He bent down towards her and she put her arms around his neck. Then he carried her up the steps, placing her gently on the floor of the pantry. He lowered the trapdoor back into place. There was a bolt that could be drawn, but he left it alone. Through the kitchen window, Emma could see that the sky had lightened and it was drizzling.

'Time to go,' Max said.

He opened the door and carried her outside. Then he locked the back door behind them and put the key in the planter next to the door.

'How did you know about the key?' asked Emma.

'Seymour Grove, you said? Let's get you home.'

Chapter Two

Sunday dawned and Aunt Florence had gone off to church, leaving Emma to sleep in and recuperate. The blow to her head was superficial, according to the doctor, and bed rest was the remedy. As far as he was concerned, Emma had come out of the experience relatively unscathed. A long, relaxing bath had washed away the grime, after her ripped and sodden clothes had been taken away to be laundered and repaired. Afterwards, Aunt Florence had tucked her into bed and ordered that she get a good sleep, but that had proved elusive. Visions of death masks had haunted her dreams.

As she sat back against the pillows, Emma read *The Argus* until Mrs Williams, the housekeeper, removed the breakfast tray. The newspaper's main articles were focused on the violent storm that had ripped Brighton apart.

She put the paper down. The consequences for her had been much more than a cut on the head and a few scratches. The storm had awakened something in her that had lain dormant for many months. She had been stricken with grief since her fiancé's death at the Somme. Even the move to Brighton had failed to transform her mood, despite the best efforts of her great-aunt to break the spell of melancholy that consumed her. Surprisingly, it was the wild weather of the previous day that had wrought the change. Fear, excitement, exhilaration, and horror had consumed her as she witnessed the terrible beauty that the storm had unleashed on Brighton Beach. She had been at the mercy of forces so much greater than she, and yet she had survived. And now, in the safety of her aunt's house, the blanket of melancholy, which had swathed her, had lifted. As she pondered the awesome force of the storm, Emma felt something new stir in her: a sense of wonder and thankfulness that she was alive.

She plumped up the pillows and lay back against them. Her thoughts turned to Max. Now there was an enigma. Remote yet kind. Brave yet fearful. Preoccupied, but by what, she did not know. He had been gentle with her despite his cold unpredictability. She wondered if they would ever meet again.

Emma pushed the blankets aside and sat on the edge of the bed, reaching for her dressing gown. She wrapped it around her and walked over to the window, taking in the view of the garden. George the gardener was sweeping up the leaves and clearing away the mess from the storm. It looked like an ordinary day but it wasn't, not for her. Everything had changed.

The death masks. They had visited her in her sleep and now they inhabited her thoughts while awake. She had never seen anything so bizarre and so extraordinary. Their fragile cold beauty made her shiver. As an artist, she could appreciate the skill of their maker, but her curiosity was drawn to their singularity. Why would anyone make such things and keep them in such a place? Max had told her to forget them but she could not. She was intrigued and she wanted to see them again.

Emma sat at her dressing table and ran a brush through her long blonde hair, taking care to avoid the cut on the back of her head. She changed into a yellow satin dress with a dropped waist and lace collar. She stood in front of the mirror. There were few other visible signs of the trauma that she had experienced, apart from some bruises on her legs and the scratch on her face.

Emma put a sketchbook and drawing implements into a bag and slung it over her shoulder, and then she let herself out of the house.

* * *

The new day was a vivid contrast to what had come the day before. The sun shone from a cloudless blue sky. If it were not for the debris strewn across

13

the road, the toppled chimneys, the roofs hastily covered with tarpaulins, one would never guess the strength of the storm that had lashed the town. Teams of workmen laboured away, clearing away rubbish, replacing tiles and slate, repairing the demolition job started by the storm.

Emma retraced her steps to South Road, passing the massive pine tree that had trapped her the previous day. Two workmen were diligently sawing through its branches and loading them onto a cart. They ignored her as she reached through the boughs to retrieve the cream canvas bag that she had been carrying. Inside was her old sketchbook, now a sodden mess.

To her right was the once stately home of the Crabtree family, which had provided sanctuary to her and Max the previous day. She had often passed it on the way to the beach, wondering why such a fine home had been allowed to fall into ruin. But today it was clear that the wild weather had delivered the final death blow.

Emma passed down the side of the house and retrieved the key from where Max had placed it. She went inside, leaving behind the cheering warmth of the day outside. It was gloomy in the kitchen. A thick layer of dust covered the kitchen table and benchtops, except for one section that had been wiped clean. Empty cans and some dirty dishes sat next to the sink, signs that someone was living there. Pools of water lay across the floor, which was filthy with muddy footprints and scuff marks.

She left her bags on the kitchen table and walked through to the main part of the house, curious to see the damage that the storm had inflicted. Just off the hallway was the room where she and Max had first sheltered. It had once been an expensively furnished drawing-room, but now was a shadow of its former self. Its plaster ceiling was badly damaged, parts of it hanging untidily from a large gaping hole through which could be seen the blue of the sky. A magnificent mahogany table, its dust cover lying on the floor, had been gouged by slate roof tiles. Dirt and leaves had blown in. Pools of filthy water lay on the polished floorboards, while the Turkish rug was sodden and covered in debris.

The remains of the chimney had been strewn across the floor. Peeping through the bricks was the frame of the portrait that she had noticed above the mantelpiece the day before. She cleared away the rubble and studied the painting. The subject was a distinguished-looking man in his prime, wearing a three-piece suit with a wing collar and striped tie. He was standing next to a wicker chair, holding his pocket watch in his right hand. His black hair was combed flat and his thick waxed moustache, tinged with grey, was neatly trimmed. His face was arresting, severe and unyielding, with eyes cold and dark. The painter had not flattered the sitter; here was a man to be reckoned with, the portrait said. Attached to the bottom of the frame was a small brass plaque which read: *Thomas Crabtree 1879.* This was the patriarch of the Crabtree family, she thought. At least he wasn't still here to see what had become of his beautiful home.

On the adjoining wall was a family portrait, hanging crookedly from the picture rail. She straightened it and stood back to admire it. Sitting on a chair was Thomas Crabtree. His moustache was greyer. Behind him stood a beautiful young woman, her hand resting on his shoulder. She had soft blue eyes and blonde hair pulled back at the sides. A cluster of ringlets cascaded onto her shoulders. An elaborate blouse of ivory lace and a skirt of thick black satin showed off her tiny waist to perfection. To her left was a young blond-haired boy in a sailor suit, with the same soft blue eyes as the woman. To her right was a dark-haired lad of about seven, whose head was slightly tilted to gaze up at his mother. The painting was beautifully executed and showed great skill and composition. She looked carefully at the signature. She'd heard of him: he had been a renowned artist whose specialty was portraits of those in high society.

Emma glanced into the other rooms on the ground floor. There was nothing more of note to see here. What she was really keen to revisit was the cellar. She collected her bags from the kitchen table and went into the pantry. She opened the trapdoor and rested it back on its hinges. Down she went, step by step, until she touched the cellar floor. The soil of the earthen floor had been compacted so that it was as hard as concrete.

The smell struck her, a thick, earthy smell, musty yet cloying as if a touch of something sweet had been released into the air. She had not noticed it the previous day.

The paraffin lamp was where Max had left it. She struck a match and lit the lantern, watching in awe as light filled the space.

On the table, next to the basin and water jug, was the shaving kit. It included a mug, a stick of soap, a brush and comb, a pair of scissors, a mirror, and two cut-throat razors which glinted in the light. She picked up one and touched the blade tentatively. Blood oozed from her finger. She licked it off.

The atmosphere of the cellar was oppressive. It weighed her down. The smell. The lack of ventilation. The strange shaving paraphernalia. The claustrophobia of being below ground. The thought came, unbidden, that this was a place of suffering. She shut out her fears and looked up. The open trapdoor offered her escape. She took stock of the situation and derided herself for giving in to her imagination. 'I'm fine. There's nothing to worry about,' she assured herself.

Emma sat on the bottom step and studied the three heads. The death masks returned her gaze. She found them unsettling but even so, she was drawn to them. Beautiful. Pale. Smooth. Flawless. Highly polished. Reminiscent of the sculptures in marble and alabaster that she had marvelled at in art catalogues. It occurred to her that a photograph or a portrait could reflect the way the subject wished to be remembered, but a death mask captured the accurate physical appearance of the departed. Three-dimensional rather than two-dimensional. There could be no dissembling. Emma realised that what she was witnessing was the way these women had looked as their souls departed their bodies. She shivered at the thought.

Whoever had made these was an artist, just as she was. But there the similarity ended. Her subjects, although beautiful to her eye, were prosaic and commonplace. This person's preoccupation bordered on the bizarre.

She emptied her bag of drawing tools and studied the faces carefully, noting the differences in shape and structure. Then she took up her pencil and began, devoting a page to each one. She aimed for realism rather than her response to the subject, eschewing the emotions that they evoked in her. Her approach was a clinical depiction of their appearance: the bone structure of the face, the shape of the jaw, the arch of the eyebrows, the curve of the lips.

Finally, she put her sketchpad and pencils away and allowed her imagination to run free. She touched the first death mask. What a kind face she had; there was softness there. Her nose was upturned and her thick full lips were slightly apart as if she were taking her last breath. Emma studied the second death mask. The woman looked like she was dozing and would awaken in a moment. Her mouth was relaxed and calm, her eyes closed. Emma marvelled at the smoothness of the plaster cast, the shape of the skull, and the high cheekbones. The third woman had an oval face, large eyes whose lids were half-closed, and distinctive well-shaped brows. Her lips were drawn back, as if she were grimacing. Emma looked closer. Two short hairs protruded from one eyelid. Was it possible that they were real eyelashes, she wondered?

She returned to the first death mask, her artist's eye comparing it with the other two. It was, perhaps, not as well constructed. There was a ridge where the two sections of the mould had been joined together. A slightly reddish discoloration was visible in the plaster. The second and third masks were better made. The sculptor had become more accomplished with each one, if indeed he were responsible for the creation of all three.

Although each woman had different characteristics, they appeared to be of a similar age, in their twenties. All were beautiful in their own way. And all were bald.

She was baffled. Who were these women? How had they died? Where were their bodies buried? More to the point, why were they here? Perhaps Max was right. They must have been made years ago because no other explanation made sense.

She sniffed the air. The smell was still there.

'Did you suffer?' Emma asked the third woman, touching her cheek. 'I feel that you did.'

She was about to take up her bags when she heard the sound of the kitchen door opening. Heavy footsteps resonated across the polished floorboards as someone passed into the main part of the house. Emma froze, unsure of what she should do. She had no right to be there. Should she climb the steps and risk being confronted by a stranger? Should she conceal herself and wait until he left?

She made her decision. She moved quickly to the centre of the room and turned down the wick on the lantern, then cupped her hands around the glass and blew out the flame. The cellar was plunged into darkness. She reached out and felt for the scissors, grasping them in her right hand. Shrinking back against the wall, she waited, trembling in anticipation.

Too soon she heard the sound of footsteps returning. They stopped. Her heart was pounding. She held her breath. Above her, the boards creaked as he stepped into the pantry. Beads of perspiration broke out on her forehead as she waited. She could sense his presence and hear him breathing, as he stood over the opening and peered down into the inky blackness of the cellar. She heard him sniff. There was a low hiss as he let out his breath. She raised the scissors.

The trapdoor slammed shut. The bolt was rammed into place. The footsteps moved away. The kitchen door closed with a thud.

Emma dropped the scissors and flew up the steps, reaching up to push the trapdoor open. It wouldn't budge. She cried out in despair but there was no one to hear her. Tears formed in her eyes. She was trapped.

Chapter Three

Florence Darrow returned from church to an empty house. Empty of her great-niece, Emma Hart. The staff was none the wiser about the young woman's whereabouts. They had assumed that after breakfast she had stayed in bed, resting after her traumatic experience the day before. It appeared that she had gone out, but where, no one knew.

'Perhaps she's gone sketching, ma'am,' suggested the housekeeper.

'Silly girl,' exclaimed the elderly woman. 'I'll have words with her once she's home.'

Aunt Florence settled into a comfortable armchair in the parlour and looked up at the portrait of her father, which took pride of place above the mantelpiece.

'What would you do with her, Daddy? She's not what I expected. Stubborn, opinionated, headstrong.

'I know what you're thinking. She's just like me.' She shook her head. 'Maybe I shouldn't have taken her in.' She sighed and picked up her knitting.

* * *

Florence Darrow née Brown was the daughter of a wealthy Scottish merchant who had made his money on the Ballarat goldfields. Eoin Brown invested wisely. He built a fine house for his wife and daughter in Brighton, about nine miles from Melbourne, choosing the suburb for its generous building sites and the prospect of sea-bathing. Florence's father invested both time and money in his only child's academic and intellectual pursuits, for she was the apple of his eye. She was educated by a private governess, becoming proficient in arithmetic, geography, the sciences and Latin. Tutors schooled her in music and painting. It was, to say the least, a most unusual education for a girl in the 1860s. Her mother, who favoured a more traditional role for her daughter, was keen to see Florence settle down, but there were few suitors for the headstrong and talented Miss Brown.

In her late twenties, Florence married her father's business partner, Fingal Darrow. On the surface it appeared an odd match but, in practice, it suited both parties well. A widower in his early forties, Fingal wanted a companion for his old age and thought the feisty and opinionated daughter of his business partner would be an interesting diversion. He was an obliging man, with a tendency to laziness, but he had money and lots of it.

Florence, for her part, was pragmatic. Marriage would give her financial stability and social standing. Although she did not love him, she endeavoured to be a good wife to her husband. In return, Fingal gave Florence the freedom to pursue interests that were not conventional in a wife: politics and women's suffrage. Her home became the venue for many meetings of like-minded women.

At the age of sixty-nine, Fingal went to his grave. Shortly after, Eoin Brown died. It was for her father that Florence reserved the bulk of her grief. He had been devoted to her and she missed his steadfastness and single-mindedness. Poor Fingal left her few memories but much wealth.

Florence Darrow became a philanthropist. It gave her life meaning and direction, but privately she was lonely. As she approached her mid-sixties, childless and lacking close friends, Florence looked to her extended family for a companion.

She wrote to relatives in Donald, enquiring as to whether Emma, their nineteen-year-old daughter, might be interested in coming to live with her. It would give the girl a change of scene after the loss of her fiancé, Clive Atkins, on the Western Front.

However, Florence Darrow was unprepared for the chilly reception she was given. On her arrival in Brighton, Emma had spoken little and had retired to her bedroom to unpack. An hour passed and she had not come down. Meanwhile, in the dining-room, Aunt Florence waited impatiently for her great-niece to join her for dinner, and when this did not occur, she sent the housekeeper up to fetch her.

Once Emma entered the room, Aunt Florence pounced. 'If you think I'm going to have a companion who stays in her room, you are sadly mistaken.'

Emma was shocked. Tears formed in her eyes as she stared dolefully at the little bundle of energy that inhabited the chair opposite her.

'I miss Clive. Can't I have a tray in my room?'

Aunt Florence studied her great-niece. She was a pretty girl, tall and willowy. Thick blonde hair cascaded down her back almost reaching to her waist. To all appearances, she looked the picture of health, but her pale complexion and the air of fragility that she exuded belied that.

'Fiddlesticks. How long is it since he died? Two years? Time for you to rejoin the human race.'

She was shocked at Emma's reaction. Her great-niece ran from the room in tears.

Aunt Florence considered her options. She could put the young woman on the morning train and send her back to Donald. But she had never backed away from a contest and this was definitely one. And there was the simple fact that Emma was family.

She climbed the stairs and knocked on the door to Emma's bedroom.

'I'm coming in. We need to talk.'

She opened the door and entered the room. Emma was lying on the bed, her face turned to the wall. Aunt Florence sat beside her.

'Your mother never elaborated on your situation. Now I understand why. She thought I wouldn't take you.' She reached out and touched Emma's arm. 'Talk to me.'

Emma sat up and wiped the tears away.

'I'm sorry, I thought you knew.'

Under Mrs Darrow's steadfast gaze, Emma revealed the heartache and guilt that had gripped her since she had heard the news of Clive's death.

'People blamed me. They said that he joined up because of me.'

Aunt Florence let out a heavy sigh. 'I doubt if he did it to please you. He would have seen his friends enlisting and decided to do it too. This didn't only happen in Donald. It happened in Melbourne as well. The patriotic marches. The white feathers. Defending King and Country. All that talk about it being over by the end of the year. How naïve we were.'

'So, you agree that it's not my fault?'

'We were all at fault, Emma. We have to take responsibility for embracing the call to war.'

Tears rolled down Emma's face, but her great-aunt was unmoved.

'Stop feeling sorry for yourself, Emma. I refuse to indulge you. From tomorrow I expect you to join me for meals.'

'I can't. Please let me stay up here,' she pleaded.

'Fiddlesticks. It's time to throw off your grief. Your mother said that you can draw. There's a beautiful beach at the end of South Road. Go down there tomorrow and sketch something.' She walked to the door and looked back at her great-niece. 'Goodnight, Emma. I will see you for breakfast in the morning.'

Chapter Four

Emma had no idea how much time had passed since she'd been locked in. Claustrophobic from being in the darkness, she lit the lamp and let the glow consume the shadows in the cellar. The ghostly visages of the three death masks stared back at her. She shivered. Her satin dress was no protection against the chill that was seeping into her bones.

'Why did I hide down here?' she asked herself.

The minutes ticked by slowly. She looked up at the locked trapdoor.

'Aunt Florence will come looking for me.'

But that was unlikely. In recounting her experiences in the storm, she had omitted mention of the Crabtree house, its cellar, and the death masks. As far as Aunt Florence was concerned, Emma had been trapped by a falling tree and rescued by Max, who had brought her straight home. It was a pity that she had allowed herself to be persuaded by Max to keep their discovery a secret. Why had he discouraged her from talking about it?

Of one thing she was sure. Her great-aunt would be home from church and wondering where she was.

Her stomach rumbled. It would be lunchtime in the Darrow household. Roast beef with potatoes, pumpkin, and home-grown beans. Lashings of gravy. Her mouth watered. Was there anything to eat in the cellar? She looked around. No food. Just a jug of water, three-quarters full. She would need to ration it. And the paraffin in the lamp.

She turned down the lantern. The women's faces took on a corpse-like appearance, pallid and ghostly in the half-light. Emma turned away but the thought came unbidden. She would end up being buried alive with them.

She closed her eyes and let her head drop onto her chest.

The back door banged. Someone was coming inside. There was no hesitation this time. Emma clambered up the steps unsteadily, her limbs numb from the cold. She banged on the trapdoor and screamed at the top of her lungs.

'Help!'

Footsteps rang out on the polished boards above. There was the sound of the bolt being drawn back. The trapdoor was slung back on its hinges. Above her was the outline of a man looking down into the opening.

'Bloody hell!' he exclaimed as she emerged from the cellar. 'Emma. What on earth are you doing down there?'

'Max. Thank God it's you.'

'Yes, it's me. Come and sit down. You look frozen.' Max took off his coat and put it around her shoulders. 'You seem to have a talent for getting into trouble. I told you not to come back here.'

'You don't understand. He locked me in.'

'Who's *he*?'

'I don't know. I was in the cellar looking at the death masks when someone came and closed the trapdoor. I thought I was going to die.' She looked at him, puzzled. 'Why are you here?'

'I thought I left my hat behind.'

'I never noticed a hat. When were you wearing a hat?'

'I made a mistake. It flew off in the storm. Let's get you home.'

'Could you get my bags, please? I can't go down there again.'

'As long as *you* don't lock *me* in.'

For the first time, Max cracked a smile. Emma thought how different he looked. Not like the overly serious young man she had first met in the storm. She was struck by how handsome he was, with his muscular but thin frame and the straggly lock of fair hair that had fallen over his brow. His face was arresting. Pale eyelashes framed a pair of unusually light green eyes. She guessed that he was in his late twenties. But there were dark circles beneath his eyes, which hinted at sleepless nights.

He was so different from Clive, she thought. She dropped her head, ashamed of herself. Fancy comparing this stranger to her dead fiancé.

'Are you alright?' he asked.

'Yes, I'm fine.' She raised her head, a sad smile on her lips. 'Sometimes it's hard to let go of the past.'

He gave her a long, intense stare then he went down into the cellar, extinguished the lantern, and came back up, holding her two canvas bags.

'What are they for?' he asked as he handed them over.

'Nothing special. Could we go now, please? And I'd appreciate it if you don't tell Aunt Florence about this. She'll never let me out again.'

* * *

Max paused outside Mrs Darrow's magnificent house in Seymour Grove. Emma could see that he was impressed by its architectural elegance.

'What a beautiful house,' he said. 'I never noticed it yesterday. I was too intent on you.'

The home was late Victorian in design, built in the grand style, with scalloped slate roof tiles, a multi-coloured solid brick exterior, a tower, and a parapet of decorative shells and urns.

He smiled down at her and she felt a frisson of excitement.

'Why don't you come in and meet Aunt Florence properly?' she suggested. 'I'm sure she'd like to thank you for helping me yesterday. And remember, not a word about today.'

Mrs Williams, the housekeeper, answered her knock. 'Miss Emma. I didn't realise that you'd gone out. Mrs Darrow has been very concerned.'

'I wanted some fresh air. Sorry.'

'Not at all. Can I take your hat, sir? Mrs Darrow's in the library.'

She stood aside and let the young woman and her companion go past. The pleasant smell of freshly baked bread wafted through from the kitchen, making Emma feel ravenous.

Max followed Emma into the library, her favourite room in the house. Two walls were lined with oak bookshelves, filled with leather-bound first editions and reference books, while the polished floorboards were covered by an enormous Turkish carpet. A massive stone fireplace dominated the room, a gilded French Empire clock taking pride of place on the mantelpiece.

Emma's Aunt Florence rose from her armchair. She was a small rotund woman, with silver hair pulled into a bun at the top of her head. She wore a grey and cream striped dress. Around her neck hung a long string of pearls, which she twirled with her fingers. It was clear that she was irate.

The scent of frangipani wafting in from the open bay window did nothing to alleviate the mood in the room.

'Where have you been? You've missed lunch.' Her gaze turned on Max. 'Mr Rushforth. I never expected to see you again.' Aunt Florence raised her pince-nez and eyed him up and down, noting the slightly wrinkled brown suit with its mismatched light grey checked shirt.

'I ran into Emma, out in South Road.'

Mrs Darrow frowned at her great-niece. 'You were supposed to rest.'

'I'm sorry, Aunt. I wanted to see what the storm had done.'

'I was worried sick about you.'

'There was nothing to worry about.' She exchanged a look with Max who raised an eyebrow at her.

Mrs Darrow turned back to Max. 'As I said yesterday, thank you for rescuing her, Mr Rushforth. I hope that you're not expecting a reward?'

Emma blushed. 'That's very unfair. We owe him thanks, not insults.'

'I'll go,' said Max, taking a step towards the door.

'Please don't,' said Emma. 'I like to sketch. Perhaps I could draw you some time, by way of thanks.' A mischievous glint was in her eye. 'Maybe I'll depict you as Perseus rescuing Andromeda when she was chained naked to a rock in the sea.'

Max stifled a laugh.

'Behave, Emma,' said Aunt Florence. She turned to Max. 'Please excuse my great-niece. She's from the country. All the manners of a farm girl.' She shook her head in despair. 'You've seen what effect the storm had on Brighton. You'll notice that my home is untouched. My dear departed husband knew how to build a house.'

Max nodded. 'It's very well-constructed. I studied engineering at university.'

'Perhaps I have been a bit hasty in my opinion of you, Mr Rushforth. If so, I apologise. I am grateful that you saved her. I've had such a business getting her out of this house and a storm nearly does away with her.'

'Please, Aunt Florence. Max doesn't want to hear about my problems.'

'Fiddlesticks! You've caused your parents a lot of pain, my dear.' She addressed Max. 'Her fiancé died and she refused to leave her room. That's why she's in Brighton. To live again.'

Emma turned away, blushing violently.

'I'm sorry to hear about your fiancé.'

'He died in France,' explained Aunt Florence. 'At the Somme.'

Max moved over towards the fireplace and leaned against the mantelpiece.

'And what do you do for a living, Mr Rushforth?'

'I work at the St Kilda Road Barracks. The Department of Defence. Clerical duties.'

'Have you seen service?'

'I have. I came home in May last year.'

'You were wounded?'

'You could call it that.'

There was an uneasy silence. Max looked down, studying the carpet. He put a cigarette between his lips and lit it, then inhaled deeply and stared out the window.

'What news of the storm, Emma?' asked Aunt Florence.

'*The Argus* says that at least two storms converged over Brighton.'

'Two storms?'

'Actually, three. One in a north-easterly direction hitting Brighton Beach. Another struck Wellington Street moving eastwards and a third hit Chatsworth Avenue, all three crossing Halifax Street. They say the winds reached two hundred miles per hour.'

'My goodness. You're a fund of information!' exclaimed Aunt Florence, eyes shining.

The housekeeper appeared at the door. 'Mrs Darrow, your knitting group is starting to arrive. I've taken them into the parlour.'

'Thank you. Let Cook know that afternoon tea should be served at three o'clock.'

Aunt Florence looked in the mirror and smoothed her hair. 'Well, I must go. Socks and scarves await. One can only hope that this war is over soon.' She addressed Max. 'Mrs Williams will show you out when Emma's finished with you.'

She turned to leave but changed her mind. 'I'm having a garden party on Saturday, the 17th of February. It starts at two o'clock. We're raising money for our blind soldiers. Why don't you join us?'

'I'll see if I can come. Thank you.'

She left the room, closing the door behind her.

Max sat down. 'Your aunt is a confident woman.'

'That's an understatement.'

'Have you lived here long?'

Emma smiled. 'About two months. I'm from Donald. My aunt wanted a companion. I didn't want to come but Mum insisted.' She looked out of the window. 'It's true what Aunt Florence said. I took Clive's death badly.'

'Good people died. Some of us lived. I'm not sure who was better off.'

The front door slammed. Max started at the sound then sat back in the chair. Emma watched him carefully.

'Are you alright? You seem a bit jumpy.'

'I'm fine.' He stood up. 'I must go. Take care of yourself, Emma. Give my best wishes to your aunt.'

'Will you come to the garden party?'

'Perhaps.'

Emma trailed him out of the library and stood at the front door, watching him as he walked slowly down the front path. He was a strange one, that was for sure. One minute friendly, the next remote. She didn't know what to make of him. He was nothing like Clive.

Chapter Five

A week after the storm that had devastated much of Brighton, Aunt Florence was sitting in the library, contemplating the arrangements for her garden party. There would be bunting and streamers, a three-piece band, stalls selling crafts and home produce, with a lavish afternoon tea to follow. Dignitaries, including the mayor, had been invited. It was hoped that significant funds would be raised to help support the rehabilitation of wounded and blind ex-soldiers, some of whom would attend. She was confident that it would be as successful as her recent efforts in collecting good, used clothing for the Presbyterian Widows and Orphans Fund.

On the side table was Emma's sketchbook. Aunt Florence flipped through some of the drawings, admiring her great-niece's talent. If she could just encourage Emma to take her hobby seriously. Art lessons, or perhaps the possibility of a trip overseas to view the European masters when this war was over, might spark some enthusiasm. So far, Emma had shown no interest. Idleness and apathy were characteristics that Aunt Florence detested and although there had been an improvement in Emma's attitude, it was still not enough for her. In her view, it was time for Emma to embrace life again.

There were the usual sketches of seascapes and beach boxes, with studies of fishermen thrown in for good measure. All quite predictable and well-executed.

On the next page was the first of three portraits of women. Emma had written beneath each one: 'February 3, 1918: In the cellar.'

They were extraordinary, bordering on the bizarre. Each woman was bald. It begged the question: who were they? What cellar? The sketches were most disturbing.

'Aunt. Have you seen my sketchbook?' Emma was standing in the doorway. Her eyes fell on the open book lying on the elderly woman's lap. She strode across the room and snatched it away.

'I can't believe that you would look at my drawings without my permission.'

'Who are those women?'

'I don't know.'

There was a caginess in her expression that suggested an explanation would not be extracted easily.

'I can tell when someone is lying. Where did you see these?'

Emma's mouth set in an obstinate line.

'Tell me, Emma.' Still, there was silence. 'If you don't speak to me, I swear, I will put you on the first train back to Donald and you can try and explain *that* to your parents.'

Emma was shocked. When she had first arrived in Brighton, she had longed to return to the isolation of her country home, with its endless fields, gum trees, and simple uncomplicated life. The noise and the frenetic pace of city life were foreign to her. However, as the weeks had passed and she had put distance between herself and the situation she had found herself in after Clive's death, she had come to realise that life in Donald was not so simple after all. Small town living could be claustrophobic. She would always be Clive Atkins' fiancée if she stayed there. At least in Brighton few knew her or judged her; she had a chance for a fresh start.

Aunt Florence had also been responsible for her change of heart. The elderly lady was a force to be reckoned with. Emma did not dare disobey her insistence that they dine together and that Emma spend time outdoors. George, the gardener cum chauffeur, would have described Emma as a crocus or tulip that closes its flower at night to protect itself, then opens its petals to embrace the sun in the morning. Emma was emerging from her self-imposed isolation to embrace life again. And she was taking pleasure in her new environment.

'I want to stay.'

'I thought you didn't like it here.'

'No, that's not true. I realise that you're trying to help me although you do demand a lot of me.'

Aunt Florence laughed, then her face softened. 'Alright, miss. Perhaps I won't send you back. Where did these drawings come from?'

'It's a long story.'

'I have time. Now sit down.'

The elderly woman patted the seat next to her. Emma sat, avoiding her gaze. Aunt Florence raised her pince-nez, took her great-niece's chin between her fingers, and turned Emma's face so that they were eye to eye.

'Start at the beginning.' She let go and waited.

Emma sighed and nodded her head.

'It began with the storm.'

She told her about the Crabtree mansion and how Max and she had sheltered in the cellar.

Aunt Florence took an intake of breath. 'He didn't bring you straight home? When you were in the cellar, he didn't interfere with you?'

Emma was shocked. 'Oh no. Max was a perfect gentleman. But there were three death masks in the cellar.'

'You said "three death masks"?'

'That's right. You heard me correctly. They are the women in my sketches. After the storm passed over, we left the cellar and he brought me home.'

'The Crabtree mansion?'

'Yes. That's what Max called it.'

Aunt Florence looked out the window, lost in thought. 'I moved here in 1880. The Crabtree house was one of the premier homes in the district at the time. You should have seen it in its prime. The best of everything. It was beautiful.'

She paused. 'I only knew the family for a short time before tragedy struck. Thomas Crabtree was a gold prospector and successful banker. He built that house in the late 1860s. It became the home of Thomas and Matilda and their two sons.'

Her eyes filled with sadness. 'The younger one died suddenly. Matilda

31

was inconsolable. She took her own life shortly after. Poor Thomas. I don't think he could handle the loss. A tragic business.'

'I saw a portrait of them in the drawing-room.'

'Then you know how beautiful Matilda was.'

'What happened to the father and son?'

'I don't know about the boy. Sent away to boarding school, I suppose. Thomas died over ten years ago. There was no will. Most of the inheritance has been eaten up by legal squabbling between his relatives.'

She sighed and looked at Emma. 'You say you went down to the cellar. Three death masks, you said?'

Emma nodded.

Aunt Florence shook her head. 'Death masks. The Victorians had an unhealthy obsession with death. Hair of the dead in lockets and brooches. They even said that Queen Victoria had her servants lay out Albert's clothes each day after he died. So morbid.'

She gazed out the window, lost in thought, and then she turned her attention back to Emma. 'You drew them?'

'I went back last Sunday.'

'When I was at church? So that's where you went.' Aunt Florence shook her head. 'Why didn't you tell me about the death masks to begin with?'

'Max said we shouldn't.'

'Then Max was wrong. I'll send for the local constabulary. If someone is living in the Crabtree mansion, we should find out exactly who they are and what they're doing there. Death masks indeed.'

'There's something more. When I went back there on Sunday, someone locked me in the cellar.'

'I beg your pardon?'

'I was about to leave when I heard someone in the house. I turned down the lamp and kept quiet because the trapdoor was open. He bolted it shut. I called out but he'd gone.'

'Who's *he*?'

'I don't know.'

'You shouldn't have gone back there. If I'd known about these death masks,

I would have forbidden it. How did you get out?'

'Max came and got me out.'

'How did Max know you were there?'

'He didn't. I called out when I heard him come into the house.'

'Why was he there?'

'I honestly don't know.'

'I don't like this at all, Emma. What do you know about this Max?'

'He saved my life.'

'Indeed, he did. Has it occurred to you that Max might be the person who locked you in the cellar?'

Emma flushed with anger. 'Don't be ridiculous. Max wouldn't do that.'

'You seem rather taken with him. I ask you to consider your relationship with him carefully.'

'I may never see him again,' she replied, a slight tremor in her voice.

'Perhaps that's for the best. I'll send for Sergeant O'Toole. This business needs to be dealt with properly. Now take your sketchbook and head down the beach for an hour. You need some fresh air.' She wagged her finger at her great-niece. 'And no more secrets. Understood?'

Emma nodded and left the room, shutting the door quietly behind her.

Aunt Florence rang for Mrs Williams.

'Could you ask George to go to the police station this afternoon, please? See if Sergeant O'Toole can return with him.'

Mrs Williams nodded and went out in search of the chauffeur.

Aunt Florence sat back in her chair, pondering the relationship between her great-niece and Max Rushforth. Emma was a naïve country girl, unworldly and gullible. Max, on the other hand, had experienced life on the Western Front and, from her observation, had not escaped unscathed. She suspected that psychological issues rather than physical wounds had brought him back home. He was handsome too, likely to turn the head of a girl who had cloistered herself for the last two years in her bedroom with little to distract her. A girl who was now emerging into womanhood.

Should she have invited Max Rushforth to her garden party? After what she'd been told, she regretted her decision, but there was little she could do to reverse it. With a bit of luck, he might not come, she thought. But then he just might. What she needed was an insurance policy against Emma getting too involved with him, but what that was she did not know.

Chapter Six

Sergeant Séamus O'Toole stood on the doorstep of Florence Darrow's Victorian mansion. He was an impressive figure in his navy-blue trousers and jacket, with brass buttons done up to the neck and his Wolseley-style leather helmet. He had large hairy hands and a mangled nose, that suggested familiarity with police association boxing matches. He rapped on the massive oak door and waited, his sharp eyes sweeping his surroundings as if he were searching for clues. He was admitted into the house by Mrs Williams and shown into the parlour.

Aunt Florence was sitting next to the fireplace. O'Toole's eyes were drawn to the painting above the mantelpiece. It was of a rather severe-looking gentleman in his sixties, wearing a black frock coat and a grey-striped cravat with a white shirt.

'My father,' she said, by way of explanation. She introduced the sergeant to Emma, who was seated close by.

'Mrs Darrow, it's good to see you looking so well,' he said, a hint of Irish lilt in his voice.

'Keeping active is the key, Sergeant O'Toole.'

'Thank you again for your generous donation to Constable Howard's widow.'

'To be taken so young by typhoid. His poor wife: two children under three and no husband.' She tut-tutted. 'Please take a seat.'

'Thank you, ma'am. How can I be of service today?'

'My great-niece has a most unusual story to tell you.'

'Indeed.' O'Toole took out a notebook and pencil and waited. He listened

35

carefully, taking notes as Emma recounted her experiences on the day of the storm. Occasionally he would interrupt to ask a question but, in the main, he let her speak. By the time she described her encounter with the death masks, he was scribbling frantically. Emma reached the end of her tale and sat back.

O'Toole scratched his head and studied the two women sitting opposite him.

'Death masks in Brighton. Hard to believe.'

'It's true, sir,' said Emma. 'I could show you if you like?'

'Certainly. Will you accompany us, Mrs Darrow?'

'Emma is quite capable of showing you the way.' She smiled at her great-niece and took up her knitting.

The policeman put on his helmet and followed Emma out into Seymour Grove. They turned left into New Street then right into South Road and continued on until they stood in front of the former home of Thomas Crabtree.

'We went around the back,' said Emma, indicating the way. 'There's a key in the pot plant next to the back door.'

'How did you know about the key?'

'Max knew.'

O'Toole slid the key in the lock and opened the door. It was dim and musty in the kitchen. He walked through into the front section of the house, which was illuminated by the gash in the roof above the drawing-room. Dust motes floated in the air, lit by the stream of sunlight that penetrated the gloom. Slate tiles from the collapsed roof had dug deep grooves into the polished boards. On one side of the room were the fallen bricks of the chimney, covered in dust and broken mortar. The sergeant took in the ruin of the storm which had drenched the carpets and drapes, leaving behind a distinct smell of mildew.

'And to think that this has been allowed to happen, because of the greed of men. Fancy fighting over an inheritance,' he said, shaking his head. 'Best get on. Now show me this cellar.'

He followed her back through the kitchen and into the pantry. Emma pointed to the trapdoor.

'Down there. That's where they are.'

The policeman took off his helmet and put it on the floor. Then he lifted the latch and pulled the door back onto its hinges.

'You said that there's a lantern down there?' She nodded. 'Wait here, miss.'

Emma watched as the portly figure of Sergeant O'Toole disappeared slowly down into the cellar. The lantern was lit and light streamed out through the open trapdoor.

'Could you come down here please?' he called.

She made her way tentatively down the steps until she stood on solid earth. The light extended into the far corners of the cellar.

'Where are these death masks?' the policeman asked.

'Over there,' she said, pointing at the shelves.

But they were empty. She glanced around. They weren't the only things missing. The basin, pitcher, towels, and shaving implements were gone too. Only the table and chairs remained.

'They were there. The death masks were there!'

'They aren't there now.'

O'Toole climbed the steps, retrieved his helmet, and led the way out of the house. Emma followed him, lost in thought. Only the previous week, she had seen the death masks for a second time and in the interim, they had disappeared. The only explanation was that whoever had put them there had removed them.

Aunt Florence was shocked to hear the outcome of their visit. 'My great-niece would never make up such a story.'

'I have no reason to disbelieve her, ma'am. There are signs of habitation.' He turned to Emma. 'Could you give me a few details about your companion? This man, Max?'

'Max Rushforth. He was a soldier. He works at the Barracks in St. Kilda Road.'

'His address?'

'Somewhere in North Brighton. I hardly know him.'

'Is it possible that he would have removed the death masks?'

Emma shrugged her shoulders. 'I don't believe so.'

O'Toole put his notebook away and put on his helmet. 'I will put in a report, but without seeing the death masks myself, there is nothing I can do. Ladies, I will take my leave of you.'

'Your drawings, Emma,' suggested Aunt Florence.

'That's right. I'll just be a minute.' She rushed out the door.

Sergeant O'Toole placed his helmet back on the table. He looked questioningly at Mrs Darrow but she was giving nothing away.

Emma returned and thrust the sketchpad into the policeman's hands. 'Here, Sergeant. Look at these.'

O'Toole took a seat. He flipped through the pages of the book, and then slowly perused the drawings of each of the women whose death masks had been displayed in the cellar.

'Where did you get these?' he asked, addressing Emma as she looked on.

'I drew them. I went back there the day after the storm.'

The sergeant was silent, staring at the third drawing. He raised his eyes and met those of Emma.

'You have a talent, Miss Hart.' He took a deep breath and tapped the sketch with a large hairy finger. 'This last one has a strong likeness to a woman who was found dead in September last year. Agnes Reason. She lived a mile from here. And her husband is in Pentridge Prison serving a life sentence for her murder.'

Chapter Seven

Florence Darrow's knitting group gathered in the parlour at Seymour Grove, a few days prior to the garden party. It had been formed in late 1916 when the elderly lady had read about the heavy rains that the troops on the Western Front had encountered in November. A letter had been published in *The Argus*, written by a lieutenant on active duty. He described how the men in the trenches had to wear thigh-high rubber boots to stop the water coming in. Each day the soldiers rubbed their feet with whale oil to prevent frostbite and trench foot, changing their socks daily and having the dirty ones washed and dried. The muddy conditions caused the feet to blister or become infected and gangrenous, requiring amputation.

Aunt Florence had been horrified. It spurred her into action. She rallied the ladies in her neighbourhood, and each week they met in her parlour, knitting socks, balaclavas, and scarves for the boys at the Front. The added benefit was that it provided a social outlet for widows and those whose menfolk had enlisted.

As they knitted khaki socks for the troops, Florence Darrow was preoccupied. Her thoughts turned to her conversation with Emma the previous day.

'I can't believe what Sergeant O'Toole told us,' Emma had said, as they ate their supper. 'I thought that those death masks were old.'

'It certainly is a concern that a crime has been committed so close to home.'

'He said that whoever made those masks had a hand in the murder of one of them. I can't help but wonder whether the murderer locked me in the cellar.'

'To think that you might have been trapped down there. It doesn't bear thinking about it.'

'If it hadn't been for Max—'

'You really should consider whether Mr Rushforth is involved in this business with the death masks. It's quite possible he removed them.'

Emma crossed her arms defensively. 'I don't think so.'

'He told you to forget about them. It didn't stop *him* from going back.'

'Just as well. I would have been trapped in the cellar.'

Aunt Florence raised her pince-nez and studied her great-niece. 'You're deliberately missing the point, Emma. You go back to the cellar a second time. Someone locks you in. Max fortuitously arrives and frees you. The death masks disappear. Doesn't that strike you as an odd coincidence?'

'Max wouldn't do that.'

'Fiddlesticks! You hardly know him. You said so yourself.'

Emma replied coolly. 'You're being unreasonable, Aunt Florence.'

'Me?' She wagged her finger at her great-niece. 'Sergeant O'Toole asked the same question. You have to take this seriously, my girl.'

Her arguments were to no avail. It was clear that Emma was not prepared to consider that Max Rushforth was involved in murder.

A voice penetrated her thoughts.

'Florence, you seem rather distracted.' Mavis da Costa was staring at her hostess with a look of concern on her face. 'Is everything alright, my dear?'

'Of course. My mind was on other things. I apologise. Where were we?'

'We were discussing the plight of soldiers returning home.'

'You are involved in so many good causes, Florence,' said Iris Watts, smiling ingratiatingly at her hostess. 'This garden party of yours will be most beneficial in assisting our blind boys.'

'Thank you,' Mrs Darrow replied, her concentration restored. 'I couldn't do it without the help of friends such as you.' She eyed the workmanship of the group. 'Two knit, two purl, Gladys. You keep dropping stitches. Our boys' toes will be peeping out through those holes. And Iris, start decreasing now, unless you want to knit socks that will fit someone the size of Goliath.'

'Are you expecting many of our boys to come?' asked Mavis.

'I've invited several of our blind soldiers to sit on the podium. Then there's the mayor's son and a friend of Emma's.'

Mavis's curiosity was piqued. 'Your great-niece has a young man?'

Florence Darrow let out a sigh and her brow puckered. 'Not if I have anything to say about it.'

The ladies leaned in, eager to grasp a morsel of gossip. Mrs Darrow continued, oblivious to the interest she had generated. 'You see, I invited him to the garden party and now I regret it. He was sent home from the Western Front. Why, I'm not sure. But some strange things have happened since Emma met him.'

'What strange things?' asked Mavis, curiosity getting the better of her.

Florence Darrow waved her question away, as if she were swatting a fly. 'I've said too much. Suffice it to say, my great-niece is showing a little too much interest in him.'

'Is a distraction required?' volunteered one of the other women. 'I know a young man who is charming and well-connected: Eric Loader.'

'Really Ava, he's just announced his engagement to the Zukor girl,' said Mavis. 'Now my son is an eligible young man.'

Mavis had a son, Reggie, who was a crime reporter with *The Argus*. He associated with the police, the legal profession, and those who could keep him informed about Melbourne's criminal underworld. His exploits made for lively conversations in Florence Darrow's parlour, because Mavis loved to share the excitement of her son's occupation.

Mavis was keen for him to make a good marriage but, to her dismay, Reggie had shown a desire to pursue the good things of life rather than settle down. His chief preoccupations were clothes, cars, travel, and his reputation as a crime reporter. Not for him the constraints of marriage to a wealthy but unattractive woman. If he were going to marry, then money, beauty, and a submissive personality were his main requirements in a wife.

There had been dalliances with older (married) women, short-lived liaisons with young (and willing) young ladies, and many nights enjoying a bachelor-style existence. Reggie was well on the way to acquiring a reputation as a *bon vivant*. Despite the best efforts of his mother to convince him to settle down, Reggie was disinclined to follow her advice. Rumours about his lifestyle had filtered through to Mrs Darrow's knitting group.

Iris looked unconvinced at Mavis's suggestion that her son would make a suitable partner for Mrs Darrow's great-niece. 'I've heard that Reggie is rather wild.'

'Not my Reggie,' said Mavis, looking alarmed. 'In fact, just last night he told me that he is keen to settle down, if he can find the right girl. And Florence,' she added, reaching across and placing her hand on Mrs Darrow's knee, 'it would be the distraction that Ava recommended. It would stop Emma from embarking on an inappropriate relationship.'

'Hmmm,' said Florence, drumming her fingers on the side table. 'It's worth trying. Mavis, you may invite your son to the garden party.'

Mavis da Costa could barely contain her excitement. 'You won't be sorry. My son is a perfect gentleman.'

'We shall see.'

Later, in the afternoon, as Mrs Darrow sipped a cup of tea, she wondered whether she had compounded one mistake with another. On paper, Reggie da Costa offered the perfect foil to Max Rushforth. He was, by all accounts, urbane, confident and experienced in the ways of the world. Although he was not independently wealthy, he mixed in the right social circles. As a practising Presbyterian, Florence Darrow did not approve of licentious behaviour, but she had no proof that Reggie followed that path. She was at an impasse. She had invited Max to the garden party on impulse. It was imperative that she find someone to distract her great-niece from Max. The only candidate, it appeared, was Reggie da Costa.

Chapter Eight

The sun was shining down on Mrs Darrow's garden party as Reginald da Costa parked his new 1917 Dodge Roadster outside her stately home in Seymour Grove. He assisted his mother as she got out of the car and then paused. There was an errant spot of dirt on the highly polished bonnet. He pulled out his handkerchief and cleaned it away. That was better. His flashy two-seater automobile with its wooden steering wheel, black paintwork, and shiny large headlamps was his pride and joy. He had paid a small fortune for it and it was worth every penny.

Taking his mother by the arm, Reggie strode up the circular driveway.

'Be good,' his mother murmured in his ear.

The Victorian mansion was very impressive, he thought, and spoke of money. They stepped up onto the verandah. Above the front door was a magnificent stained-glass window with a fleur-de-lys design in green, lilac, red, and blue. Reggie moved so that he could see his reflection in the side window. He straightened his collar and smiled inwardly at the sight of his impeccably cut linen suit, high-collared cream shirt, and green striped tie.

The door was answered by the housekeeper. Reggie and his mother were shown into a grand entry hall lined with dark wainscoting and flocked wallpaper. He caught his reflection in an elaborately framed mirror and ran his fingers through his shock of thick black hair. They followed the housekeeper past the staircase and down the hallway into the backyard.

Bunting and Chinese lanterns were strung from the trees, a string trio was playing on a raised bandstand, and trestle tables had been set up, displaying a multitude of goods for sale. 'All proceeds to aid blind soldiers' a sign read.

To the side of the stage sat three servicemen, one with a bandage covering his eyes, a second with considerable scarring across his face, and a third in a wheelchair wearing dark glasses. A fourth leaned heavily on a wooden crutch, his right leg amputated below the knee. Several ladies were chatting with them and serving them drinks.

On the far side of the lawn, stalls had been set up laden with foodstuffs, cakes, jars of preserves, craft items, and potted plants for sale. On another trestle table, women were serving cups of tea with scones, jam, and lashings of clotted cream for a sixpence.

Reggie was not happy. All around him were well-dressed Brighton matrons, not one of them under the age of thirty. There was not an attractive young woman in sight. But his mother had made it abundantly clear that he must attend. After all, his company had been requested by none other than Mrs Florence Darrow herself, his mother told him, and it would be social suicide to refuse. Apparently, the doyenne of Brighton society was keen for him to meet her companion and great-niece, Miss Emma Hart.

Reggie shuddered at the thought. His mother had explained that she was a country girl, from Donald in the Mallee-Wimmera. It was expected that she would inherit Mrs Darrow's millions, which presented an opportunity not to be missed for an eligible bachelor in need of funds.

A country girl. He grimaced at the thought. Calloused hands from milking cows. A ruddy complexion from working out in the sun. Conversation about crops and the weather. Likely to be a strait-laced spinster with poor dress sense and no looks.

'Where's the beer?' he asked his mother.

'Mrs Darrow's Presbyterian,' Mavis hissed.

Reggie rolled his eyes. He wondered how long he would have to stay before he could escape. It would be necessary to be introduced to the formidable Mrs Darrow and her dowdy relative and then perhaps he could make his excuses.

His mother broke away and was making conversation with a plump, well-dressed woman in black taffeta. Her dress was embellished with a collar of expensive white lace. A strategically placed pince-nez hung around her neck on a black velvet ribbon. Mavis pointed to Reggie and the two women came over to him. Introductions followed and he found himself face to face with the hostess herself.

'So pleased you could come, Mr da Costa.' Mrs Darrow raised her pince-nez and proceeded to give Reggie the once-over. He was sure that she would be impressed with his immaculate beige suit and matching accessories.

'There's someone I want you to meet,' she added, beckoning him to follow. She led him over to the summer house where a small group of women stood in a circle. There was a thin woman with her back to them, dressed in a severe grey suit with her hair pulled back into a bun at the nape of her neck. Reggie took a deep breath.

'Emma, dear, come and meet Mr da Costa.'

The woman in the grey suit stepped aside and made way for a pretty young woman. Emma Hart was a delightful surprise. Not a thirtyish spinster off the farm but a fresh, achingly attractive beauty in the first flush of womanhood. Her fashionable dress was of the finest quality organza in shades of soft apricot and Wedgwood blue. Two thin ribbons were tied at the waist, with the hemline falling to mid-calf. Her thick blonde hair fell in waves down her back, all the way to her waist. Little frizzy ringlets framed her face, complemented by a fashionable, wide-brimmed straw hat. Her complexion was smooth and flawless, like that of the Goddess of Love whose statuettes Reggie had admired on a trip to Italy before the War. And when she looked up at him, he was struck by the coolness of her clear blue eyes, the colour of cornflowers. Miss Hart took his breath away.

'Hello,' she said in a mellifluous voice.

And for the first time in his thirty years, Reggie da Costa, man about town and eligible bachelor, was rendered speechless.

Emma looked away; her attention caught by the sight of a tall, well-built man with untidy, fair hair who was making his way through the throng towards her. He stopped to speak to the soldiers near the stage.

'Who's that?' Reggie asked Mrs Darrow.

'Mr Max Rushforth,' she replied, a brittle edge to her voice. 'Excuse me. I need to check the afternoon tea.'

Mrs Darrow headed off in the direction of the trestle tables. Reggie now had the opportunity to scrutinise the new arrival. He was in his late twenties and appeared ill-at-ease, glancing distractedly at the people milling around him. Reggie compared his own outfit with the slightly wrinkled appearance of Rushforth's cheap suit. If this were a rival, Reggie thought, he had nothing to be concerned about.

Emma performed the introductions then addressed Reggie.

'You have come to support the fundraising efforts, Mr da Costa?'

'Reggie. Call me Reggie. In actual fact, I came to support my mother. She asked me to accompany her. I don't wish to denigrate those who served,' he said, lowering his voice and indicating the four wounded men in uniform, 'but I won't pretend that I believe in war.'

Max blinked at Reggie through pale lashes. 'I served on the Western Front.'

'That was your prerogative. I believe that the Australian public now sees the War for what it was: British capitalist interests defending their markets against the growth of Germany as a world power. Invading Belgium and France would give Germany control of the ports along the English Channel. The British realised that the Berlin-Baghdad railway would allow the Huns to control oilfields in the Persian Gulf, the Caucasus and British India.'

'You see this as an economic war?'

Da Costa frowned, his thick black brows knitting together. 'I do. The politicians misled people with their appeals to patriotism. Young men marched off to war, not knowing what they were fighting for. Those who encouraged and cajoled them were complicit in the murder of a generation of young men.'

Emma interjected. 'That's strong language. You'd condemn those who encouraged young men to join up when war was declared?'

'Indeed, I would.'

'Steady on,' remarked Max. 'That's extreme. I don't for one moment blame anybody else for my enlistment. It was my decision and I take full responsibility for what happened to me. No one else.'

'Those people that you condemn so easily didn't want their loved ones to die,' argued Emma, her face ashen.

Reggie sensed that she was upset. 'I'm sorry. I get carried away sometimes. It's the waste of human life that I can't stand. That and the failure of politicians to be honest.'

A voice came from behind him. 'You have strong opinions.'

Aunt Florence had returned. Reggie made way for her. She raised her pince-nez and eyed him intently. He understood what it must feel like to be a butterfly pinned to a display board. Reggie had entered dangerous territory and he knew it. If he were going to keep in the good books of both the lovely Miss Hart and her intimidating great-aunt, he would have to lighten the mood.

'Mother thought that I'd get myself into trouble today. She warned me not to use your garden party as a soapbox.'

'You should listen to her more often. We are honouring our wounded today.'

'I apologise, Mrs Darrow. I meant no harm.'

'On the other hand, I myself have sometimes been out of step with conventional society. My opinions have been regarded as revolutionary although certainly not socialist. You are a socialist, are you not?'

Reggie sidestepped the question. 'Mother said that if I jeopardised her relationship with you, she would personally pay my ship's passage to Russia.'

'She said that, did she? In my opinion, you and Russia are not well-matched.'

'Why is that?'

'Your suit. If I'm not wrong, I'd say it's from Savile Row. Your shirt and tie are undoubtedly made by Wallace, Buck and Goodes of Queens Walk.'

'Mother said you were sharp. You have skewered me. I confess that you have identified my one weakness.'

'Only one?'

Reggie da Costa roared with laughter, relieved that the conversation had moved to safer ground. He was pleased to see that the lovely Miss Hart was smiling.

'You are forthright, Mrs Darrow. Mother said that you were the Brighton equivalent of Emmeline Pankhurst.'

'Fiddlesticks! I've never heard your mother express such an opinion.'

Mrs Darrow was staring at him through her pince-nez. Reggie felt a few beads of sweat break out on his brow. Fortuitously, the string trio started to play a lovely piece by Scott Joplin, called 'The entertainer, ragtime.' Everyone stopped to listen, enjoying the melody. By the time the band had finished, the awkward moment had passed. Reggie took the opportunity to address Emma.

'Are you aware that I am chief crime reporter with *The Argus*, Miss Hart? You may have read some of my articles in the newspaper.'

'I believe I have,' said Emma, her interest piqued. 'You'd meet all manner of people.'

Reggie glowed with pleasure. 'Indeed, I do.' He tapped each finger of his hand as he listed them. 'Police, lawyers, and informants, of course. And then you have murderers, gangs, thugs, and hoodlums. Melbourne's criminal underworld is extensive.'

'It sounds rather exciting.'

'It can be. A successful crime reporter, such as myself, needs a good memory, investigative skills, and excellent contacts. Of course, one must have a way with words.'

'You appear to use words as weapons,' commented Max.

'At least mine don't kill.'

'Time for afternoon tea.' Aunt Florence took Reggie's arm. 'Come Mr da Costa, I believe your mother wants you.'

Reggie allowed himself to be steered away. Reunited with his mother, he whispered in her ear, 'Why didn't you tell me Emma Hart was a beauty?'

'I did,' she replied, 'but you never listen to me. I've been telling you that you need to meet her. She's one of the most eligible young ladies in Brighton and you're letting her get away. Miss Hart is the heiress to the Darrow fortune. Her great-aunt has no children.'

Reggie glanced back at Emma, now deep in conversation with Max Rushforth. Next time, he would get the lovely Miss Hart alone. She had the two prerequisites for a wife: money and beauty. Reggie felt that he couldn't compromise his standards by sacrificing one for the other. He was indeed fortunate that compromise would not be necessary when it came to Emma Hart. She was young too, malleable in the hands of an experienced man of the world such as himself.

* * *

Emma was glad that Reggie had moved away. Although she had been initially impressed with his good looks and dapper appearance, she suspected that Reggie was too preoccupied with himself and his own opinions. His lack of subtlety had upset her, implying that she was responsible for Clive's death. Max, on the other hand, had a depth to his personality. He interested her even though she knew that it might take some time to draw him out.

The string trio was putting their instruments away. The maids were removing the dirty dishes from the afternoon tea in preparation for the official part of the garden party's program: the speeches, thanks, and the announcement of how much money had been raised. The guests were making their way towards the temporary stage as Aunt Florence accompanied the dignitaries to their seats. A lull had come over the assembled company.

Max turned to Emma. 'You look so different.'

'Is that a compliment?'

'I suppose it is.'

'It's hard to look beautiful when you've been battered by a gale, trapped by a fallen tree, and drenched by rain.' Emma laughed at the surprised expression on Max's face. 'Sorry. I tend to be a bit blunt. My aunt says that I have no manners.'

'You are beautiful.'

Emma blushed despite herself. It had been a long time since a man had complimented her. She found it hard to meet his gaze and changed the subject abruptly.

'I find city life so different from the country.' She lowered her voice. 'It's been difficult adjusting to living with Aunt Florence. Not that I'm not grateful, of course. She's been very generous to me.'

'Did you tell her about the death masks?' Max asked, looking at her intently.

Emma took a deep breath. 'There's something I have to tell you. I found out—'

Behind Emma and Max, there was an almighty crash. One of the maids had dropped a tray full of empty glasses and jugs of lemonade. The smashing of glass and the clang of the tray as it hit the ground were deafening. Immediately Max threw himself to the ground, covering his head with his hands.

Emma stood, looking on in shock, as he whimpered on the floor of the summer house, while those who were close by moved away, eyes averted. Putting aside her initial reaction, Emma kneeled down beside him and put her hand on his shoulder.

'It's alright, Max.'

He slowly got to his feet and leaned against the wall of the summer house, breathing heavily. One of the wounded soldiers, the amputee, hobbled down the path towards them.

'Are you okay, cobber?' he asked, a look of deep concern on his face. Max nodded slowly. The serviceman turned to Emma. 'I've seen this before, miss. Shell shock. Take him inside. Somewhere quiet.' He patted Max on the shoulder. 'She'll be right, mate. Give it time.'

He touched his cap and walked away, back towards where the day's proceedings were beginning. The mayor was speaking, drawing the attention of the crowd away from the stricken man. Polite applause rippled through the audience as the mayor went on to thank Mrs Darrow.

'Come with me,' whispered Emma.

She took Max's arm and guided him towards the house. Reggie da Costa watched as they passed by, a smile hovering on his lips. Mrs Darrow, too, was watching their progress, although her expression was one of apprehension.

They found a quiet spot in the library. Emma poured him a glass of water and put it to his lips, insisting that he drink. He was shivering, but the worst of his reaction had dissipated.

'I'd like t– t– to go home,' he stuttered. He lit a cigarette and took a long, slow draw of it. 'I'm sorry, Emma.'

'Don't apologise.' She rang for the maid. 'Ask George to bring the car around.'

They made their way out onto the verandah as Mrs Darrow's black Model T Ford pulled up at the bottom of the steps.

'I'll come with you,' said Emma.

'I'd rather you didn't,' said Max.

'You're still in shock. I couldn't possibly let you go alone.'

Max was too exhausted to argue. Emma took the empty seat next to him and soon George was driving them towards Max's home in North Brighton.

'Do you want to talk about it?' she asked softly.

Max sighed deeply. 'I suppose I owe you an explanation.' He mopped his brow with his handkerchief. 'The War, you know.'

Emma nodded. 'Where did they send you?'

'Flanders. It was June 1916. A little village called Fromelles.'

'Was it bad?'

'Pure hell. We were right on the German frontline. Half of us were raw beginners, the other half Gallipoli survivors. If I close my eyes, I can still hear those bullets whistling through the air.'

He took a last puff of his cigarette and flicked it out the window.

'Did many die?'

'It was a slaughterhouse. More than five thousand casualties in one night. The 59th and 60th battalions were practically wiped out.' Max sighed and gazed out the window. His voice was soft and uncertain. 'I was almost buried alive. They sent me to field hospital.'

'It must be hard to get over an experience like that.'

'It is. Loud noises. They bring back memories.'

Max shut his eyes and sank back into the seat.

'It's understandable that you've been affected by it.'

Max shook his head. 'I don't want to talk about it.'

'I felt like that too. In the end, bottling things up doesn't help.'

He looked at her intently. 'I'm so much better now. I really am.'

Emma nodded. 'We've both been touched by war. I know I can't compare my situation with yours, but it's affected me too. People blamed me for Clive's death. They said that if I hadn't encouraged him to join up, he might still be here. Even Clive's mum wouldn't talk to me.'

'Clive's mother lost her son. She had to blame someone. In the end people make their own decisions, your fiancé included.'

The car pulled up outside Max's house in Durrant Street. It was a little weatherboard terrace with a small front yard and a picket fence.

'This is where you live?'

Max nodded. 'It's enough.'

'Perhaps I'll see you soon?'

'Perhaps.'

Max got out of the car, then leaned in through the open window. 'Thank you, Emma.'

He paused at the front gate, and then lifted his hand in farewell.

Emma was preoccupied as George drove the car back to Seymour Grove. Max Rushforth's war wounds were not visible, like those of the soldiers who had attended Aunt Florence's garden party, but they were just as debilitating. 'Shell shock' the soldier had called it. Despite Max's assurances that he was 'so much better now,' she doubted that he was. In truth, she was not sure whether he was trying to convince himself, as well as her.

Putting aside the fact that he had saved her life, in the face of his fear of the storm, she realised that she was more than interested in him. He intrigued her. And she realised that he was the first person that she had willingly shared her feelings with regarding Clive's death, despite the fact she hardly knew him. But she despaired that she would ever see Max again and that thought made her feel unexpectedly sad.

And then she heard Aunt Florence's voice as if she were sitting next to her.

'Stop feeling sorry for yourself, Emma.'

Meeting Max was making her understand that she had spent too much time looking inward when there were others who were suffering too. There were truths that she would have to face, particularly with regard to herself. She needed to be strong and take control of her life again, not wallow in self-pity. And, if she saw Max again, she would have to be sensible and keep a hold on her emotions, until she knew what she was really dealing with.

Chapter Nine

GRUESOME DISCOVERY AT BRIGHTON BEACH
COLD-BLOODED MURDER

By REGGIE DA COSTA, Senior Crime Reporter

An unidentified woman was found dead yesterday alongside the railway line at Brighton Beach station. A person walking his dog made the gruesome discovery when he found a body buried in a shallow grave. Mr Eric Ingram Smith, of Roslyn Street, Brighton, said his dog became excited and began to dig, revealing a hand protruding from the dirt. Mr Ingram Smith contacted the police.

She was bald!

The victim is presumed to have been in her late twenties and was wearing a grey woollen dress. She had been strangled and her head shaved.

Preliminary examination of the scene suggests that the body may have been dumped within the last forty-eight hours. No weapon has been found.

Residents in the streets surrounding Brighton Beach, who may have witnessed events of a suspicious nature on Saturday night or Sunday morning, are asked to contact Detective Inspector Wasp of the Criminal Investigation Branch. The

54

body has been removed to the Morgue, and a post-mortem examination will be held today. No clue as to the identity of the murderer has as yet been discovered.

Police are investigating. A thorough search of the railway tracks is underway today.

[*The Argus* February 22, 1918]

Chapter Ten

Max Rushforth presented himself at the Brighton police station in response to a telegram that had been delivered to his office at the St Kilda Road Barracks. He wagged it in the face of the constable at the front desk.

'What's this about?' he demanded.

The constable took it from him and read it:

'Mr Maxwell Rushforth c/- St Kilda Barracks
   Urgent STOP report to Brighton Police Station Friday 1 March
   9:00 a.m. sharp
   STOP Employer has been advised of your absence STOP
   Sergeant O'Toole
   Officer in charge'

'Take a seat, please.'

The constable disappeared into the back room. Two minutes later he emerged.

'Follow me.'

Max was placed in an interview room off the main corridor. It was sparsely furnished, with three chairs and a table in the centre and a high window that was covered in a grille. The walls were a faded green, in need of paint.

The door opened and a stout man in a sergeant's uniform strode in. He stood aside as another man entered the room. This man was in plain clothes, small and neat in appearance, about fifty years of age, with thinning hair and sharp features. He sat in the chair on one side of the table while the sergeant took up his position next to the door.

'Good morning, Mr Rushforth. Please be seated. I am Detective Inspector Felix Wasp. This is Sergeant Séamus O'Toole.' He leaned forward. 'The interview will commence once our other witness arrives.' He drummed his fingers on the table then sat back, crossing his feet in front of him.

The door opened again and a young woman was ushered into the room. Max looked startled. 'Emma, what are you doing here?'

Before she could answer, Detective Inspector Wasp spoke. 'All will be revealed. Be patient, Mr Rushforth.'

The introductions were repeated and the policeman got down to business.

'Sergeant O'Toole has drawn our attention to a report that he made on Wednesday, the 13th of February. It concerns the discovery of death masks in a house in South Road, Brighton. You appear to be the only witnesses to this odd situation.' He cleared his throat and stared at Max. 'According to Miss Hart, you knew of the existence of a cellar at the Crabtree house. Could you elaborate please?'

Max flashed an angry look at the young woman beside him.

'If I must. As a child, I stayed with my cousins. They lived a few doors down from the Crabtrees.'

'Where the Crabtrees *used* to live,' corrected Wasp.

'Yes, where they *used* to live.' Max shifted in his seat. 'It was common knowledge that there was a cellar. I never went there myself.'

'Interesting that you should say that. Yet you knew about the key.'

'My aunt cleaned for the old man. He left the key in the planter so that she could let herself in. Mr Crabtree didn't like to be bothered.'

'Your aunt can vouch for this?'

'She died a few years ago.'

'That's convenient. Now, moving on. You rescue Miss Hart from the storm and rather than take her to the safety of her house in Seymour Grove, some three hundred yards from where the tree fell, you take her to a cellar. Why did you do that?'

Emma could contain herself no longer. 'You seem to be suggesting that

Max had some evil plan in store for me. He acted like a total gentleman at all times.'

'Please don't interrupt. Could you answer the question, Mr Rushforth?'

'It was a matter of safety. The Crabtree house was close by. We needed to get in out of the storm.'

Wasp smirked. 'If you say so.' He leaned forward. 'Why were you standing out in the storm? Were you waiting for Miss Hart?'

'Of course not. I didn't know her. I heard the tree fall and saw Emma in its path.'

'Have you seen these death masks before?'

'I have not. As I said, it was the first time I'd been in the house.'

'And yet you knew where the cellar was.'

Max was silent. He looked up at the barred window.

Wasp sat back, his arms akimbo. Then he leaned forward, his eyes fixed on Max.

'Why were you sent home from the War?'

Max took out a cigarette and lit it, his hands shaking.

Wasp continued. 'I have your medical files from the Defence Department here. They state that you saw a psychiatrist while in service. Are you on medication?'

Max's shoulders sagged. 'I have had problems, I don't deny it, but I am so much better now.' He looked sideways at Emma.

'You haven't answered my question.'

Emma stood up. 'I'm leaving. This is none of my business.'

'Sit down, Miss Hart. If I'm going to get to the bottom of this matter, you need to stay.'

She reluctantly took her seat, unable to look at Max.

Wasp continued. 'I reiterate. You saw a psychiatrist when you were repatriated from the Western Front. It says so in your records.'

He opened a manilla folder, removed a document from the top, and started to read:

'Medical file: Private Maxwell Clifford Rushforth

30th July, 1916: The patient was admitted suffering from war neurosis manifest in the forms of mutism and inability to walk. Exhibits repressed aggressive behaviour. Other symptoms include nightmares, insomnia, heart palpitations, dizziness, depression and disorientation.

4th August, 1916: 1st course electroshock therapy. Applied to pharynx.

10th August, 1916: 2nd course electroshock therapy. Applied to spine.'

Max put his head in his hands.

The detective inspector continued. 'Your file speaks of a general improvement in physical symptoms but not in mental function. The diagnosis was that you had suffered some form of mental breakdown. It was recommended that you were unfit for duty and should be returned to Australia.

'When did you return, Mr Rushforth?'

'You know the answer to that. May 1917.'

Sweat broke out on Max's forehead. He stubbed out his cigarette then glanced Emma's way. He addressed the policeman in a trembling voice.

'It's true that I've been unwell, but those death masks have nothing to do with me.'

'Now, now. You're jumping to conclusions. I never said that you were connected to the death masks. But it does seem strange to me that after you took Miss Hart to the cellar, they disappeared.'

'Disappeared? They've gone?' Max looked between Wasp and Emma.

'Yes, they've gone,' said Emma. 'Someone has removed them.'

'Do you swear that you had nothing to do with that?' Detective Inspector Wasp eyed Max sceptically.

'I haven't been back there since that Sunday.'

'We will check up on your movements.' He studied a document in front of him. 'Did you know a woman called Agnes Reason?'

'I don't understand,' said Max, brushing back the lock of sandy-coloured hair that had fallen over his brow. 'Who's Agnes Reason?'

'She was found murdered in September last year. Her death mask was in the Crabtree mansion.'

'I'm confused. If these death masks are missing, how do you know that one of them was of this Agnes woman?'

'Did you bring your sketchbook, Miss Hart?'

Emma reluctantly handed it over and watched as the detective opened it to the drawing of Agnes Reason.

'Do you know her?'

Max glanced at the sketch and pushed it away. 'I don't.' He looked questioningly at Emma. 'Where did this come from?'

'As you know, I went back the next day,' she explained. 'I wanted to see them for myself again. I sketched them. By the time Sergeant O'Toole visited the cellar they'd gone, so I showed him my drawings.'

Max rubbed his forehead. 'I've had enough of this. If you have no further questions, I'm leaving.'

'Sit down, Mr Rushforth. You can leave when you've answered one last question. Were you in the vicinity of Brighton Beach railway station on Thursday, the 21st of February?'

'Of course not. Why would I be?'

'Because the body of a woman was found there. Her head had been shaved. Rather a coincidence, don't you think?'

Max squared his shoulders and stood up suddenly, knocking his chair over. He loomed over the policeman. 'Charge me, otherwise, I'm leaving.'

'You're free to go but we may need to speak to you again.'

Max glared at Wasp then stormed out of the office, slamming the door behind him.

'Bit of a temper, miss? I'd be careful if I were you.'

Emma rose and studied the impassive face of the detective.

'You have no right to treat him like that. You should be ashamed of yourself.'

Wasp didn't flinch. 'It's only the start of our enquiries, Miss Hart. Thank you for attending today.'

Emma took her sketchbook and put it back in her bag. Then, with a withering look at the detective and his sergeant, she left the police station.

* * *

Wasp leaned back in his chair and stretched his arms. 'What do you think, O'Toole?'

'I'd suggest that Rushforth is a person of interest, sir.'

'Oh yes, he is. But we need to rule out the Crabtree family first. I'd like you to see if they know about the existence of these death masks. Find out if any of them has visited the old home lately.'

'I'll get onto it straight away, sir.'

Wasp tapped Max Rushforth's medical file. 'My instincts tell me that the answer lies here.'

* * *

Out on the street, Emma saw Max up ahead, walking towards the railway station. Close by, Aunt Florence's driver, George, was leaning up against the Ford. He tipped his hat to her and went to open the door.

She hesitated. Should she heed the advice of Detective Inspector Wasp and avoid Max? The interview had raised serious doubts about his mental state. It was hard to ignore the facts. If she only considered what she had just heard, that Max was psychologically unstable and had suffered a nervous breakdown, she should sever her connection with him immediately.

'Am I wrong about him?' she said, voicing the seed of doubt that Wasp had planted in her mind.

She considered her personal experience with him and couldn't recall a time when she had felt threatened by him. The fact was that Max had saved her life, and she owed him her support in return.

Emma made her decision.

'Wait for me, George. I'll be back shortly.' She called out, 'Max, please stop! Max!'

He turned at her voice and waited, his face red and angry. 'What do you want? Haven't you done enough?'

'What do you mean? What have I done?'

'Calling in the police.'

He started to walk away from her but she grabbed his arm. He pushed her hand away and faced her.

'Well?'

'Aunt Florence contacted the police, not me. We need to talk about this.'

'What for?'

'Because they think you had something to do with that murder.'

'Is that what you think?'

'Of course not, although you do have a temper.'

Max took a deep breath. Emma noticed that his hands were trembling.

'What can I do?' he asked, in exasperation. 'I'm not responsible for any of this.'

He turned on her, his fists clenched. 'I wish I'd never met you. My past has been dredged up, my personal problems made public and now I'm a suspect in a murder investigation. Thanks very much.'

Emma's temper flared. 'It's not my fault and you know it. I'm not the enemy.'

She paused. Max, in his old navy suit and white shirt, slumped visibly. He shrugged his shoulders, the fight gone out of him.

'It's hard to know who to trust.'

'Use your intuition. You need friends. If you give in now, Inspector Wasp will win.'

'What do you suggest?'

'Prove you had nothing to do with it.'

'Easier said than done.'

Emma bit her lip and tried to control her temper. 'Do you get time off work?'

'Mondays and Thursday afternoons. Why do you ask?'

'Aunt Florence wants me to volunteer with the Red Cross. Their headquarters are in Melbourne. Where are the Barracks?'

'St Kilda Road. South side of the Yarra River.'

'I'll meet you there at noon next Thursday.'

'What are you talking about? How will that help me?'

'The death masks. Let's start with them. You mentioned a waxworks when we met.'

'Kreitmayer's? It closed down.'

'Is there anyone else we can talk to?'

Max Rushforth was wavering. 'One of Kreitmayer's assistants was a friend of the family. Dr Silas Bacon. He works at the Melbourne Museum, next to the State Library.'

'There you are: a starting point. Will he remember you?'

'No doubt.'

'Thursday at noon. Outside the Barracks.' She clapped her hands then turned away, hurrying back towards her aunt's automobile. She had no intention of giving Max any chance to change his mind.

Chapter Eleven

Melbourne was a hive of activity. Now, under the clocks of Flinders Street station, Emma watched in awe as hundreds of people crowded the footpaths, people she would never know or see again. Cyclists dodged horses and carts, and automobiles on Swanston and Flinders Streets. Car horns tooted. Engines roared. Cable trams rumbled and screeched as metal wheels ground against metal tracks. It was, to Emma, a country girl, a cacophony of sound.

What a contrast to Donald, her hometown. Now that was a close-knit community, she thought. Everyone knew everybody. And everyone knew everybody else's business. The occasional car was lost amongst the proliferation of horses and carts along Woods Street, the main thoroughfare. People didn't rush; they stopped to chat. Life was slow and familiar. Unlike Melbourne.

At nine o'clock sharp, Emma presented herself at the Red Cross head-quarters. She was assigned various jobs: spinning wool, sifting flour for cakes, and rolling bandages. Despite the mundane nature of the tasks, she enjoyed herself. There were plenty of women to chat with, and she realised how isolated she was in Brighton. One of the women in charge commended her for making a useful contribution to the war effort. It made her feel good. Surprisingly, her trip to Melbourne was giving her more than the opportunity to see Max. Joining the Red Cross might just offer some variety to her life.

It was midday when Emma Hart stood outside the Barracks on St Kilda Road. She was waiting for Max, who was due to finish work around that time. She smoothed her dress and fixed her hair. Emma had dressed with considerable care that morning, selecting a frock of deep green silk, one of a range that Aunt Florence's dressmaker had made for her. It had a thick waistband and layered skirt down to mid-calf. Fortunately, the Red Cross apron had protected it while she worked there. Her blonde hair was tied back with a large black velvet ribbon and on her head, she wore a jaunty straw hat trimmed in green satin. She tapped her foot and checked her watch. He was late.

At last, Max emerged from the bluestone building which housed the Department of Defence. He was wearing a brown check jacket and plain trousers, both of which required a press. Oddly enough, Emma found his appearance rather endearing.

They stepped forward to greet each other, hesitating as to whether they should shake hands or stay apart.

'There's the tram,' said Max. They climbed on board and found seats in the open section.

'Does Dr Bacon know we're coming?' asked Emma.

'I haven't had a chance to contact him.'

'Tell me about him. Is he a good friend of your family?'

'He helped organise my parents' funeral.'

'I'm very sorry. I didn't realise.'

'You will find Silas rather unusual.'

'How so?'

'He has certain preoccupations. Scientific, in the main.'

The tram lurched up Swanston Street past the Town Hall, finally depositing them outside the Melbourne Public Library. The impressive statue of Sir Redmond Barry, the founder of the library and a former Chancellor of the University of Melbourne, took pride of place on the front lawn. Emma and Max strolled up La Trobe Street and entered the new National Museum through the Russell Street entrance. The temperature dropped as they left the street behind.

Emma gazed around her in wonder. McCoy Hall was lit by a series of skylights. Glass cases filled with animals frozen in time were dotted throughout the main space, interspersed with their skeletons, displayed on raised platforms. Prehistoric birds, which had in a past life ruled the skies, were now restrained by wires that were suspended from the ceiling. Glassy-eyed seals, saved from decay by the work of the taxidermist, were perched on fake rocks.

Time had stood still for a range of wild animals—lions, elephants, coyotes, wild boar, and bears, amongst others—their sole purpose in death to educate and amaze the visitors to the museum. Above the main exhibition hall was a balcony on four sides, which contained more glass cases, skeletons, and illustrations of prehistoric animals. A host of butterflies and moths were pinned to large boards along the side walls, their scientific names printed carefully beneath them.

A small group of children was finishing up their tour. Emma was surprised to see the guide making his way towards them. He shook hands with Emma's companion.

'Max Rushforth. It's been years. What are you doing here?'

'We're here to see you,' replied Max. He performed the introductions.

Silas Bacon smiled. 'I heard that you were back from the War. How are you?'

'Let's just say that I'm glad to be home.'

'You were injured?'

'I'm much better now. I have a job at the Barracks.'

Silas turned to Emma who was staring at the skeleton of a giraffe. 'Do you have an interest in natural history, Miss Hart?'

'This is certainly a most interesting place,' Emma replied politely.

'Let me give you a brief tour.' Silas led them over to a glass cabinet containing an African elephant. 'This is an example of taxidermy at its best. The animal looks real. Note the naturalness and texture of the hide.'

Silas steepled his fingers as he paused. Emma noticed that they were unusually long and finely boned. They were almost feminine, she thought.

'Taxidermy is the art of preparing and preserving animals using their skins in a lifelike manner. The practice goes back hundreds of years when people such as the Ancient Egyptians mummified their dogs and cats when they died. Some of those animals were actually buried with their owners.'

'I doubt if I'd want my blue heeler buried with me,' commented Emma. Max stifled a laugh.

Silas looked at her intently then smiled. 'You're making a joke.' He continued, slightly disconcerted. 'In the early days, a taxidermist would treat the tanned hide of the animal like they would an upholstered chair, sewing it up and stuffing it with whatever was available, such as rags or sawdust. You can imagine that some of those animals didn't look real at all, out of shape, sagging in all the wrong places.'

He removed a horned owl from a case, warming to his subject. 'Later, taxidermists took more notice of the shape of their subject. They made a frame or model that was anatomically correct and covered it with the hide. You still had to stuff it to give it a lifelike shape, like this bird.'

Emma noted Silas Bacon's large ears and the broad sweep of his forehead. He would make an unusual subject for a portrait.

He glanced up at the clock. 'Oh, dear. I didn't realise what time it was. Unfortunately, I need to prepare for the next tour. Perhaps we could meet on the lawn of the library at one o'clock and we can chat then. Would that suit you?'

'You're more than generous,' replied Max. He watched as his friend walked away. 'Unusual man, but very special. Such a good scientific mind.' He glanced at the lifeless eyes of the animals and birds that formed the displays. 'Let's go, Emma. Death is all around us.'

* * *

The sun shone down on Max and Emma as they sat on the lawns of the Melbourne Public Library, watching the cable trams rumble past down Swanston Street. Emma upended her canvas bag and picked out the sketchbook and pencil that she always carried with her. On a new sheet of paper, she wrote the date and title of her next drawing: 'March 7, 1918: Melbourne on a Thursday.'

Max lit a cigarette and leaned back on the grass, watching the people passing by. From time to time he checked Emma's progress as she sketched the scene before her. She started with a rough outline of the buildings and the road in front of them, then skilfully added detail: trams, cyclists, and automobiles, a gaggle of people rushing every which way. She took her time checking the perspective of the composition, rubbing out and adding in elements to produce a pleasing cityscape. Next, she created shadows and depth by shading and crosshatching. All through the process Emma was totally absorbed, seemingly oblivious to her companion who was now watching her intently. Finally, she put her pencil down and held the sketch out in front of her, examining it critically.

Max smiled. 'You're very good. You've studied art?'

'I did think about it once,' she replied.

Their eyes met.

'Your hair's come loose.'

He tucked a strand of hair behind her ear. She turned away, blushing.

'Here comes Dr Bacon,' she said.

Silas had come around behind them. He hoisted his trouser legs up a few inches before he sat down on the grass next to Emma. She noticed that his legs were hairless.

He addressed Max. 'I was trying to remember when I last saw you. I think it was at your graduation.'

'That's right.' Max turned to Emma. 'Silas was a good friend to me after my parents' accident. I'm not sure that I would have finished university without his support.'

'Your sister stood by you, too,' added Silas. 'Do you see much of her?'

'She lives in Townsville. She has her own family to look after, but we do write.'

'Give her my regards. Now, why did you want to see me today? It can't be my good looks and personality alone.'

Silas smiled warmly and leaned in towards Emma. Despite herself, she recoiled slightly. She put her sketchbook back in her bag.

Max stubbed out his cigarette. 'It's a strange story. Do you remember the storm that struck Brighton a month ago?'

'I read about it in *The Argus*. Quite a singular event weather-wise. Three storms all converging on a single geographic point. But what does that have to do with me?'

'We were sheltering from the storm in a derelict house, not far from my cousins' place in South Road. The roof gave way and we went down into the cellar. There were three death masks of women on a shelf.'

'Death masks of women? That's most unusual. Most death masks are of males, although my previous employer, Maximilian Kreitmayer, did make likenesses of famous women. You remember his waxworks in Bourke Street?'

Max nodded. He offered Silas a cigarette then lit up another one. 'I doubt that these were famous women.'

Emma had been listening to their conversation. She interrupted them. 'One mask was of a woman murdered late last year. The police are involved.'

'A murdered woman? That's even more unusual.'

Emma looked intently at Silas. 'I know little about death masks. How are they made?'

'This is a rather delicate subject. I'm not sure that female sensitivities can cope with the crude details of the process.'

'I'm made of sterner stuff than that. I'm a country girl.'

Silas smiled. 'Well, if you insist. There are two types of death masks: either a representation of a face or an entire head.

'Death masks were often made of hanged felons. The impression or mask was taken directly from the corpse. After execution, the body was cut down and usually placed in a chair. The hair and beard were shaved off, as in the case of Ned Kelly, but women's hair was usually left intact.'

'Why was that?'

'Strangely, they didn't think it was nice to remove a woman's hair.'

'These three death masks. The women were bald,' said Emma.

'Again, unusual,' remarked Silas, raising his eyebrows. 'The process of making them is fairly simple but requires skill. First, you shave the head, smear oil over the skull, apply layers of wax or plaster and allow them to set. The next stage is the hard part. You remove the cast by cutting it into sections, then join them together again using liquid plaster. The mould is now complete. Pour liquid plaster in through the neck, remove the mould once it's hardened, and *voilà*, the death mask is revealed.'

'They only made masks of people who were hanged?' asked Emma.

Silas Bacon smiled. He was enjoying himself. 'Not at all. Famous people too: politicians, artists, soldiers, and writers. Lord Nelson. Napoleon Bonaparte. Sir Thomas More.'

Max interrupted. 'That's very informative, Silas. But why would three death masks be in a Brighton cellar?'

Silas shrugged his shoulders. 'I have no idea. I dislike indulging in speculation. Perhaps the owner didn't feel at ease displaying them in a more public place? Outsiders might misinterpret it as being a macabre preoccupation.'

'I heard once that death masks were made for another purpose, but I can't remember what it was called,' said Max.

'Quite right. Death masks were also made to prove the theories behind phrenology.'

'Phrenology? What's that?' asked Emma.

'A pseudo-scientific theory relating a person's character to the shape of his head.'

'I don't understand,' admitted Emma.

'I knew someone once who used phrenology in his work. It's been discredited for a number of years now.' Silas looked at his watch. 'I'd love to go into more detail but time has got away from me. I have another tour. I'd like to see you again, Max, and hear more about what you experienced in France.'

Max shook his head. 'Death masks are a much more interesting topic of conversation. Thank you so much, Silas. You've been very helpful.'

'Goodbye, my friend. And you too, Miss Hart.'

Silas Bacon touched his brow in farewell and stood up. Then he adjusted his trouser legs, brushed off the grass, and strode back into the building.

'You were right when you said that Silas is unusual,' said Emma. 'I don't think I've ever met anyone quite like him. Why would a doctor work in a wax museum? And why isn't he practising medicine now?'

'He was working in a hospital for a while then he left suddenly. There were rumours about him.'

'What rumours?'

'I'd rather not say.'

'I don't think that Silas would be your average doctor.' Her eyes shone as a thought crossed her mind. 'Honestly, I'd love to sketch him. His forehead is so broad and his ears are fascinating. And those long thin fingers.'

'People should be judged by who they are, not by appearances.'

Emma blushed. 'I didn't mean to criticise. He's your friend, after all. I was looking at him as an artist does.' She looked away. 'It's true what you say. People should be judged by what's in their hearts.'

Max took Emma's arm and helped her to her feet. 'I tend to be a bit too serious these days. Take no notice.' He smiled at her. 'Let's catch that tram.'

They stepped up into the cable tram and found a couple of spare seats.

'I'm not sure that we made any progress with those death masks,' conceded Emma, 'but at least I understand why and how they were made. What I don't understand is why a man would murder his wife and then make a death mask. It makes no sense.'

Max shrugged his shoulders. 'Perhaps he was in the War and it pushed him to the edge.'

'But what if Agnes Reason's husband isn't the murderer and he's been wrongly convicted? There were two other masks in that cellar. Who were those women?' Emma stared out the window, lost in thought.

The cable tram trundled past Flinders Street station. A large banner had been hung above the entrance, advertising the latest war loan, calling on the public to invest in bonds that would help finance the war effort.

Emma turned to Max. 'Don't you wish it was over? The War?'

'Most definitely.'

'Do you have plans for the future?'

He considered her question carefully. 'I haven't thought much about it, but I'd like to get back into engineering one day. Make a contribution to rebuilding this world of ours, after all this destruction. And I want a garden.

To grow things.'

'It's true what Detective Inspector Wasp said?' asked Emma abruptly. 'Did they really do that to you? Shock treatment?'

Max nodded slowly. His thick pale lashes fringed sad green eyes. 'It nearly broke me. That doctor was a sadist. I probably would have committed suicide if they hadn't shifted me to another rehabilitation hospital.'

'What was different there?'

'They didn't punish us for having shell shock. We weren't made to feel like cowards. One of the doctors told me that everyone had a breaking point. The War scared everyone, he said, but not everyone could cope with it. I was one of those.'

He had confirmed what the wounded soldier had said on the day of the garden party. His reaction to loud noises was the result of what was termed 'shell shock.' Emma had never met anyone suffering from it, until Max. Thunder and lightning, even the crash of the tray at the garden party, reminded Max of the sounds and flashes of gunfire and cannon on the battlefield. What he had seen on the Western Front had stayed with him.

The tram rumbled past the Town Hall. 'Mine's the next stop,' said Emma. 'Are you catching the train back to Brighton?'

'No. I have to catch up with some work. I'll head back to the Barracks.'

'In that case,' she said, 'this is for you.' She reached into her bag and handed him a piece of paper tied with a green ribbon.

'What's this?' Max asked. He untied the ribbon and unrolled the paper. It was a sketch of him in Aunt Florence's library, leaning against the mantelpiece and staring off into the distance. It was a good likeness.

'Is this how you see me? You make me look—'

'What?'

'Substantial. Like someone with a future.'

'Isn't that what you are?'

The tram ground to a halt outside Flinders Street station. Emma jumped down and turned back. Max was still staring at her portrait of him.

Chapter Twelve

Aunt Florence heard the front door close and walked out into the hallway. The grandfather clock was striking half-past four. Emma was hanging her canvas bag on the hatstand and avoided her great-aunt's questioning look.

'Why so late?'

Emma started to climb the stairs. 'I don't know what you mean.'

'Don't lie to me. No more secrets, remember? I'll see you in the parlour in five minutes.'

In her bedroom, Emma stared at herself in the mirror. 'She's right. I promised. No more secrets.' She took off her hat and changed into a simple white blouse and navy skirt, then brushed her hair and descended the staircase.

Mrs Darrow was seated in the parlour, reading the newspaper. She put it down and gave her great-niece her full attention. Emma sat opposite her.

'Well?'

Emma took a deep breath and then confessed that she had rendezvoused with Max in the city. She went on to describe their meeting with Dr Silas Bacon. When she had finished, she sat back and waited.

'You feel that the police might implicate Max in the murder of Agnes Reason? Is that why you're gathering information about death masks?'

'Exactly. I believe Max is innocent. We have to start somewhere.'

'You saw his behaviour at the garden party. You still think he's perfectly sane?'

'He has problems but he's never raised a hand against me. He saved my

73

life, putting himself in danger.'

'What about his medical records? He doesn't sound stable.'

'He needs help.' She wagged a finger at her aunt. 'I know what you're going to say, Aunt Florence, but I want to do this. I want to help him. I can't believe that he had anything to do with Agnes Reason's murder.'

'Admit it, Emma. You like him.'

'Perhaps I do.'

'You've had nothing but trouble since you met Max. Finding death masks. Being locked in the cellar. And then there's the indignity of being questioned by the police. You seem incapable of admitting that he might have something to do with murder.' She relented slightly, seeing the stricken look on the face of her great-niece. 'However, there's no doubt, from what you told me, that Detective Inspector Wasp overstepped the mark. There appears to be no evidence connecting Max with this murdered woman.'

'You've been a supporter of causes for most of your life,' said Emma. 'Can't you make Max one of them?'

Florence Darrow was weakening. 'You are a manipulative little minx. If I help you, will you promise me that you'll avoid getting too friendly with Max?'

Emma nodded in agreement, a smile breaking out across her face. 'I've been thinking about what we should do next. Could we ask Reggie da Costa for information on Agnes Reason's death? After all, he is a crime reporter.'

Aunt Florence studied her great-niece. 'What are you saying? You want to play Sherlock Holmes? This is real life, not fantasy.'

'What if Agnes Reason wasn't killed by her husband? What if the maker of the death masks did it?'

'You don't know that.'

'But I'd like to find out the truth. You can't let a man die in prison when he did nothing.'

Aunt Florence raised her eyes to heaven and then nodded slowly.

'Does that mean you'll help me?' said Emma.

'Against my better judgment, I will.' Mrs Darrow consulted her social calendar. 'We'll have Mr da Costa over for dinner on the 16th of March.

Invite Max too. Tell him that George will drive him home.'

Emma kissed her aunt on the cheek. 'You are rather wonderful, you know.'

'Fiddlesticks. Go and get ready for dinner.'

When she had gone, Florence Darrow stared up at her father's portrait, hanging above the mantelpiece.

'What do you think, Daddy? Have I done the right thing?'

Eoin Brown looked off into the distance, somewhere above her head, but it seemed to Florence that his expression was one of approval.

Chapter Thirteen

S ilas Bacon was troubled. After Max and Emma's visit, he had been preoccupied with his work, but now that he had time to think, he realised the peculiarity of their discovery. During his time at Max Kreitmayer's waxworks, Silas had met his fair share of unusual people who exhibited an unhealthy fixation with death and its customs. But he had never heard of a person who collected death masks for a hobby or who secreted them away in a derelict house. And there was the alarming fact that one of them was of a murdered woman.

Silas caught the tram along Victoria Parade and dismounted close to Young Street in Fitzroy. He lived in a small terrace house in Napier Street between the footwear factory and the Presbyterian Church. As he walked along the footpath, he thought about the likelihood that someone had created those masks using deceased persons, but dismissed it out of hand. Wax likenesses were celebrations of the famous and the infamous, not the ghoulish preoccupation of disturbed people. But that still begged the question: why would anyone keep such items in the way that Max and Emma had described?

Silas put such thoughts aside as he opened the gate to the little front yard of the home he had shared with his parents when they were alive. He looked at the paint peeling off the weatherboards and the mass of weeds in the overgrown garden. One of the posts holding up the porch was rotting at the base. He must fix that some time. He opened the screen door and stepped into the dim hallway. The bedroom to the right had been his mother's study. In his mind's eye, he could still see her corpulent figure hunched over a large volume on ancient history.

His bedroom was next along. On the window ledge was a stuffed raven, its beady eyes fixed on a point on the other side of the room. Silas dropped his bag on the bed and removed the books that he had borrowed from the museum library. He placed them carefully on the bookshelf above his desk and then put his bag in its usual place next to the wardrobe. He hung up his coat and then walked through into the kitchen, opened the back door, and proceeded out to the shed, which occupied most of the space along the back of the block. His father had been an inventor and the shed had been his domain.

Silas went inside and examined some of the items that his father had invented. There was an artificial hand made from wood with two mechanical fingers that could grasp objects, a hearing aid shaped like a small horn that attached to the ear, a 'bicycle' with four wheels instead of two for those with balance problems, and a kettle that, in theory, wouldn't boil dry. All were spectacular failures.

Despite this, Silas's father had been so absorbed in his work that he had made up a bed in the corner of the shed so that, whenever inspiration struck him, he could work without disturbing his wife or son. It was a strange arrangement, but Silas had grown used to it.

Both his parents were dead now and the house seemed empty without them.

Silas returned to his bedroom and reached for the porcelain skull that he kept on the shelf above his desk. It was L.N. Fowler's phrenology bust. Emma and Max's visit had triggered memories of a time in his life when he had subscribed to the theory that the shape of the skull was an indication of character traits and mental faculties. Those days were long gone. He traced his fingers over the named character and mental abilities that divided the brain into twenty-seven different organs. Silas had committed them to memory and could still recall them. He replaced the model on the shelf and took a well-thumbed volume: Wells' *A New Illustrated Hand-book of Phrenology, Physiology and Physiognomy* from his bookshelf. He shook his head in disbelief. How could he have ever believed in phrenology? How could he have been so gullible?

* * *

After he had finished dinner, he took his jacket from the hall cupboard, and then stepped outside. Napier Street came alive in the evenings and Silas savoured the experience of watching life from a distance. Night shift workers on bicycles were heading off to toil in the factories that dotted the suburb. Children played in the street. Mothers talked over side fences to their neighbours, while their husbands sipped beer and sat relaxing on the porches. Their arms linked together, young girls promenaded up and down the road deep in conversation, never missing the opportunity to size up an eligible male. Poverty was all around, but the simple pleasures were there to be enjoyed.

This particular evening there was a purpose to Silas's walk. He was intending to visit a colleague from the days of Maximilian Kreitmayer's Wax Museum. Walter Eames had worked alongside Silas as a wax modeller, retiring when Kreitmayer died in 1906. Without the genius at the helm, Walter had said, there's no point continuing. Silas had stayed on until 1910, when a position had opened up for him at the Melbourne Museum. In the same year Kreitmayer's widow, Harriett, closed the wax museum and re-opened the business as a cinema.

Although Eames lived close by, Silas avoided him. Walter Eames was a chatterbox and Silas found him exhausting. But it was necessary to talk to him about Max Rushforth's discovery. Walter was the only other person he knew who might be able to shine a light on the creator of those death masks. He found the man bending the ear of his neighbour, who was attempting to withdraw into his house but was failing to make any headway. A look of relief passed over the neighbour's face when he noticed Silas standing at the gate.

'Must go. You have a visitor.' He darted inside the house leaving Eames in mid-sentence.

'Walter Eames. Good to see you again.' Silas stood patiently, waiting for the look of recognition.

'Silas Bacon. I haven't seen you for twelve years. Come inside and have a drink with me. We have so much to catch up on.'

Eames opened the door and led Silas into a small front room full of overstuffed floral armchairs.

'Please sit down.' He stood leaning up against the mantelpiece as his former colleague sank into the soft cushions of the couch.

'Do you mind if I smoke, Walter?'

'Not at all.'

Silas offered him a cigarette, but Walter refused. 'I gave up six months ago,' he explained.

'I was thinking about the waxworks the other day and here you are! Such a coincidence. What a shame Harriett closed it down. It was an institution, a Melbourne institution.' He shook his head in wonder, his eyes shining. 'Those wax models. Queen Victoria on her throne, Fat Fred and Stout Sarah, the fattest boy and girl in the world, little Tom Thumb and Pope Pius X. And what about Li Huang Ling, the Chinese giant?'

He pointed at Silas. 'Do you remember Sacco, the man they couldn't starve? In that glass room for six weeks, just spa water and cigarettes and he was in the peak of condition when they let him out. Amazing.'

Eames paused for breath.

Silas interrupted him. 'I remember it all. I was there, you know. I need to ask you about something,' he said, silencing Eames by raising a long, thin finger to his lips. 'A friend of mine found three death masks of women in a Brighton house about a month ago. Do you know anything about them?'

Walter Eames was dumbfounded. 'No, I don't.'

'One of the masks was of a woman who was murdered late last year.'

'That's strange. There are few people with the expertise. You and I, Desiderio Cristofani in Sydney and, of course, our dear departed Maximilian were all skilled in wax modelling. I don't know who would have made them.'

'I'll never forget my first death mask,' said Walter, his eyes shining. 'He was a murderer. They finally caught up with him as he was about to despatch his fifth victim.'

As Walter talked on, Silas remembered how Max Kreitmayer had taken him through the process of creating death masks, in his first days at the wax museum. Their subject had been executed two hours earlier and had been carried out to the Dead House in the courtyard next to the Melbourne Jail. He had been propped up in a chair. Silas remembered the impression of the rope on the man's neck, the chalky appearance of his skin, the detachment in his expression. While Kreitmayer prepared the plaster, Silas trimmed the man's hair till it was little more than stubble. Then, as he slowly and methodically sharpened the razor, a chant rose unbidden from the deep recesses of his memory. He shaved the dead man's skull and, as he worked, he intoned under his breath:

'A razor must be straight.

A razor must be polished.

A razor must be sharp.'

'What are you saying, Silas?' Kreitmayer had asked him.

'Something from my past,' replied Silas. 'Something I would rather forget.'

* * *

Walter Eames' voice brought him back to the present.

'Now you speak of it, a man came to see me about nine months ago. He was a strange one. He'd been to see Harriett Kreitmayer first. When she couldn't help him, she sent him to me.'

'What did he want?'

'It was an odd request. He wanted to know how to make death masks. I spoke to him for perhaps an hour or two and then he left.'

'Did he say who he was?'

'He never did.'

'You haven't seen him again?'

'No, I haven't.'

'Why did you think he was strange?'

'It was what he wanted from me. He asked me if I'd ever created a death mask while the subject was still alive. I explained that on a technical level the mould would be ruined if the face were not immobile. The plaster has to set. And then it dawned on me what he was suggesting. I was appalled, to be honest. A person would suffocate in the circumstances unless straws were put in the nostrils. I asked him if that were the case but he wouldn't answer. It brought our conversation to an end. He left immediately.'

'Do you remember what he looked like?'

'Tall, fair, unhealthy looking. Sallow skin.' Eames shook his head. 'Do you think he has something to do with those death masks?'

'I don't know. It's hard to believe that a sane man would consider using a live person as a model. It doesn't bear thinking about.' Silas Bacon stood.

'I wonder if I did the right thing, telling him about the process. I tend to get carried away discussing my craft.' Walter frowned and followed Silas to the door, and then he touched his arm. 'There was something else that struck me as strange. I had the distinct impression that he was wearing a wig.'

'A wig?'

'That's right. What about that drink? Can't you stay a little longer?'

Silas shook his head. What Walter had told him was disturbing and he needed time to himself to consider the implications of the stranger's visit, if indeed there were any. He made his farewells and shut the gate behind him.

As Silas strolled home in the dark, his uneasiness grew. As a scientist and a doctor, he valued logic, reason, and facts. His visit with Walter had made him recollect a part of his life that he'd prefer to forget. A time when he had believed in phrenology. A time when he had believed that some people were born evil, a belief at odds with his current thinking. But Walter's encounter with the mysterious stranger showed that there was a dark side to the human personality where evil dwelled. He shuddered involuntarily. What he wished for most of all was that the past should stay where it was: in the past.

Chapter Fourteen

The keys to being a successful crime reporter were, as Reggie had said, a good memory, investigative skills, and excellent contacts. It was the latter that *The Argus's* intrepid journalist drew on after he received Mrs Darrow's invitation to dine with her and her great-niece. Apparently, the ladies were eager to know the finer points of the Agnes Reason murder and hoped that Reggie would be able to enlighten them as to the facts of the case. His curiosity was aroused by the strange request.

Suspecting that there was more to this than a detached interest, he contacted Detective Sergeant Blain, his primary source of information about police matters. Fortuitously, the detective had been involved in the Agnes Reason case and was partial to Scotch whisky. Blain would be waiting at The Duke of Wellington Hotel on the corner of Flinders and Russell Streets.

It was ten forty-five. Reggie put on his hat and coat and headed out into the street. The first hint of autumn was in the air, as a cool wind whipped around his ankles. He wrapped a muffler around his neck to keep out the chill. As he walked up Collins Street, he glanced in the shop windows and was dismayed at the drab colours of the clothing favoured in the war years. Not for him the grey worsted suit. He turned into Russell Street and headed down the hill to the familiar two-storey pub, said to be the oldest in Melbourne.

'The Duke,' as it was called, was a workingmen's pub, with its well-worn furniture, the familiar smell of grog ingrained into the bare boards, and the slight odour of urine emanating from the toilets.

Detective Sergeant Clary Blain was waiting, leaning up against the bar. His bulbous nose and blotchy face were covered in spidery red veins, speaking of over-indulgence and lack of exercise. Reggie noted with a sly grin that the policeman hadn't ordered a drink. If *The Argus*'s chief reporter on crime wanted information, he would pay for it in alcohol.

'Clary, my friend, the well is dry,' he observed.

'Not for long.' He leaned over the bar and beckoned to the publican. 'Scotch. One of your best.'

'A beer for me,' said Reggie. 'Let's find a table.'

Once Clary had a whisky in front of him, Reggie got down to business. 'I've been hearing that some new evidence has turned up on the Agnes Reason case. Is that true?' He phrased his question in general terms, hoping that Blain would not realise that he was fishing for information.

'You amaze me, Reggie,' said Clary. The policeman had taken the hook. 'The Agnes Reason murder has hit a snag. You remember that her husband was tried and convicted just before Christmas?'

'Of course. Ex-soldier. Violent. A wife-basher. Straightforward case.'

'Not so anymore.' Clary sculled the drink. Reggie raised his hand and the bartender responded by refilling the policeman's glass. 'Detective Inspector Wasp is buzzing around about the discovery of some death masks in Brighton.'

'Death masks? What's that got to do with Agnes Reason?'

'One of them looks like her.'

'You're joking?'

'Nah. Anyways. The masks went missing but the girl that saw them drew them. Wasp saw the sketches and reckons one's Agnes. He thinks that the bloke that was with her is involved. Another ex-soldier. Could be a connection, he thinks.'

'What? A connection with Christian Reason?'

'Wasp has an itch and he likes to scratch it. He's looking into it, he says.'

'Who's the bloke? Any names?'

'Rushforth. Maxwell Rushforth.'

Reggie sat back in his chair. 'I think I'll have a scotch too.' He signalled to the bartender. 'And the girl?'

'She lives with some wealthy aunt in Brighton.'

Reggie took a swig of his drink.

Clary continued. 'Wasp sent a team to the Crabtree house where these death masks were kept. The cellar had been stripped of evidence but, in the backyard, they found a bag of hair buried in the garden. Some animal had dug it up. Wasp reckons that it's female hair. Long and blonde but looks like it came from multiple sources. Agnes was blonde. We've got some forensic blokes looking at it.'

'Not such a straightforward case after all. This means that Reason had an accomplice.'

'Looks that way, don't it?' Clary raised his glass to the bartender. 'One more, my friend.' He leaned in towards Reggie. 'I've another bit of information for you too. The woman who was found dead near Brighton Beach? Strangled. Head shaved. Remember her?'

'Of course. I wrote about it.'

'We've identified her. Bessie Cartwright.'

Reggie grabbed his hat. 'Thanks, my friend. You might have just given me the biggest story in my career.'

'Don't quote me, Reggie. I'll deny everything,' Clary called after him.

Detective Sergeant Clary Blain scratched his nose and smiled. He lifted the glass and studied the amber liquid, swirled it around, and sculled it, smacking his lips in satisfaction.

* * *

Reggie had stopped in at the offices of *The Argus* after meeting with Clary Blain, to collect his file on the Agnes Reason case before driving home. He bathed, dressed with care, choosing one of his best suits, ran brushes through his thick black hair, and, after bidding farewell to his mother, jumped into his Dodge Roadster and pointed it towards Seymour Grove. From long experience in the journalistic world, he knew that the abiding wisdom was to strike while the iron was hot. Armed with inside information from Emma Hart and Max Rushforth, Reggie would jump the gun on the opposition and publish before they got wind of the story. It was rare that a reporter had a relationship, albeit a slight one, with a witness to a murder case. He was excited at the prospect.

Mrs Williams answered the door and hung Reggie's hat and coat on the hall stand. Reggie checked his reflection in the mirror then followed the housekeeper into the parlour, where the hostess and her great-niece were waiting. Max Rushforth was sitting in the corner. Reggie drew himself up to his full height and shook hands with Mrs Darrow and Emma Hart, his hand lingering in that of the beautiful young woman.

'It's so good to see you again, ladies.' He ignored Max.

'Greetings, Mr da Costa,' said Florence Darrow. 'You're late. We'll go straight into the dining-room.'

Reggie muttered his apologies and followed the formidable Aunt Florence into a lavishly decorated room with a highly polished, black oak floor, covered with a deep blue and crimson Turkish rug. The walls were wainscoted with oak, with wallpaper featuring golden vases containing garlands of flowers on a bright Nile blue and cream background. Two bay windows of ruby and amber stained leadlight were framed by deep blue velvet curtains.

In the middle of the room, an antique dining table was set for four. Against the wall stood an elaborately carved sideboard of black oak, on which was placed an expensive collection of silverware including an ornate tea set and tray. Reggie calculated that the silverware alone would pay for another of his overseas jaunts.

Reggie took his seat at the bottom of the table opposite Aunt Florence, with Emma and Max facing each other along the sides. After saying a prayer of thanks, Mrs Darrow instructed the cook to serve dinner.

As they were savouring a succulent roast chicken, Reggie took the opportunity to ask his hostess why she desired information about the death of Agnes Reason.

'Let's do justice to our meal first,' replied Aunt Florence, pursing her lips. 'A murder is not an appropriate subject when we are eating dinner.'

Suitably chastened, Reggie da Costa selected a slightly less salacious topic of conversation and referred instead to the state of the War and the noticeable reduction in enlistments.

'Have you heard that the military are changing the rules for those who enlist?'

'Are they indeed?' asked Mrs Darrow.

'Instead of the usual twelve weeks' training in Australia, recruits will be sent to Egypt or England and then undergo preparation for the War.'

'They want to boost numbers,' Max commented.

Reggie looked at him in surprise. 'Quite right. Only one hundred and nine men enlisted in Victoria this week, compared to one hundred and sixty-six the previous week.'

'And even less will join up now, because they'll be afraid that they won't be trained properly before they're sent to the Western Front,' added Max.

Reggie raised his eyebrows in surprise. 'I thought you'd be in favour of the changes.'

'If they knew what they were going to see, no one would enlist.'

'How's that?' said Reggie with a smile. 'We actually agree on something.'

'Don't count on it,' muttered Max, casting his eyes in Emma's direction.

* * *

Dinner finished and the plates removed, Aunt Florence addressed Reggie. 'I've invited you tonight for a particular purpose. We were hoping that you could enlighten us as to the circumstances surrounding the death of Mrs Agnes Reason.'

'I can do that, Mrs Darrow.'

'When you have finished, we will provide you with some information in return. In a manner of speaking, I have wined and dined you, Mr da Costa, and now you must pay.'

'Indeed, I always pay my debts.' Reggie stood and searched through his brown leather Gladstone bag, removing an envelope and spreading its contents on the dining table. There were about a dozen newspaper clippings, some notes, and a few sheets of paper that appeared to be police reports.

'May I have the floor?'

'I thought you already had it.'

He began to read from his notes. 'Mrs Agnes Mary Reason, of Were Street, Brighton, was reported missing by her sister, Mrs Sally Lineham, in late August 1917. She had not heard from Agnes in two weeks which she said was most unusual. Mrs Lineham had attempted to visit her sister but the door was blocked by her husband, Christian William Reason, an unemployed ex-soldier. She reported that she could hear their little boy crying inside the house. That same day she visited the police station and asked them to investigate.

'The police attended and were met by Mr Reason who claimed that his wife had run off, possibly with another man. The neighbours were interviewed and they confirmed that they had not seen Mrs Reason since mid-August. The house was searched but no evidence of foul play was discovered. They also confirmed what the sister had claimed, that Mr Reason was a heavy drinker and beat his wife. One neighbour thought that she had seen Agnes Reason leaving the house on the 15th of August, around the time that she disappeared, but she couldn't be sure. Another person said that he'd seen her talking to a man at the beach.'

Reggie glanced at Emma. She was listening intently. 'Mrs Reason was initially classified as a missing person. On the 10th of September, her body was found at Green Point on the Brighton foreshore. That was about a mile from her home.'

'Did they determine how she died?' asked Emma.

'Decomposition was well-advanced but she'd been strangled. They identified Mrs Reason from the St Christopher medal she wore around her neck.'

He referred to his notes again. 'Christian William Reason was the main suspect. He was remanded into custody. Within two months of the discovery of Agnes's body, Christian Reason was found guilty of murder and sentenced to life in prison.'

'Did the police have any other suspects?' asked Emma.

'According to my sources, no.'

'What was the evidence against him?'

'It was overwhelming: arguments overheard by neighbours and excessive drinking. The man had a temper.'

'Did he admit to the crime?'

'He protested his innocence. Reason admitted that he had sometimes struck his wife, but it was only when he was under the influence of alcohol.'

'He sounds like an awful man,' commented Mrs Darrow.

'I don't disagree with you.'

'Why would he kill her? Was she intending to run off with another man?' asked Emma.

'That's what the defence claimed but there was no indication of that. Her clothes and possessions were all accounted for. The only things missing were what she was wearing on the day.'

'Did the sister testify?'

'She sealed the case for the prosecution. She said that her brother-in-law had a temper and drank too much. She also claimed that her sister would never have abandoned her little boy.'

'What's happened to the child?' asked Aunt Florence.

'He was given over to Agnes's family.'

'Poor thing.'

'What about Reason's war record?' asked Max. 'Was that taken into consideration?'

'He was part of the Gallipoli campaign in April 1915. He spent four and a half months there before being sent on to France. It probably saved him from being hanged.'

'Did they find any physical proof of his guilt? A weapon perhaps?'

'Agnes was strangled. By the time they found her, it was difficult to tell what he'd used.'

'What did Mrs Reason look like?' asked Emma, thinking back to the death mask.

'Average height, blonde, slim, very attractive by all accounts. Twenty-four years old.'

Emma leaned in. 'Was there anything odd about the body?'

'Odd? I'm not sure what you mean.'

'Anything unusual about her appearance?'

Reggie grinned. 'Now you mention it, there was.' He checked through the police reports and tapped his finger on the page. 'Bald. She was bald.'

Emma sat back and looked at Aunt Florence then Max, seeking confirmation. 'So that means that she was killed shortly before the death mask was made.'

Reggie played the innocent. 'What death mask are we talking about?'

Emma spoke up. 'Two months ago, a storm lashed Brighton.'

'How could one forget that?' said Reggie. 'It was headline news.'

'I was caught in the storm and was trapped under a fallen tree. Max rescued me.' She glanced at the sandy-haired man sitting across from her. 'We sheltered in the Crabtree mansion in South Road. The roof fell in and we went down into the cellar.'

'What did you see?' Reggie asked, licking his lips.

'Three death masks. All of women.'

'Go on.'

'I went back the next day. I suppose I had trouble believing what I'd seen. I took my sketchbook and drew their faces. Aunt Florence called in the police once I told her about it. When we went back there, the death masks had gone. I had to show my sketches otherwise the sergeant would have thought I was making it up.'

'And this policeman identified one of the women as Agnes Reason. Am I right?'

'Indeed, you are.'

'Can I see your drawings?'

'Certainly.' She reached over and opened up her art folio, which she had brought with her into the dining-room. 'Here they are.'

Reggie da Costa turned over the pages of the sketchbook, studying each face intently.

'You're quite the artist.' He stabbed a finger at one. 'That's Agnes Reason. Oval face, big eyes. No doubt about it. Did the police check the other two drawings against other murders or missing persons?'

'They glanced at them,' replied Emma. 'They never asked to keep the sketches.'

'Then they were negligent.' He held up the second drawing. 'If they had made enquiries, they would have recognised Lillian Broderick of East Brighton. Disappeared November 1917.'

'She's dead?'

'Missing. Body never found.'

'How do you know about her?' asked Aunt Florence, raising her pince-nez to view the picture.

'I know her parents. They called me when the police failed to follow up on her disappearance.'

Silence fell as the gravity of the situation descended on them. Two of the three death masks identified. Two women murdered; one body not found. Lillian Broderick's parents were soon to face the distinct possibility that their daughter was dead.

'What do we do now?' asked Emma.

'Call in Detective Inspector Wasp,' said Aunt Florence.

'Do we have to?' asked Max, looking pained.

Reggie flashed him a look. 'Is there a problem?'

'Wasp seems to think that I might have something to do with Agnes Reason's murder.'

'Ridiculous,' said Emma.

'Why would he think that?' asked Reggie.

'He surmised that because I knew about the existence of the cellar, I must know something about the death masks.'

'If he had firm evidence you'd be behind bars. I know Wasp. He'll leave no stone unturned to get his man. If he gets you in his sights, you're in trouble.'

Max went pale. Reggie noticed that his hands were shaking. If this man were involved in the murders, then he must have another side to his personality, which he was keeping well hidden. On the surface, he was a weak, withdrawn man suffering from shell shock. He was definitely unstable, of that Reggie was sure. He only had to think back to the garden party to prove that.

Emma, her aunt, and Max had lapsed into silence. Reggie, however, was in his element. 'Let me have another look at the first woman.' He took back the sketchbook and studied the portrait. 'I'll go through the archives and see if there's a woman, missing or dead, who fits her description. She's not a recent case.' A thought struck him. 'There's something else I should tell you.'

'What's that?' asked Aunt Florence.

'A recent death. You might have read about it. A woman strangled near Brighton Beach railway station. She was identified last week as Mrs Bessie Cartwright, although that piece of information hasn't been officially released yet. Someone had shaved her head.'

'You think that the killer was going to make a death mask of her too?' asked Emma.

'I don't know.'

'This just gets worse.'

'I've never seen anything like this,' said Reggie, unable to suppress the exhilaration he was feeling. 'It's unique. I can only assume that these death masks are a kind of trophy.'

'What do you mean by "trophy"?' asked Aunt Florence.

'A keepsake. Murderers sometimes like to have a memento to remind them of a kill. A piece of jewellery, a lock of hair. This is the first time that I've seen a death mask made for this purpose.'

Aunt Florence was distinctly rattled. 'Trophies? Killers? What are we involved in here?'

'Murder, pure and simple. But, on second thoughts, not so simple.'

It was time to go. Reggie had completed his part of the bargain and, in return, had been gifted the story of the decade. It had all the hallmarks of murder most foul: three female victims (one unknown), possibly four, plucked from their day-to-day existence and subjected to a terrifying death at the hands of a sinister and sadistic killer. It called into question Christian Reason's guilt and shone a light on the scrappy investigation techniques of the police force. If the deaths of all four women were connected, Melbourne had a killer on the loose.

Reggie almost salivated at the effect that his report would have on his readers. They would be shocked, intrigued, and begging for more. Nothing inspired interest like the news that there was a crazed murderer out there. He retrieved his notes and the newspaper articles and slid them back in his bag.

'Mr da Costa,' said Aunt Florence, 'you understand where your loyalties lie in relation to what we have told you tonight?'

'I am very aware where my loyalties lie,' he assured her. 'Thank you for a magnificent dinner and a most interesting evening. I'll be off now.' He shook hands with Max and took one last long look at Emma. 'It's been a pleasure meeting you again, Miss Hart. I look forward to our next encounter.'

As he left the house, he rationalised his position. His dinner companions would have to understand that he was a journalist first and foremost. What they had told him was now in the public domain. He was a man with scruples but sometimes it was necessary to sacrifice them for the greater good. And his readers were the greater good. It would be the biggest crime story to hit the headlines in months. It might even stop the War being the main item. Reggie had the urge to run such was his excitement, but he managed to show restraint and left the house at a sedate pace.

* * *

After Reggie and Max had left, Aunt Florence and Emma sat in the library discussing the revelations of the evening.

'Max was very quiet,' commented Aunt Florence.

'I think he'll be very worried after what Reggie said about Wasp.'

'Reggie's an interesting man. He's a little old for you but that didn't stop me marrying Mr Darrow. People say he's ambitious. You could do much worse. On the other hand, Mr Rushforth is a dark horse. We don't know much about him at all.'

Emma's eyes narrowed. 'I'm not sure I like or trust Reggie. He's so sure of himself.'

'That's his Italian heritage. He takes after his father. Very flamboyant. Although he has excellent taste in clothing, whereas your friend always looks rather crumpled.'

She leaned in towards Emma. 'Mr da Costa, his father. He left Mavis. He ran away with another woman. The maid, in fact. Quite shocking.' She took a sip of water. 'Reginald da Costa doesn't miss much. I think he likes you.' She smoothed her dress. 'It really is time for you to forget the past. Your mother didn't send you here just to be my companion.'

Emma sighed. 'I'm tired. This evening has been rather exhausting.' She stood and went to the door. 'Sleep well, Aunt Florence.'

The elderly woman put down her glass and gave some thought to what she should do next. It would be counter-productive to ban Emma from seeing Max. Her great-niece was a stubborn young woman and would align herself more with the damaged ex-soldier just to spite her. It was a safer course of action to empathise with her and be her confidante. This would give Reggie da Costa the time and opportunity to woo her. Hopefully, Emma would ultimately show a preference for *The Argus's* senior crime reporter.

And if she didn't, and it turned out that Max was complicit in the crimes, Aunt Florence promised herself that she would be there to pick up the pieces.

Chapter Fifteen

DEATH MASK MURDERER ON THE LOOSE IN BRIGHTON
Bizarre discovery in cellar

By REGGIE DA COSTA, Senior Crime Reporter

It was only two months ago that a severe storm ripped through the bayside suburb of Brighton, wreaking havoc and leaving two people dead in its wake. But last week another twist to this strange tale was added that has left our law enforcement officers baffled.

A young couple, seeking shelter from the storm on that day in February, descended into the cellar of a derelict mansion in South Road, the former home of wealthy Thomas Crabtree, now deceased. To their astonishment, Miss Emma Hart, an aspiring artist, and Mr Maxwell Rushforth, a former soldier, discovered three death masks displayed on a shelf. The plaster casts were of women. When the police came to investigate, the masks had disappeared!

Two women identified

Using sketches that Miss Hart had made of the death masks, the police identified one of them as Mrs Agnes Mary Reason, whose body was found at Green Point, Brighton on the 10th of September, 1917. Her husband is presently serving a life sentence in Pentridge Prison for her murder.

Faced with the inaction of the police to further identify the remaining death masks, Miss Hart and Mr Rushforth turned to *The Argus*'s senior crime reporter, Reginald da Costa, for assistance. He was able to identify a second victim, Miss Lillian Broderick of East Brighton. She disappeared in November 1917. Police had listed the twenty-year-old as a missing person even though her parents suspected foul play. Her body has not been recovered. The identity of the third death mask remains unknown.

Police are now looking into the possibility that the death of yet another woman may be connected. She has recently been identified as Mrs Bessie Cartwright of Gardenvale, aged twenty-eight, mother of two children. She was found strangled to death alongside the railway tracks near Brighton Beach station in late February.

In a bizarre twist, it can now be revealed that Mrs Agnes Reason's head had been shaved prior to her death and that a similar attempt was made with regard to Mrs Bessie Cartwright. Sources reveal that a bag of blonde hair was found buried in the backyard of the Crabtree mansion. It is likely therefore that the persons who committed the murders and prepared the death masks were working in tandem, unless they are one and the same. All three women resided in the Brighton area.

Yesterday *The Argus* approached Detective Inspector Felix Wasp, who oversaw the Agnes Reason case and prosecution. He was asked to comment on his failure to identify Miss Broderick from the drawings that Miss Hart made of the death masks. At the time of going to press, *The Argus* had not received a response. We invite our readers to scrutinise the sketches of the three women, which are reproduced below.

It appears that the Death Mask Murderer has been active in the southern suburbs of Melbourne since mid-1917. Anyone with information, which might assist with the investigation of these heinous crimes, should contact either *The Argus* or the Victoria Police.

[*The Argus* March 21, 1918]

Chapter Sixteen

Emma was in Melbourne, working at the Red Cross Headquarters. She was making up 'comfort' parcels to supplement the Australian soldiers' army rations. Into each went sardines, tea, biscuits, tobacco, soap, salt and pepper, chocolates, prunes, raisins, powdered milk, corned beef, salmon, tinned butter, cheese, and sugar. A veritable feast compared to the soldiers' staple diet of bully beef and biscuits.

While she worked, she listened in to the women complaining about the sharp increase in the cost of food and groceries, which was well ahead of the rise in wages.

'Meat costs five shillings more than before the War,' one woman said. 'The government should do something about it.'

Emma had to admit that living with Aunt Florence had its advantages. Her great-aunt didn't skimp when it came to food but she also made sure that the poor benefitted from her good fortune. She frequently sent food parcels to families who were struggling.

It was two o'clock and Emma had finished for the day. As she removed her mob cap and hung up her apron, she heard a voice call out behind her, 'Emma Hart. I didn't expect to see you here.'

She turned around and stopped dead. In front of her was a pretty young woman with curly black hair, well-shaped eyebrows, and a curvaceous figure. It was her best friend from school, Sophie Fitzgibbon. While other girls in Donald had been preoccupied with boys, sport, and babies, Emma and Sophie had been devoted to art and music, respectively.

They had drifted apart after Emma's engagement to Clive Atkins, but the fatal blow to their friendship came with Clive's death. When she was finally persuaded to run an errand for her mother in town, the first person that Emma met was Sophie. Whether it was over-sensitivity on Emma's part or awkwardness on Sophie's, the former came away with the feeling that her friend was blaming her for Clive's death: if she had not encouraged him to enlist, he still might be alive.

It was over two years since Clive Atkins had died at the Somme. And now Emma and Sophie stood face to face, in the headquarters of the Red Cross. The atmosphere was tense.

'I didn't realise you were in Melbourne too,' said Emma, not looking directly at her former friend.

Sophie smiled bleakly. 'It's been a month now.'

'Are you still playing the violin?'

'As a matter of fact, no.'

'What do you mean "no"?'

'I caught my hand in some farm machinery. I can't play anymore.' Sophie held out her right hand, a thin red scar snaking down her little finger.

Emma recoiled in horror. 'How awful. When did that happen?'

'Just after you left Donald.'

Emma's anger dissipated. She took a deep breath. 'Let's find somewhere to talk.'

They found a café nearby and ordered tea, then sat and talked for what seemed hours. It was as if the years were peeled away, back to the times when they had been adolescent girls, full of hope for the future and an optimistic belief that they could conquer the world. And then the conversation moved to the obstacles that had come between them and their dreams, and how they were dealing with them.

'I moved down to Melbourne,' said Sophie. 'I needed to get away and find a life for myself. It's too stifling at home. Everyone feels sorry for me.'

'A fresh start. I needed that too, although I didn't realise it at the time.'

'I really am sorry about Clive. I never meant to imply that you were responsible for his death. To be honest, Emma, I saw you here last week but wasn't sure whether you'd want to speak to me.'

'I'm sorry that I treated you that way. I was overwrought. I wasn't sleeping. I needed a friend; I just didn't know it.'

Sophie scribbled down her address and handed it to Emma. 'This is where I'm living now. I start at the Melba Memorial Conservatorium of Music next month. I made a decision: if I can't play then I'll compose.'

Emma smiled broadly. 'You're amazing.'

'So are you.' She studied her friend. 'Those drawings you made of those death masks are truly exceptional.'

'What are you talking about?'

'Today's *Argus*. The article about you and the ex-soldier in the cellar. It's an amazing story.' She took a newspaper out of her bag. 'Headline news.' Seeing Emma's horrified expression, she added, 'You didn't know?'

Emma grabbed the newspaper and skimmed the report then read it more slowly. 'I knew I couldn't trust him,' she muttered under her breath. Emma was flushed with anger. 'I wonder if Aunt Florence has seen this? She'll skin Reggie da Costa alive. And what about Max? Poor Max.'

Sophie Fitzgibbon sat silently, watching her friend's reaction. 'I'm sorry if I've upset you. I thought you'd seen it.'

Emma shook her head. 'Don't blame yourself. It's not your fault.' She smiled and hugged her friend. 'I've missed you. Let's meet again soon.'

As she walked away, Emma's emotions threatened to overwhelm her. She reflected on the extremes that life could throw up in one day. On the one hand, she was overjoyed to reconnect with her old friend. On the other, she had seen her privacy invaded and an episode in her life splashed across the pages of a Melbourne newspaper. Not only was her part in this sordid drama public knowledge, but the article implied that she and Max were in a relationship, which could be very embarrassing for them both. Her mouth set in a grim line. Emma promised herself that Reggie da Costa would soon learn that there were repercussions for betraying trust.

* * *

'You're a stupid boy,' cried Mavis da Costa. 'You're just like your father!

Fancy publishing that outrageous rubbish about a "death mask murderer" without telling Mrs Darrow. I've just got back from a tongue-lashing at her house when I was expecting a quiet afternoon knitting with the cream of Brighton society. It's taken me years to establish myself after your cad of a father took off. You've ruined it in one day.' She shook her head in fury. 'Tell me now. What are you going to do to make this right?'

Reggie was used to tirades from his mother, but this was different. He had certainly sailed close to the wind in some of his more outrageous exploits, but he'd always been able to talk his way out. Today her reaction took him aback. He had crossed the line.

'I'm sorry. I will go directly and apologise.'

Mavis was furious. 'You may have ruined your chances with Miss Hart. Apparently, journalists from *The Age* turned up at her door wanting an interview. You silly, silly boy.'

Reggie rallied against his mother's harsh criticism. 'Emma's a bit too assertive for my liking. She needs to be more submissive. Always stating her opinions, as if they matter.'

'You amaze me, Reggie. As if her personality is important. She's worth millions.'

'Alright. I hear you.'

She stabbed her finger at his chest. 'Just like your father! Why couldn't you take after the English side of the family?'

'Mother, please, you're being melodramatic. I can fix this.'

'Apologise. Tell Mrs Darrow you've made a terrible mistake.'

'Give me twenty-four hours and I'll have both of them eating out of my hand.'

Mavis muttered in disgust, 'I'm going up to bed. I've lost my appetite.'

Chapter Seventeen

Reggie da Costa was true to his word when he presented himself at Seymour Grove. He checked his appearance in the hall mirror and followed Mrs Williams into the parlour. Five minutes elapsed before the entrance of the formidable and most displeased Mrs Florence Darrow.

Despite himself, Reggie was not quite as confident as he had professed to be to his mother, and was threatening to strangle the bunch of flowers that he held in his grasp.

'I'm surprised that you should have the audacity to come here,' said Mrs Darrow.

'I bring these most unworthy flowers as a peace offering to you and Miss Hart,' said Reggie, looking appropriately deferential and meek. 'It is extremely kind of you to see me after I appeared to breach your trust.'

'Appeared? Appeared? There's no appearance here. You breached our trust.'

'If I could explain?'

Aunt Florence studied him through her pince-nez. 'I confess, I'd like to hear this.'

'Thank you. May I sit down? No? As you wish. Well, I was sitting at my desk last Monday, checking through clippings from *The Argus* on women who were missing or who had died over the last two years, to see if any woman resembled Miss Hart's first sketch.'

'Hurry up. I'm a busy woman.'

'My sub-editor is a man who likes to keep abreast of the stories we are working on and he had been watching me surreptitiously. I had to tell him what I was investigating.'

'You *had* to tell him?'

'He's not the kind of man you try to bamboozle.'

'Bamboozle?'

'Trick. Mislead.'

'No need to explain the English language to me, young man.'

'I told him everything. I had to. It was either that or dismissal.'

Aunt Florence took a step back, raised her pince-nez then fixed him with a stare. 'They would sack you?'

'They would.'

Reggie concentrated on holding eye contact. The wait seemed interminable. At last Mrs Darrow blinked.

'I am not happy. My great-niece's reputation has been smeared. We have had reporters on our doorstep. What have you got to say?'

Reggie looked suitably contrite. 'I'm so sorry. I feel terrible. I have betrayed your trust although, as I have explained, it was not willingly done. I hope that you and your delightful great-niece can forgive me.'

He held out the flowers and Aunt Florence took them, albeit reluctantly. She weighed up her options then deliberated. 'One more chance. I do this for your mother rather than you. I remind you that you are on notice. You will not publish anything unless I say so. Is that understood?'

Reggie smiled unevenly. 'Certainly. I wouldn't dream of distressing you a second time. One last thing. Is Emma here? I would like to apologise to her as well.'

'She's about to go out. I doubt if she would want to speak to you.' Mrs Darrow waved her hand in the air dismissively. 'Give your mother my best wishes. I look forward to seeing her next week. You can show yourself out, Mr da Costa.'

Florence Darrow swept out of the room, leaving the bedraggled bouquet of flowers lying on the side table. Reggie sighed. Ingratiating himself with Emma's great-aunt was proving more challenging than he'd expected.

* * *

Emma was in the hallway, listening in to the conversation between Reggie and her great-aunt. By the time Reggie left, she was sitting in the library reading a book. Aunt Florence entered the room and raised her eyebrows at the sight of Emma engrossed in the pages of John Buchan's *Greenmantle*.

'You don't like that author. Admit it, you were listening in.'

'Why shouldn't I? The man's a scoundrel. As if he were threatened with the sack? I don't believe it.'

'I'm not sure that I do either.'

Emma put the book aside. 'I wish there was something I could do to help Max.'

'But what if he's involved in these deaths?'

'I don't believe it.'

'How can you be so sure?'

Emma wrung her hands. 'I just know.' She looked appealingly at her great-aunt. 'You must understand what I'm saying? You loved Mr Darrow. You would have done anything to help him.'

'I hate to disillusion you, my dear, but I didn't love my husband. Ours was a marriage of convenience.' She paused, registering the look of shock on Emma's face. 'Don't be alarmed. Both of us gained much from the marriage. He wanted a companion and someone to run his household. I wanted what money and marriage can give a woman: social standing and the means to pursue my causes. I could never have achieved anything if I stayed a spinster. Before you accuse me of being mercenary, I will say that I liked and respected my husband and I never betrayed his trust.'

'You're suggesting that I should marry for money?'

'You can do better than Max.'

'You mean Reggie?'

'Not necessarily. Principles are important. But money is too.'

'I'd rather stay a spinster than marry Reggie.'

'If that's the case, you have to make something of your life. What do you want?'

'I don't know.'

'Then I'll make two suggestions. Firstly, you need to deal with this Clive business. You need to take responsibility for what happened to him. Face up to it and get on with your life. Secondly, a lifetime's experience has shown me that you can't fix someone. Don't try and fix Max. When you're older you'll realise that people have to help themselves, you included.'

Emma shrugged her shoulders, a sulky expression on her face. 'Why can't you leave me alone? I did alright without you.'

'I doubt that very much,' said Aunt Florence, exasperated. 'Why don't you go down the beach and do some drawing. You need some fresh air.'

* * *

Emma stood outside the house, her face red with anger. 'Wretched woman,' she muttered under her breath.

She looked up and scowled. The last person she wanted to see was leaning against a Dodge Roadster, fiddling with his hat.

'Damn,' she said. She stalked up to Reggie da Costa. 'You're not waiting for me, are you?'

'I was told that you were going out.'

'You're not my favourite person, you know.'

'Did your aunt explain everything to you?'

'Oh yes. I understand your predicament completely. Self-interest triumphs over principles every time.'

Reggie laughed. 'Anger makes your cheeks a pretty peach colour.'

'Don't patronise me. You've embarrassed me and invaded my privacy.'

'I am truly sorry.' His smirk gave the lie to his apology. 'As I explained to Mrs Darrow, I had no choice.'

Emma tied her hat firmly under her chin. 'Goodbye, Mr da Costa.'

'One minute of your time, please,' Reggie said.

Emma stopped and glared at him. 'Well?'

'I should warn you. Your reputation will be in tatters if you become involved with Max Rushforth. You can do much better than him.'

Emma glared at him. 'How dare you!'

'The truth is that I adore you.'

'I find that hard to believe. Look in the mirror. You'll see the object of your affections there.'

'If you won't see sense, then consider this. I know that you have an excessive interest in these murders. And that you are protective of your friend, Mr Rushforth. So, as a sign of my deep respect and high regard for you, I bring you a peace offering.'

'And that is?'

'I will visit Christian Reason in Pentridge Prison and see if he can shed any light on who really committed his wife's murder. I can't promise anything but I will do my best.'

Emma paused, looking at him intently. 'You would do that, for me?'

'I will.'

'Then take Max with you. He has so much to lose if they accuse him of being involved in those murders.'

'Is that really necessary?'

'If you mean what you say, then you'll do it.'

Reggie put on his hat. 'Very well, I'll take him, if you insist.' He frowned, a note of anger rippling beneath the surface. 'You should take my advice and forget him.'

Emma turned on her heel and was soon in South Road heading towards the beach. She watched Reggie drive past but didn't acknowledge him.

* * *

Down by the beach, Emma sat on the sand. Two children were running up and down, stopping every now and then to gather shells, while their mother followed behind them. A fisherman was sitting on the pier, his line dangling into the water. Seagulls were squawking at each other, fighting over some fish bait that had been left behind. It was a relief to be out of the house.

She looked around her. The change in the seasons had come and gone. The sun was still warm on her skin but lacked the intensity of summer.

An autumn breeze was whipping up the little waves that splashed against the shoreline. It seemed like an eternity since the storm had savaged the beachfront.

Emma took a pencil out of her bag and opened her sketchpad. She wrote the date and title of the picture she was about to draw: 'March 23, 1918: Brighton Beach.'

The You Yangs were obscured by a misty blue haze on the other side of Port Phillip Bay, while the skyline of Melbourne was just visible. It was a beautiful day. She started to sketch a panorama, from the little weatherboard bathing boxes that lined the beach on one side to the fishing boats that bobbed up and down on the waves on the other.

'That looks good.'

The voice came from behind her. She looked up to see who was speaking. The sun was behind him and it was hard to see his features. She shaded her eyes with her hand and smiled up at the tall man in a black hat and coat.

'Thank you,' she replied. 'Is that you, Lewis?'

'It is, Miss Hart.'

'Enjoy your walk.'

'I will. It will be all the better for seeing you.' He tipped his hat and walked on.

Alone again, she went back to her drawing.

Chapter Eighteen

Silas Bacon read Reggie da Costa's report about the Death Mask Murders with a mixture of fascination and repulsion. He was no closer to understanding why three death masks of women should be kept hidden away. However, he feared that their existence pointed to a murderer at large, a man who had met with his former colleague, Walter Eames, some nine months before. A man who had questioned him about the making of death masks and horrifically, whether one could make them pre- as well as post-mortem.

And now the authorities had discovered that not one, but possibly two of the death masks were of women who had been killed recently. What if this man had used the information, that Walter had so innocently shared with him, to do vile and unspeakable acts? What if the anonymous man were the Death Mask Murderer?

He was disgusted with himself. He was a scientist first and foremost, a man who put analysis, rationality, and evidence before nonsensical speculation. Emotion should never take precedence over logic. The fact was that there was no proof that the man who had met with Walter had anything to do with these murders. It could have been an innocent enquiry, nothing more. In Silas's opinion, it would be premature and hasty to take his suspicions to the police without evidence to support them.

But his lack of action would come back to haunt him. Silas picked up the Tuesday edition of *The Argus* and scanned the news. The usual reports on the War: twenty-six young women had arrived in Melbourne, having married Australian servicemen in London; a Sixth War Loan was being raised by the

Commonwealth Bank; Paris was being shelled again.

In a small paragraph at the bottom of page four, he saw the headline 'Man dies in Fitzroy house fire.' He read how Walter Eames, aged sixty-eight years, former wax modeller at Kreitmayer's Waxworks Museum, had been found dead. It was suggested that Mr Eames was smoking in bed and had fallen asleep. But Walter didn't smoke.

Silas laid aside the newspaper and stared up at the ceiling. Four days after Reggie da Costa had published his report on the Death Mask Murders, Walter Eames was dead. As a scientist, Silas didn't believe in coincidence. What if Walter's anonymous visitor had taken steps to eliminate a potential witness?

Filled with unease, Silas met with Maximilian Kreitmayer's widow, Harriett, on the Tuesday after Easter. Together they commiserated with each other over the loss of their former colleague.

'I visited Walter recently,' said Silas. 'He told me that you had a visitor who enquired about making death masks. You referred him to Walter.'

'That's right, but it was months ago. Once I told him that I had never made a death mask, he was in a hurry to be off. It was an afterthought of mine to recommend that he contact Walter.'

'What did he look like?'

'He was a strange one. When Maximilian was alive, my job was to dress the wax models. False hair, eyebrows, glass eyes, appropriate clothing. You can imagine that I can spot a wig or false beard a mile away. That's what struck me about this stranger. His hair and moustache were fake.'

'What's this all about?' she asked. 'Do you think he had something to do with Walter's death?'

'Unfortunately, I do.' Silas shook his head. 'Did you see the report on the Death Mask Murders?'

'I did,' replied Harriett. She hesitated, and then said in a trembling voice, 'You're saying there's a link between this man and the fire? That he deliberately burned down Walter's house? That he might be the person they're talking about in the papers?'

'Consider this: Walter died only a few days after this article was published.

He was a witness to this man's identity. I don't believe in coincidence.'

'That means he might come after me,' she said, noting Silas's concerned look. 'Don't worry, I'll be careful. My son-in-law, F.W. Thring, is managing director of J.C. Williamson Films. If anyone can protect me, he can. But you be careful too. Ask too many questions and this man might find his way to you.'

Silas smiled grimly. 'Death holds no fears for me. But you're different. You have family and friends. Take care, Harriett. Trust no one.'

He caught the cable tram down to the St Kilda Road Barracks. It was vital that he catch up with Max Rushforth. It was now a matter of life or death.

Chapter Nineteen

It was a fortnight since Reggie da Costa's article appeared in *The Argus*. Max and Reggie stood outside the main entrance to Pentridge Prison. On each side of the gateway was an octagonal tower, with cross-shaped slit windows and crenellated parapets, one of which was surmounted by a clock tower. Pentridge looked like a medieval fortress, made of impenetrable bluestone and, in a sense, it was.

A southerly breeze whipped leaves around the bare forecourt of the prison. Clouds scudded across the sky, hiding the sun. Warders, like birds of prey, stared down from guard towers that were positioned along the massive bluestone walls. It was a forbidding place, ugly and stark, a place one would not choose to visit except in special circumstances.

The drive to Coburg in Reggie's 1917 Dodge Roadster had been a silent one apart from one exchange at the start of the journey.

'I didn't want to bring you,' said Reggie. 'I did it for Emma.'

'Emma's the only reason I'm here,' said Max.

'We know where we stand then.'

* * *

It had not been easy for Emma to convince Max Rushforth that he should accompany Reggie da Costa. She had arrived at Max's place on Easter Monday, unannounced. Max was resistant at first to the idea of going to Pentridge. There was mutual distrust and dislike between the crime reporter and himself, he argued. Reggie's article was an exercise in betrayal, exposing both Emma and himself to public scrutiny. Emma had agreed but pointed out that the article was not the issue. Inspector Wasp had Max in his sights. Couldn't Max see that visiting Christian Reason was a necessary step in proving his own innocence? Perhaps Agnes' husband could shine a light on the real killer and, by so doing, bring him to justice? And what about Christian Reason himself? Here was an innocent man, wallowing in a prison cell, while the real culprit was out there terrorising and murdering women.

'You're right,' agreed Max. 'It's the moral thing to do.'

As he handed her back into the Ford, his hand had lingered in hers.

'You give me faith in myself,' he had said. 'You give me the strength to fight back and prove that I'm innocent.'

* * *

And thus, on a Thursday afternoon, the two rivals for Emma's affections stood before the pointed arch and timber gates of Pentridge Prison's entrance, preparing to step inside the bluestone walls.

'The guards are touchy at the moment,' said Reggie. 'Attempted escape. Bound and gagged a warder on sentry duty. They were caught trying to scale the walls.'

Reggie slipped on his overcoat as they approached the first set of gates. In his hand, he carried a letter from Christian Reason's lawyer, which would admit them into the prison. At the entrance to the jail courtyard, they submitted to a search, then passed through a second set of gates into the prison proper.

Christian Reason was being held in 'A' division. They passed through double wooden doors, which opened into the cellblock. The smell hit them: a pungent mixture of body odour and urine. Reggie gagged and covered his nose with a handkerchief. Max wrinkled his face in disgust. The doors closed behind them and they stepped into the gloom.

The cellblock was two storeys high, with cells on each side of a central gallery. Max looked around him, at the white-washed walls, the thick wooden cell doors with their heavy brass padlocks, the filtered light that guided their way along the corridor. A prisoner shuffled along the walkway above, his leg irons dragging and clanking. As the poor fellow passed the other inmates, they called out and whistled, causing the warder accompanying him to swear loudly.

'In here.' The prison officer indicated a small room to their left. He undid a large padlock and opened the barred door. Inside were two vacant chairs and a stool. A shrunken husk of a man sat behind a simple wooden table; his wrists handcuffed together. A small window high in the wall afforded some light in the gloom. 'You have ten minutes.' The warder took up his position inside the interview room and sat on a stool, looking bored.

Max and Reggie took their seats. Christian Reason raised his head. He had a purplish bruise beneath his left eye and dried blood on his ear.

'Who are you?'

'Reginald da Costa from *The Argus*. This is Max Rushforth. We would like to ask you some questions concerning your wife's murder.'

Christian looked the journalist up and down. 'You're a swell. Been to war?' Reggie shook his head. 'What about you?' he said, indicating Max.

'Western Front.'

'Poor bastard. I'll talk to you.'

Reggie and Max exchanged looks, then the journalist nodded.

'Tell me about yourself, Christian,' said Max.

'I joined the 16th Battalion A.I.F. in Perth in 1914. I done my training and sailed to Egypt. I was twenty-three years old. I was at Gallipoli in April 1915, and a few months later I joined the 1st Australian Division and was sent to the front-line trenches near Armentières.'

'When did you get back?' asked Max.

'Middle of last year. Agnes and I settled in Melbourne with our little boy. Don't see him no more.' He paused. 'Why do you want to know about Agnes?'

'About two months ago I came across three death masks in a Brighton cellar. One of them looked like your wife.'

'It was in the newspaper. One of the screws told me about it.'

'I wrote the article,' said Reggie.

'You sure it was the wife?'

'Positive,' replied Reggie. 'Do you know anything about how those death masks came to be there?'

'No.'

'Did your wife ever mention Lillian Broderick or Bessie Cartwright?'

Christian shook his head. 'Agnes didn't get out much. Just the shopping and a walk along the beach.'

'They said at the trial that you hit her. Do you think she was planning to run away? Maybe with another man?'

Christian Reason pulled a face. 'Not Agnes. She loved our little lad.' He rubbed his chin. 'I'm ashamed of what I done to that woman but I never killed her. Look at me now. In this hell hole.'

'What's it like in here?' asked Max, glancing around.

'Goes like clockwork. Up at ten past six. Washed and dressed by half-past. Breakfast. Seven o'clock I work in either the boot factory or the timber yard. Dinner then back to work at one. Get the idea?'

Max nodded. 'And the food?'

'They call it "grey death," a stew made from offal and tendons. Delicious.' He smiled grimly.

'Christian. It's important,' said Reggie. 'Did Agnes ever speak about meeting anyone when she was out walking? One of your neighbours saw her talking to a man.'

'Funny. She mentioned something about a man. His daughter had run away. That was about a week before she left.'

'What else did she say?'

'Just that it was a shame when people didn't get on. I think she was trying to tell me that I had to stop drinking. That it was ruining us. She was right. Agnes cared about us despite what I done to her. War messes you up. You know what I mean?'

'Yes, I do.' Max went silent.

'Did she say what this man looked like?' asked Reggie. 'Where he lived?'

Christian put his head down and studied the floor. He shook his head.

'Time.' The prison warder was on his feet.

'Get me out of here.' Christian Reason brushed the tears from his eyes. 'I can't stand this much longer.'

'We'll do our best,' said Max.

Reason was escorted back to his cell, dragging his shackles along the dark slate flagstones.

Max shivered. The cold was starting to work its way into his bones, despite the heavy wool coat that he was wearing. Even Reggie was feeling the effects of the chill emanating from the bluestone and slate. He blew onto his hands and rubbed them together, trying to get the warmth back into his fingers.

'Let's go,' said the prison guard. He followed them out of the cellblock into the courtyard. A bleak sun was trying to break through the clouds. Reggie and Max stared up at the bluestone walls.

'That was a bloody waste of time,' said Reggie.

'Not for Christian, it wasn't,' said Max. 'Poor bugger.'

A heavy door slammed shut somewhere behind them. One of the large timber gates of the main entrance opened and they stepped through, relieved to be outside again in the fresh air. Free.

Chapter Twenty

Detective Inspector Felix Wasp straightened up the pencils that were on his desk. He skimmed the file that he had accumulated on the case he now referred to, in private, as 'The Death Mask Murders.'

Three women were dead, three women whose heads had been clean-shaven. He was perplexed. In all his years in the police force, he had never come across such an extraordinary *modus operandi* as that of the perpetrator of these murders. Why would anyone resort to such excesses? What was their motivation? He racked his brains and couldn't come up with a simple answer.

Agnes Reason. The case against her husband had been straightforward. A violent man driven to murder by drink. The discovery of her death mask muddied the waters. It appeared that he had been in cahoots with an accomplice who had those skills, for it appeared unlikely that he had ever made one.

Lillian Broderick. The police had ignored her parents' insistence that she had met with foul play, and contended that she had left home of her own volition. In an unwelcome development for the authorities, she had been identified as the subject of a second death mask by none other than the crime reporter for *The Argus*. Wasp resented Reggie da Costa's precocious talent as an investigator, given that the reporter had scooped him on securing the identity of the second woman whose face had been immortalised in plaster. It wasn't good for the reputation of the Criminal Investigation Branch or for him personally. The police's failure to investigate Lillian's disappearance looked like incompetence. It was a bad business all around.

Bessie Cartwright. Another murdered woman with a shaved head, whose body had been found in February. And someone had leaked her identity to that wretched reporter, da Costa. If he found out who it was, he'd have their guts for garters. At this stage though, thankfully, no death mask had been located, which would have linked the case incontrovertibly with those of Agnes Reason and Lillian Broderick.

Pressure from his bosses was being applied. They had read the press coverage on the case and didn't appreciate the implied criticism. Wasp had to find a suspect, and fast.

He perused the information provided by Detective Sergeant Clary Blain and Sergeant Séamus O'Toole, both of whom had met with him the previous day.

'What is the status of Thomas Crabtree's surviving relatives, Sergeant?' he had asked O'Toole, his piercing gaze appraising the portly policeman.

O'Toole puffed out his chest, straining the brass buttons of his uniform. 'I've never seen a more money-grabbing, unprincipled lot, sir. There are two cousins, both in their sixties, as well as a nephew who owns a grocery store and Crabtree's former accountant who claims he was owed money. All of them fighting over the Crabtree estate.'

'Any suspects amongst them?'

'I think not.' He referred to his notebook. 'The nephew, Randolph Stuckey, is about to pull out of the suit. He's run out of funds to pay the legal costs. He lives in Rainbow. That's two hundred and fifty miles away. I think that counts him out.

'There are the cousins, Joseph and Archibald Crabtree, but they seemed completely bewildered when I questioned them about the cellar. They claim that they visited the house years ago when Thomas and Matilda lived there, but not since. I didn't think that they were lying.'

'And the accountant?'

'Alfred Bynes is already under investigation for fraudulent use of his clients' accounts. I think he'll be seeing the inside of a cell very soon. He seemed more unethical than deadly.'

'Have you discovered the whereabouts of the adopted son? He was seven at the time of his mother's death.'

'According to his relatives, Frederick Crabtree was sent to boarding school.'

'Which one?'

'No one could tell me. The trail's gone cold on that one.'

'Most unfortunate,' said Wasp. 'Thank you, Sergeant. Good job.'

He dismissed O'Toole with a wave of his hand.

Clary Blain was sitting in a chair in front of Wasp's desk, taking notes. He looked up as the sergeant left the room.

'I think we can rule out the family. There's little motivation or opportunity to commit murder,' he ventured.

'I agree,' said Wasp. 'Let's look at what we have.' He referred to his notes. 'Henry Crabtree, aged two, died in a tragic accident. Drowned in a fishpond. Matilda Crabtree died in 1882. It appears that she took her own life. Frederick Crabtree: sent to boarding school in 1882 after his mother's suicide. No current address known. Thomas Crabtree died in 1908.'

He leaned forward and sniffed. 'That's not alcohol on your breath, is it, Blain?'

Clary blanched. 'No, sir. My mother's cough mixture.' He cleared his throat.

Wasp paused and then lowered his eyes to his notes. 'Randolph Stuckey, nephew, lives two hundred and fifty miles away. That excludes him. Cousins, Joseph and Archibald Crabtree, claim ignorance of the cellar. Nothing there to contradict that. Accountant, Alfred Bynes, questionable reputation but no evidence to suggest involvement in the murders.'

'Where does that leave us, sir?'

Wasp tapped the file on Max Rushforth. 'That's where it leaves us. I had a telephone call from Pentridge last Thursday. Apparently, our suspect paid a visit to Christian Reason. How's that? Is it a case of the accomplice visiting his partner in crime?'

Clary Blain scratched under his arm. 'Interesting.'

'Rushforth was accompanied by Reggie da Costa.' Wasp's eyes narrowed as he spoke the reporter's name. 'I'd love to see that underhanded, egotistical hack hoisted with his own petard.'

Blain looked puzzled. 'Sorry sir, I'm not following you.'

Wasp scowled. 'I'd like to see da Costa charged with a crime. Poetic justice, Detective Sergeant.'

Blain nodded slowly and tapped his nose. 'Understood.'

'Where did he get that information on the bag of hair that we found in the Crabtree yard? And Bessie Cartwright's name? If I get my hands on the sneaky rat that passed him that information, I'll—'

'What, sir?' asked Blain, beads of perspiration breaking out on his forehead.

'Never mind.'

Clary hesitated. 'You're not going to call da Costa in for an interview, are you?'

'What's the point? He'd only lie or claim he's protecting his sources, that sort of rubbish.' Wasp tapped his fingers on the desk, his displeasure evident.

'Is there anything I can do for you, sir?'

'There is, Detective Sergeant. Rushforth and Reason. Both of them were soldiers, weren't they? Let's see if their paths crossed on the battlefield. You have contacts in the Department of Defence?'

'Yes, sir. I'll get right onto it.'

'Contact the Melbourne Museum and ask them if they know anyone with knowledge about death masks. I'd like to speak to an expert, if there is one. We need to make the link between Rushforth and death masks.'

Wasp rubbed his hands together. 'The net is tightening around Maxwell Rushforth. A little bit more evidence and we'll have him where we want him: on a charge of accessory to murder.'

Chapter Twenty-One

It was an odd group that gathered in the drawing-room of Mrs Darrow's house in Seymour Grove on a Saturday afternoon. There was Reggie da Costa, his thick black hair tamed by the liberal use of hair oil, wearing a sharply-cut tan check suit, Max Rushforth, dressed in pants and a high-waisted jacket in khaki brown, reminiscent of a serviceman's uniform, and Dr Silas Bacon, all large ears and broad brow, attired in loose-fitting grey trousers and a dusty black jacket. The doctor glanced around, glumly studying the opulence of his surroundings and the baby grand piano in the alcove.

Emma Hart poured tea while Aunt Florence greeted the menfolk. Once the introductions were completed, they sipped their drinks and helped themselves to the cakes and sandwiches that had been provided by their hostess. Conversation was rather stilted at first but slowly the men began to relax, only lapsing into silence when Mrs Darrow took the floor. Her navy dress was cut to make the best of her ample figure, assisted by corsetry that was as inflexible and unyielding as its wearer. She was the type of woman who commanded attention. She studied her guests then began.

'I've invited you here today to discuss the case that Mr da Costa has rather melodramatically dubbed "The Death Mask Murders."'

She paused, eyeing Reggie's sheepish expression.

'I have invited Dr Bacon along on Mr Rushforth's recommendation. We will hear from him later.

'Now, to the purpose of this meeting. In earlier years I supported causes that I thought worthy. Today, my great-niece has, as it were, brought me out of retirement to help her investigate an apparent miscarriage of justice.

'Emma will begin.' She nodded to her great-niece.

Emma smoothed the skirt of her blue and white sailor-style dress. 'You're all familiar with the circumstances that led to the discovery of the death masks in South Road, Brighton. We suspect that their creator may have been involved in the murder of two of the women.'

'Before you go on, I have a question,' said Reggie, interrupting her. He looked pointedly at Max. 'Why were you in South Road on that Saturday?'

Max licked his lips. 'I went to see my cousins.'

'Where exactly do they live?'

'That's none of your business.'

'Then tell me, how did you know about the cellar?'

'I don't see why I have to explain myself to you. You ask too many questions.'

'It's my job.'

Max walked over to the window and looked out at the garden. The trees had lost their leaves and stood bare against the sky. In the fork of one was a nest, now empty. He took a few deep breaths and faced the crime reporter.

'I know what you're implying. That I might be involved in this business. That I might even be a murderer.'

Reggie shifted in his chair.

'No one believes that,' said Emma, alarmed at the direction the conversation was taking.

Max gazed at her. 'Thank you. However, not everyone shares your opinion.'

He took two steps towards Reggie.

'You see everything in such simple terms. Black or white. Innocent or guilty. It must be easy for you, making accusations and hiding behind your so-called reputation as a crime reporter.'

Reggie's face went red. He was out of his chair in a flash, fists clenched.

'Stop this!' cried Mrs Darrow. 'You're like two children itching for a fight. If you can't put aside your petty squabble then I'll ask you both to leave.'

She waited. There was silence. Her tone changed. 'Emma's right. No one is calling you a murderer, Mr Rushforth.' She stared defiantly at Reggie, who sat down again, then addressed herself to Max.

'Now, tell us about your visit to Pentridge. What was your opinion of Christian Reason?'

Max took his seat. 'I think Reason was telling the truth when he said he didn't kill his wife.'

He described their interview with the convicted man, and how he had readily admitted his propensity for violence and dependence on drink.

'So, he is a violent man,' said Aunt Florence.

'War encourages violence. You can't shrug that off just because you've come home.'

'And you, Mr da Costa?'

'Reason appeared to be telling the truth,' he admitted reluctantly, avoiding eye contact with his adversary.

Throughout it all, Dr Silas Bacon sat silently, smoking a cigarette and watching the interaction between the four participants.

Max turned to him. 'Silas, you contacted me recently about the death of one of your colleagues. We should hear your story.'

Silas cleared his throat. 'Let me introduce myself,' he began, stubbing out his cigarette. 'My name is Dr Silas Bacon. I am a medical doctor, anatomist, scientist, and wax modeller. I was employed at the Kreitmayer Waxworks before I took up a position at the Melbourne Museum.

'I contacted Max recently regarding the strange business of my former colleague, Walter Eames. He met a tragic death in a fire just prior to Easter.'

He went on to tell how, some nine months earlier, Walter had been visited by a stranger, intent on learning the art of making death masks. His anonymous visitor had asked probing questions about the production of death masks, including whether they could be made pre- as well as post-mortem. Silas paused, noting Emma's questioning look.

'That is, *prior* to death as well as *after* death.'

'The world is full of peculiar people with peculiar obsessions,' commented Reggie, staring pointedly at Silas.

'Continue, Dr Bacon,' said Mrs Darrow.

'Mr da Costa published his article detailing the discovery of the death masks in *The Argus* on Thursday, the 21st of March. By Tuesday, the 26th of March, Walter Eames was dead, consumed by a fire that destroyed his home. As a scientist, I believe there is no such thing as coincidence.'

Reggie was incensed. He rose from his chair. 'Are you suggesting that I am somehow responsible for Eames' death?'

'Not directly,' replied Silas coolly, 'but your article would have reminded the killer that Walter could identify him. My former colleague died in an *accidental* fire, according to the police. I think not.'

'This is very concerning,' said Aunt Florence. 'The police are prepared to pursue this?'

'Unfortunately, no. They believe that Walter caused the fire. Detective Inspector Wasp was dismissive of my theory that Walter's visitor had killed him.'

'You've spoken to Wasp?' asked Max, leaning forward in his chair.

'The inspector required my expertise to assist him with the case of these murdered women. He asked me whether I was aware of any persons, apart from the very small fraternity of wax-modellers, who might have the ability to produce a death mask. My reply was in the negative.'

Silas nodded at Max. 'His particular interest was in you, my friend. I could not satisfy him on that score, fortunately. It's fair to say that he was unhappy with my answers.'

Max sat back, his face pale.

'We have four victims,' said Emma. 'Agnes Reason, Lillian Broderick, Bessie Cartwright, and one woman who hasn't yet been identified. We could make that five, if we include Mr Eames.'

'Unfortunately, there's one more,' added Reggie, enjoying the limelight. 'I had a visit from a Mrs Dunphy a week ago. It appears that she may have escaped the clutches of this murderer.'

Reggie referred to his notes. He recounted how Mrs Helen Dunphy, a widow, had visited his offices to report her encounter with a man at Hampton Beach. She had become alarmed when the stranger's questions became increasingly personal in nature: about her being a widow and a good mother.

'That would have scared her,' said Emma.

'It did. When she said that she was going home, he insisted on accompanying her. They went up South Road and he stopped outside an old house.'

'The Crabtree mansion?'

'She's not sure. He said he lived in the house and asked her if she'd like to come in. She refused and that's when he became angry. He argued with her. By that stage, she was becoming very frightened. Then he calmed down and tried to reason with her, assuring her that she had nothing to fear. She wasn't convinced and left. The last she saw of him, he was heading back towards the beach.'

'When did this happen?' asked Aunt Florence.

'Mid-January.'

'Did she report it to the police?'

'There was nothing to report. Nothing happened. But she also felt it would look bad that she had befriended a stranger, particularly being widowed recently. She read my article in late March. It reminded her of what happened, so she contacted me. Fair to say that Mrs Dunphy had a close shave with death,' said Reggie, smirking.

Aunt Florence ignored his jibe. 'What similarities are there between these women?'

'An interesting question, Mrs Darrow. There are some parallels. They're aged between twenty and thirty. All attractive. All lived in the Brighton Beach, Hampton area. One defining characteristic is that Lillian, Agnes, and Bessie were blonde. Helen Dunphy too. This may be a coincidence but the bag the police retrieved from the Crabtree backyard contained blonde hair.'

'Blonde, young, attractive women living in this area,' said Emma.

Reggie looked at her. 'Not unlike you, Miss Hart.'

'Really, Mr da Costa. That's uncalled for,' said Mrs Darrow, peering at him through her pince-nez. 'But there are differences, surely?'

'Of course. Widow, spinster, married, children, no children. I could go on.'

'Let's consider what we know about this man's appearance,' suggested Silas. 'Harriett Kreitmayer, my employer's wife from the waxworks, referred this alleged murderer to Walter Eames. She told me that the stranger was wearing a wig and false moustache. Walter described him to me as tall and pale.'

'Mrs Dunphy said he was tall, plump and had a thick black moustache,' added Reggie.

'So, we have a tall, plump, pale man in disguise,' concluded Emma. 'That's not very helpful. Do we know anything more about him?'

'He is skilled at making death masks,' said Max.

'Very true.' Emma addressed Silas. 'When I first met you, you told me *how* death masks were made, but you didn't have time to tell us *why* they were made.'

Silas smiled grimly. 'Most were created to celebrate the famous and the infamous, but there is another underlying reason why death masks were made. It was to prove the tenets of phrenology.'

'Could you please explain what this "phrenology" is?' asked Aunt Florence. 'Some of us are not of a scientific bent.'

Silas leaned back in his chair and steepled his fingers. 'Phrenology originated with the nineteenth-century German physician, Franz Joseph Gall. When he dissected bodies, he noticed that the nerve system didn't end in one area of the brain—it branched throughout. This formed the basis of his theory that different parts of the brain controlled different parts of one's character.' He noticed the puzzled look on Mrs Darrow's face. 'I'll simplify it for you. Gall and his followers believed that if someone was particularly caring and compassionate, that part of the brain would be used more and thus increase in size, pushing out the skull. In the same way, this person might not use the criminal element of his brain, and so it would contract, leaving a depression in the skull.'

'Fiddlesticks. Fancy suggesting that lumps and bumps show your personality,' said Mrs Darrow.

Silas was flustered by her outburst. 'I confess that I was once a believer. I was certainly not the only one, although I regret my naïvety now. In

124

phrenology's heyday, diagrams or maps of the brain were created. Theories were expounded about the link between the contours of the skull and personality. Phrenologists used a measuring tape and a craniometer to calculate the dimensions of the skull and thus analyse character. Indeed, the expressions "highbrow" and "lowbrow" derive from phrenology.' Silas chuckled nervously.

Emma was puzzled. 'You're suggesting that the Crabtree death masks were made to show the personalities of the victims. Why would the killer do that?'

'I don't have all the answers to life's little riddles. I can draw on the science for explanations but I don't have access to what goes on in the minds of murderers. I can only suggest that the man is obsessed.'

'Intriguing,' replied Reggie, 'but in my wide experience of human nature, including the basest kind, I believe that the motivation for murder comes down to four main things: love, hate, revenge, and money.'

'And this may still be true. But this man is not simple or average,' countered Silas Bacon. 'This person is psychologically damaged.'

Reggie ignored him. 'The death masks are important to this killer. He keeps them as mementos of each kill. The fact is that he shifted the death masks and his tools of trade from the Crabtree mansion to another location as soon as he realised that they had been found. That shows that he is still active and that he is capable of planning ahead.'

'That reminds me,' said Emma. 'I forgot to mention that one of the death masks was quite amateurish compared to the others. The other two were much better in execution.'

Reggie laughed. 'Nice pun.'

'There's nothing humorous about murder, Mr da Costa,' said Aunt Florence.

Reggie looked contrite. 'I apologise.' But the suggestion of a smile lingered on his lips.

'What do we do now?' asked Mrs Darrow. 'I mean no offence, Dr Bacon, but how can we go to the police with theories about death masks and phrenology?'

'We can't,' said Reggie. 'Wasp would laugh in our faces.'

'So, we let another woman die?' said Emma. 'Is that what you mean?'

'They might arrest someone,' said Reggie, his eyes fixed on Max Rushforth. The former soldier went pale. 'I have to go.'

The eyes of everyone were upon him as the tall rangy man stood. The dark circles around his light green eyes were more pronounced, contrasting as they did with his pale lashes and fair skin. There was a tightness about his expression; a strained look.

He strode out the door without another word, leaving Reggie, Silas, Mrs Darrow, and Emma staring after him.

'Now that's a strange one,' commented Reggie.

Chapter Twenty-Two

DEATH MASK MURDERER STRIKES AGAIN
PANIC IN BRIGHTON

By REGGIE DA COSTA, Senior Crime Reporter

A fifth victim of the infamous Death Mask Murderer has been found washed up on Hampton Beach. The body of Mrs Rosalind Joan Baker, aged nineteen years, was found on Tuesday morning by Mr Clancy Stewart, a local fisherman. He was collecting driftwood when he noticed a large clump of seaweed at the water's edge. On closer examination, he saw a face amongst the kelp.

She was bald!

He first thought that it was a man, but once he cleared away the rest of the kelp, he realised that it was a woman. Her head had been shaved. He immediately contacted the police.

Detective Inspector Felix Wasp, of the Criminal Investigation Branch, released a statement to the press yesterday. It said that Mrs Baker had agreed to meet her brother, Mr Joe Dobbs, on Saturday afternoon in Church Street, Brighton. When she did not arrive, Mr Dobbs contacted her husband. He had not seen her since 1:00 p.m. that afternoon.

Mrs Baker, mother of an eight-month-old baby girl, disappeared somewhere between her home in New Street, Brighton, and the Brighton Beach railway station. She was wearing a white blouse, black skirt, and a straw hat with a red ribbon.

The cause of death has not been released but it appears that Mrs Baker did not drown. Preliminary examination suggests that she was strangled. There was a ligature mark around her neck. The coroner's inquiry is to be held in two weeks.

Fifth victim?

The death of Mrs Baker follows the discovery of three death masks in a derelict Brighton mansion in February, two of which were identified as being cast from the heads of Mrs Agnes Reason and Miss Lillian Broderick. The body of the latter is still listed as missing. Mrs Reason's husband is serving a life sentence for her murder. The identity of the woman represented by the first death mask remains a mystery. A fourth victim, Mrs Bessie Cartwright, was found dead next to the Brighton Beach railway line in February. She had been strangled and her head shaved. No death mask has been found.

Arrest imminent

Detective Inspector Wasp issued a statement to the effect that police were following up all leads in the case, and that they had identified a person of interest. He concluded that an arrest is imminent. To date, no further information has been made available.

Panic in Brighton

There appears to be a killer on the loose in Brighton, particularly in the area around South Road and the Brighton Beach railway station. It is recommended that young women, in particular, remain alert and refrain from talking to strangers. Anyone with information, which might assist with the apprehension of the Death Mask Murderer, should contact either *The Argus* or the Victoria Police.

[*The Argus* April 17, 1918]

Chapter Twenty-Three

Detective Inspector Felix Wasp rolled up his shirt sleeves in preparation for his interview with Max Rushforth. It signalled that he was ready to do business. He indicated to Detective Sergeant Clary Blain that he should bring the suspect in. Wasp lined up his notebook and pencils and straightened the pile of documents that he had accumulated over the past week since the discovery of Rosalind Baker's body. He was a fastidious man, both in appearance and his approach to his job. Felix Wasp was the kind of man who dotted his i's and crossed his t's. There would be no escaping conviction due to sloppy evidence-gathering on his watch. Now he was ready to home in on the man he believed was involved in the murders of at least four Brighton women.

Max Rushforth was shown into the interview room and took his seat opposite Wasp. The detective noted that the suspect looked nervous and tired. He surmised that extracting a confession would not take long.

'Mr Rushforth. The Crimes Act of 1914 states that you may request legal representation during questioning. Do you wish to avail yourself of this?'

Max shook his head.

'Detective Sergeant Blain. Please note that the suspect indicated in the negative.' He turned to the next page of his notebook. 'Could you please state the purpose of your visit to South Road, Brighton on Saturday, the 2nd of February, 1918?'

'The day of the storm? I was visiting my cousins.'

'And how did you know the whereabouts of the key to the back door of the Crabtree home?'

'My aunt cleaned for old Thomas Crabtree after his wife died.' Max looked directly at Wasp; his eyes haggard. 'I've explained about the cellar before. My aunt told me about it.'

'Were you at all familiar with Miss Hart before the day of the storm? Did you know her by sight?'

'I did not.'

'Why were you standing outside the Crabtree house in the middle of a wild storm? Were you waiting for her?'

'Of course not. You are obviously aware that I suffer from what they call "shell shock." I don't like loud noises.'

'And yet you stayed out in the storm with lightning and thunder all around you. Surely the sensible thing would have been to seek shelter?'

'You don't understand what shell shock is like.'

'Can't say I do. Speaking of your condition, your medical file refers to an assault that you made on a senior officer.'

Max sighed. 'If I explain, maybe you'll understand. When I was on the Western Front, that officer sent us over the top in a hail of enemy bullets. He stayed in the safety of the trenches. One of my mates was brought down by German machine guns, and when I tried to go and get him, the corporal ordered me to stay put. I disobeyed orders and brought Jackie back. My mate had to have both legs amputated. Later on, I heard the corporal bragging that he'd done everything he could to rescue the injured, so I punched him.'

'You broke his jaw.'

'It was very satisfying.'

'You resort to violence to make a point?' Wasp shuffled his papers and leaned forward, his nose inches away from Max's face. 'How do you explain your assault on the nurse at the rehabilitation hospital?'

Max gasped and went pale. 'I was ill.'

'You attacked a woman. A young nurse doing her job. Not an officer whom you saw as responsible for your friend's injuries.'

Max stared up at the barred window.

'It's in your records that you had a physical and mental breakdown after Fromelles.' Wasp paused.

'We come to the garden party held by Mrs Florence Darrow in February. We have testimony from witnesses that you collapsed. Your behaviour, according to them, bordered on hysteria. We have also interviewed some of your colleagues at the Barracks. They say that you are anti-social and moody. One can safely assume that you have been psychologically damaged from your experiences on the battlefield.'

'You're a psychiatrist too?'

Wasp looked at him pointedly. 'I wouldn't be too smart, Mr Rushforth. It will work against you.' He referred to his notes again. 'You have a friend, Dr Silas Bacon. He's an expert wax modeller. No doubt he has shown you his creations and you have discussed how they were made?'

'As a matter of fact, no.'

'Hard to believe. We searched your rental house while you were at work. We found a bag of plaster in a cupboard in the outhouse. Can you explain why you had it?'

'I hardly remember. It was probably from my parents' house in Elstern-wick.'

'Your parents died in a boating accident. That must have affected you badly?'

'My sister supported me until I finished university. We survived.'

'Very touching. Let's move on, shall we?' Wasp removed an envelope from under the documents and spilled the contents onto the table in front of Max. There was a look of triumph on his face. 'What do you have to say about this?'

A gold locket lay on the table. Wasp opened the locket to reveal some strands of blonde hair, bound with a thin red ribbon.

Max blinked when he saw it.

'It was found in your desk drawer at the Barracks, underneath some files.'

'It was my mother's. A keepsake.'

'You like keepsakes? What about death masks? Do you like those too?'

Wasp leaned in, as if to share a secret. 'Forensic science. It's the latest in police methods. Microscopes. That's what I'm told. Each hair looks different under them and you can identify who they come from. How's that?' He picked up the lock of hair. 'If we can match this with either Agnes Reason, Lillian Broderick, Bessie Cartwright, or Rosalind Baker, then we have you.'

Max crossed his arms. 'You have the wrong person.'

'Let's go through some *facts*, Mr Rushforth. Fact one. Your cousins no longer live in South Road. They moved five years ago. Fact two. You intended that Miss Hart would be your next victim but, for some reason, changed your mind. Fact three. You have a friend who made death masks for a living. Fact four. Your behaviour is, to say the least, violent and unpredictable.'

'That's not true. I am so much better now.'

'Fact five. You possess a locket containing blonde hair. All the victims were blonde. Fact six. Christian Reason was shipped home on the *Wiltshire*, the same transport that brought you back to Melbourne in May 1917.'

Max slammed his fist on the table. 'What are you saying? There were hundreds of men on that ship! I never met Christian Reason before he was in Pentridge.'

'Temper, temper, Mr Rushforth. Fact seven. The murders began from the time you returned. Agnes Reason: murdered August 1917. Lillian Broderick: disappeared November 1917. Bessie Cartwright: murdered February 1918. Rosalind Baker: murdered April 1918.'

Wasp sat back in his chair. He smiled grimly and said, 'Case closed.'

Chapter Twenty-Four

THE DEATH MASK MURDERS
ACCESSORY NAMED IN AGNES REASON CASE
Ex-soldier arrested

By REGGIE DA COSTA, Senior Crime Reporter

Police have arrested Maxwell Clifford Rushforth, aged twenty-nine and a former private in the A.I.F., on suspicion of being an accessory to the murder of Mrs Agnes Reason, whose body was discovered last September at Green Point, Brighton. Her husband, Christian William Reason, is currently serving a life sentence in Pentridge Prison for her murder.

Our readers will recall that Mr Rushforth, accompanied by Miss Emma Hart, discovered three death masks in the cellar of a Brighton mansion in February this year, when they sheltered from a storm. Two of the death masks have been identified as being taken from Mrs Reason and missing person, Miss Lillian Broderick. *The Argus*'s senior crime reporter has been credited with the latter's identification.

Detective Inspector Felix Wasp, lead investigator in the Death Mask Murders case, issued the following statement:

'Private Maxwell Clifford Rushforth was declared unfit

for service on medical grounds and was repatriated from the Western Front in May 1917. The prosecution will assert that he became acquainted with Mrs Reason's husband when they were shipped home together. They then conspired to kill the unfortunate woman. We believe that Mr Rushforth was familiar with the cellar and its ghastly contents. It is possible that he intended to do away with Miss Hart when he took her there and, for reasons we are not privy to, decided against killing her. I wish to emphasise that Miss Hart is not regarded as a suspect in this case.

'This outcome is the result of meticulous and methodical detective work on the part of the Criminal Investigation Branch.'

Police are investigating whether Mr Rushforth is also involved in the disappearance of Miss Lillian Broderick and the murders of Mrs Bessie Cartwright and Mrs Rosalind Baker.

[*The Argus* April 24, 1918]

Chapter Twenty-Five

The Melbourne City Watch House was an impressive Romanesque-style building in Russell Street, dating from 1909. On one side was the Melbourne Magistrates' Court and on the other, beyond the courtyard, were the forbidding bluestone walls and barred windows of the Melbourne Jail. Within the Watch House, innocent men shared cells with drunks, murderers, pickpockets, and thieves, waiting for their cases to come before the court.

Max Rushforth had been attacked on his first night on remand. Word had soon spread that he was involved in the Death Mask Murders, prompted mainly by the article written by *The Argus*'s own crime reporter, Reginald da Costa. Max's fellow prisoners had reacted angrily, which had forced the authorities to move him into the isolation cell, situated next to the main exercise yard of the Watch House. With only iron grilles separating his small exercise yard from the main one, Max was subjected to verbal abuse and catcalls from some of the forty prisoners—petty criminals, vagrants, drunks, armed robbers, and murderers—who spent the daylight hours next to him. He was, according to the inmates, a pervert and a deviant who made death masks of the innocent young women that he had helped murder.

The constant barrage of abuse and venom directed at Max was taking its toll as he spent his seventh night under the Watch House roof. He found it hard to sleep, abetted by the numbing cold and the acrid smells of vomit and urine, which infiltrated all parts of the building. At night, he would lie on his thin mattress staring up at the ceiling of his cell, wondering if he would ever be free again.

Max turned to face the wall and traced his initials on the painted bricks. From the 'drunk tank' over the way, he could hear the sounds of retching followed by loud swearing. Poor buggers, he thought. All they had was a cold concrete floor with a drain hole in the middle. No benches, no mattresses. In the morning they'd be hosed down like animals in a stall. In the adjacent cell, he could hear muffled conversation. On the other side of the cellblock there was an argument brewing, which would be dealt with by the police sergeant in charge of the Watch House.

In some respects, Max appreciated the isolation of his protective cell but, on the other hand, it reinforced his estrangement from society, even if it were a bunch of vagrants, drunks, and criminals.

He tried to remember what it felt like to be part of something, to belong. That seemed so long ago. He had had friends and a family. Holidays at the beach with his cousins. Time with his parents until the boating accident deprived him of a mother and father. A sister who had raised him and then left to live her own life once he finished his degree. University pals. Enlistment with his mates. And then came the War. It changed everything.

Max reached down and touched the floor. Cold and hard. Prison would be more of the same, but permanent.

He now had a solicitor, John Upjohn. On hearing of Max's arrest, Emma's great-aunt had retained the services of her lawyer to represent Max. She was also paying the rent on his terrace house while he was in custody. Her generosity was overwhelming. She wasn't related to him, theirs was no longstanding friendship, and yet she was supporting him financially and emotionally. He considered himself lucky to have her and Emma in his corner.

Max lay on his back and mulled over the prosecution's case, as set out for him by John Upjohn. It was circumstantial but clear-cut. Upjohn expected that Max would be committed for trial within fourteen days. Max would go before the court, they would read the charges, he'd plead not guilty and then he'd apply for bail. His solicitor warned him that bail would, most likely, be refused. And when all of the testimony was considered at the trial, Upjohn admitted that a jury might find him guilty.

'What's the maximum sentence for being an accessory to murder?' Max had asked him.

Upjohn hesitated before answering. 'Life imprisonment.'

The odds were stacked against him. The case was built on the premise that he did know Christian Reason, having travelled back to Australia from the Western Front on the same ship. And both had arrived home in May 1917, prior to the time the murders started.

Upjohn warned him that his medical records would become public knowledge, detailing his physical and mental breakdown after Fromelles. What would damn him most, in the jury's eyes, were his assaults on a superior officer and a nurse. The overriding impression would be of a man who was psychologically unsound and prone to violence, a man capable of participating in a particularly gruesome set of murders.

The final piece of evidence would be his friendship with Silas Bacon. It proved that he knew someone who could teach him how to create the infamous death masks sighted in the Crabtree mansion.

* * *

Since his return from the War, Max had protested that his health was improving; that he was 'so much better now.' But the repetition of those words now sounded hollow to him. Here he was in the Melbourne City Watch House, awaiting trial. It was his unpredictable behaviour that had brought him to this place, rather than circumstantial evidence. And he had to admit that he wasn't coping, no matter how often he protested that he was.

Emma Hart. Chance had brought her into his life. She was the one person who had not judged him or been repulsed by his behaviour. She represented a fresh start and the possibility of happiness. But now he knew that the moment had passed. He would never woo this artistic, feisty young woman, now that he was facing life in prison. What would she think of him when she heard the prosecution assert that he had planned to target her as his next victim on the day of the storm? As if he ever intended to hurt her.

Why had he been in South Road that day, Upjohn had asked him? There were no relatives to visit. If he wanted to prove that he had not been stalking Emma Hart, he had to explain his whereabouts. Max gritted his teeth. No one would elicit from him where he had been. So much of his private life was on open display and this was one thing that would remain secret, even if it contributed to him being found guilty. Bugger them.

Max lay on his back, pulling the thin blanket up under his chin. He stared up at the ceiling. Despite everything, despite the threat of life in prison, he was feeling mentally stronger. Entering the Watch House had made him recognise that he needed to be honest with himself. If he ever saw the outside of a cell again, he would make his recovery from war neurosis a priority. And the fact that he no longer felt so alone—that Emma, Mrs Darrow, Silas, Upjohn and even Reggie (although not willingly) were in his corner—made him feel more positive about his life. If the trial went against him, then so be it, but at least he had friends who were sticking by him through thick and thin.

The quarrel in the cell across the corridor was gaining in volume. Someone yelled and swear words ripped through the chilly air of the Watch House. One of the grille gates slammed, metal grating on metal. The officers were coming to break up the fight. No sleep tonight. Max traced his initials on the wall and pulled the blanket up over his head.

Chapter Twenty-Six

When the news reached Emma of Max's arrest, she was bewildered and upset. Her immediate response was undeniably selfish and she knew it: first Clive, now she was about to lose Max. She chided herself severely and shed tears of grief and outrage. Max, who had saved her life and who had suffered so badly in the War, was to face trial for crimes she knew he had not committed.

When had life grown so grim? Why couldn't she return to those carefree days back in Donald before the Great War had ruined everything?

Emma took out one of her old sketchbooks from the drawer in her bedroom. She flipped through the pages. There was her farm on Sheep Hills Road, about five miles out of town, with its large rambling homestead and fields as far as the eye could see; sheep grazing contentedly, chewing on the lush grass after the spring rains. Another drawing was of her father, Joe Hart, a big gruff country farmer, his arms all hairy and tanned. When she was little, he would wrap his arms around her and spin her until she was dizzy. A man of few words, his smile spoke volumes. And here was her mother, Jenny Hart, a petite, simply dressed woman with blonde, curly hair beneath a broad-brimmed hat, in her vegetable garden.

The last portrait was of her beloved brother David, a loud, boisterous man in his early thirties, protective of his 'little sis.' Sometimes when the tasks around the farm were completed for the day, he would accompany her on long rides into the countryside. It might be south towards St Arnaud. Other times it was north to Watchem. East was Charlton. Some days they only went as far as Lake Buloke, circling the large stretch of water that was home to a wide variety of birdlife. And David would watch proudly as Emma took out her sketchbook and, with a few deft strokes, portray the landscape that gave them so much pleasure.

She was about to put the sketchbook away when a piece of paper fluttered to the floor. Emma picked it up and froze. It was a portrait of Clive. His face stared back at her, his eyes with those little wrinkles at the side when he smiled. There was the lopsided grin that had first attracted her to him, and the mop of curly hair that defied the comb. How she missed him.

She had been incapable of drawing him since he had died. Sometimes she had even found it hard to remember what he looked like. Staring at his face now was challenging for her. She wished she could go back in time to the conversation that had changed everything.

'I don't want to join up, Emma. Mum will be on her own. How will she manage the farm without me?'

'Don't be silly. People in Donald band together and help each other out. Anyway, you'll be back within a few months. They say the War will be over by the end of the year.'

Clive had looked doubtful. 'I don't know, Emma.'

'People say you're a coward. I've heard them talk behind your back.'

'I don't care what people say.'

'I do.' She folded her arms, her mouth set in a pout.

He touched her lips gently and smiled. 'I'll enlist if you agree to marry me when I get back.'

Emma kissed him then snuggled into his arms. 'It's a deal. I always knew you'd do the right thing.'

How she regretted her words now. Clive was gone and Max, enigmatic and troubled Max, was facing an uncertain future. She placed Clive's portrait back in the sketchbook and put it in the drawer.

She missed her family badly. Once she would have caught the first train home, but she wasn't the same person that she was six months ago. Instinctively, she knew that running away from her problems solved nothing.

Now, in Brighton, Emma had come to understand that life was complicated; that actions had consequences. With Max's arrest, she realised that this too was a situation from which she could not escape. She cared about Max and she had to do something. She went downstairs.

Aunt Florence was in the parlour. She looked up when she saw Emma enter the room. The girl's face was pale and strained.

'Are you going home?' she asked.

'I'm staying here. Max is in trouble and he needs help.'

'Bravo, my dear. I'm proud of you.'

Emma stood uncertainly in the middle of the room. 'I've had this thought floating around in my head for a while now. Do you want to hear it?'

'I'm listening.'

'It's something that Detective Inspector Wasp said back in March. At the interview with Max and me. He implied that Max was a suspect because he knew about the cellar in the Crabtree mansion. But what if the real murderer, whoever he is, knows the Crabtree mansion too? It's not chance that he chose it. He *knows* it.'

'You're saying - what?'

'It's the link. Why did the killer choose it as his base?'

Mrs Darrow rang the bell. Emma frowned. 'You want tea *now*?'

'Don't be ridiculous.'

Mrs Williams stood in the doorway. 'Tea, Mrs Darrow?'

'Not yet, thank you. Please come in and sit down.' Mrs Williams looked surprised but did as she was told. 'When were you first employed here?'

'I was housekeeper to Mr Darrow from 1879, two years before your marriage, ma'am.'

'Did you mix much with the staff at the Crabtree mansion?'

'Indeed, I did. My husband worked there as head gardener before he died, so I knew them well.'

'Do you still see anyone from the house?'

'As you know, Mr and Mrs Crabtree have passed on. But every Christmas, I visit Miss O'Connell. She was their housekeeper. She lives in a home for elderly ladies in Cheltenham.'

'Is she doing well?'

'She's a chipper little thing. Quite happy.'

'Did she ever talk about the Crabtrees when she worked there?'

'Never. That's a requirement of being a housekeeper. You keep confidences if you want to keep your job.'

'Well said. That will be all, thank you. You can serve the tea now.'

The housekeeper left the room.

Emma was confused. 'What was that all about?'

'Pay Miss O'Connell a visit. Find out about the Crabtree family. It's a long shot, Emma. There may be no link between the killer and the Crabtree house, but Miss O'Connell may remember something useful. She has no need to be circumspect about what she says anymore.'

'Aunt Florence, you're a genius.'

'Highly intelligent but hardly a genius.'

And despite the seriousness of the situation, Emma and Aunt Florence shared a laugh.

Chapter Twenty-Seven

The Melbourne Benevolent Asylum, in Warrigal Road, Cheltenham, was a most impressive building, a charitable home for the aged and infirm. Opened in 1911, it was a two-storey red brick construction with an arched portico, artificial lake, and ornamental trees set in more than 140 acres of parkland. It was now home to Miss O'Connell, former housekeeper to the Crabtree family. The sudden death of her employer had left the old lady homeless and penniless, necessitating her move to a relative's home until a vacancy arose at the asylum.

As George guided the automobile up the gravel driveway, the words of Silas Bacon rang in Emma's ears: 'I believe there is no such thing as coincidence.' Why had the Death Mask Murderer chosen the Crabtree mansion as the location for his nefarious deeds? Was it more than chance at work?

While George waited beside the car, Emma was shown to a four-bed ward housing Miss O'Connell. It was a cheerful room, clean and bright. She lay back against the pillows, a little shrivelled husk of a woman, wearing a nightdress covered by a crochet shawl. Her hair was sparse, her arms withered and her face was a mass of wrinkles, but her eyes sparkled when she saw Emma cross to her side of the room.

'I don't remember you,' she said in a sing-song voice.

Emma introduced herself and sat next to the bed, chatting about the things they had in common: life in Brighton, her aunt's housekeeper, and Mrs Florence Darrow. After a while, Emma broached the subject that had brought her there in the first place.

'My aunt has told me a bit about the Crabtrees. Can you tell me more about them, please?'

'Help me sit up first.'

Once she was comfortable, Miss O'Connell described life at the Crabtree mansion, with its opulent accommodation, large staff of maids, footmen, and gardeners, overseen by the formidable and exacting Mr Thomas Crabtree.

'He was a hard man but he loved his wife to distraction. She was the only person who could wrap him around her little finger. When she died, he lost interest in everything.'

'What happened exactly?'

'They had two children. Master Frederick was adopted then Mrs Crabtree had a little one, Master Henry. They didn't think they could have children at first, you see, so her having a baby unexpectedly was a pleasant surprise. She was over the moon, Mrs Crabtree. Loved that little boy to bits.'

'What did Mrs Crabtree look like?'

'She was a beautiful woman, still young when she had Master Henry. Like an angel to look at. Golden hair, pale skin.'

Her face clouded. 'The little boy died. Only two years old. They found him in the fishpond. He fell and drowned. Must have wandered away from the nanny. The mistress was inconsolable. She didn't leave her room for weeks.'

'How awful.'

'Poor Master Frederick was motherless. He would stand at her bedroom door bashing it with his hands, wanting to come in. She wouldn't let him. Even Mr Crabtree couldn't do anything for her. They called the doctor, sedated her but it was like she withdrew into herself. Do you know what I mean?'

'I do. I can understand that,' Emma said.

'I suppose we shouldn't have been surprised when she died.'

'How did Mr Crabtree cope?'

She looked up at Emma, her eyes dimmed with sadness. 'The way men do.' He put on a brave face. But underneath it all, he wasn't the same man. Poor Master Frederick lost a mother and a father the same day. Mr Crabtree sent him away.'

'When did this happen?'

Miss O'Connell screwed up her face in concentration and then she nodded. '1882.'

'Where did Master Frederick go?'

'A boarding school up the country. Only seven years old too. But he never came home for holidays. I never saw him again.'

'He never came home?'

'He never did.'

'Do you know what school it was?'

'Mr Crabtree never mentioned a name.' She looked intently at Emma. 'I've never said this before, but I did wonder.'

'What did you wonder?'

'Whether the rumours were true. You see, it was said that little Henry didn't drown accidentally, it was Master Frederick who held him under. No one said anything in public, of course.' She fiddled with her shawl. 'I'm rather tired. I think I'd like to take a little nap now, if it's not too much trouble.'

'Of course not. Thank you so much for seeing me today. I hope it wasn't an imposition.'

'Not at all. I like to talk about the past, but some things are best forgotten.'

As she drove away from the Melbourne Benevolent Asylum, Emma pondered what she had learned. Thomas Crabtree's family had suffered enormous grief - the loss of a son and wife. And what if the older boy had really killed his brother? It was a truly tragic story.

Chapter Twenty-Eight

Detective Sergeant Clary Blain was leaning on the bar of The Duke of Wellington Hotel when Reggie da Costa walked in. He scratched his nose when he saw the reporter and smiled.

'Reggie. Join me in a scotch?'

'A beer thanks. You wanted to see me?' Reggie pulled up a stool and sat next to the detective. He glanced around at the half-dozen or so drinkers who were occupying the public bar. They were a down-at-heel lot, working-class to their bootstraps.

Clary nodded and sculled his drink. He beckoned to the bartender. 'Another.'

'Let's have it.'

Clary leaned in towards Reggie. He smelled of alcohol and body odour. He undid the top button of his shirt and belched.

'Sorry, mate. Not feeling so great today. I've been burning the candle at both ends with this Death Mask Murders case. Wasp's flying around trying to stitch up the evidence against Rushforth and he's like a dog scratching a flea. Won't let up until he's got Maxxy behind bars permanently.'

Reggie looked impatiently at the door. 'I don't have much time, Clary. Is there anything else? Can we cut to the chase?'

'There's been another murder. This morning the body of a woman was found in the scrub near Mair Street in Brighton.'

'I heard about it before I came,' said Reggie. 'The word is that it's a crime of passion. Someone she knew well.'

Clary Blain shook his head and wagged a finger at Reggie. 'Nah. Shouldn't believe everything you read or hear.' He laughed at his little joke.

'Are you saying—?'

'That's right. The Death Mask Murderer. His *modus operandi*.'

'But I heard her face was slashed.'

'True, but her head was partially shaved. She had a nasty old scar on the back of her head. The razor must have hit it and the killer went berserk. Likes his ladies smooth. Then he used the blade on her face.'

'Any idea who she was?'

'Nah. Hard to tell after he got through with her. She was a mess. Looks like the killer lost control. To be honest, she looked like a lump of meat in a slaughterhouse, there was so much blood. I nearly lost my breakfast.'

Clary's blotchy face had gone pale. He clutched his glass then noticed it was empty. He waved it in the air and the bartender filled it again. 'Makes a man turn to drink, it does, seeing stuff like that.' He gulped it down and stared at Reggie. 'What's the world coming to?'

'Sorry, Clary. Must have been hard. Yet, you say Wasp reckons it's not the real thing?'

'Wasp wants Max Rushforth for the Agnes Reason case. This crime complicates things. And Maxxy can't be blamed for it if he's in the City Watch House, can he? He can't be in two places at once. Once the coroner's report is public, Wasp will claim it's a crime of passion, done by someone who knew the victim well. Not the work of the Death Mask Murderer. Wasp is right in one sense though: there are discrepancies between this one and the deaths of Reason, Cartwright, and Baker.'

'Such as?'

'Not strangulation like the others. Throat cut. Face slashed.' Blain paused and eyed his empty glass. 'I think it's as plain as the nose on my face that it *is* him. Razor. Shaved head. Another blonde. Brighton area. But I won't be arguing with Wasp. Not if I want to keep my job.' He scratched under his arm.

Reggie sat back and took a swig of his beer. 'He's escalating.'

'Who? Wasp?'

'No. The Death Mask Murderer. And if Wasp ignores the real killer so that he can put Rushforth away, then more women will die.' He studied Clary Blain. 'Another one?'

'Nah. Trying to cut down.' Clary wiped his mouth with the back of his hand. 'One more thing. Here's a tip for you. There's a petty criminal out there: Joseph Theodore Leslie Taylor. What a mouthful. Calls himself "Squizzy." Keep an eye on him. I reckon he's destined for big things.'

'I've been following his career. Theft, assault, inciting to resist arrest, offensive language, and vagrancy. Only a little man too. Ex-jockey. Involved in the murders of Arthur Trotter and William Haines. Found not guilty.'

'You're amazing, Reggie. You're destined for bigger things too.'

'I'm working on that.'

Clary checked his watch. 'Better get on. One thing, Reggie, you protect your sources, don't you?'

'Of course.'

'That's a relief. I wouldn't want Wasp getting the wrong idea about me. You shouldn't have published that story about Bessie Cartwright. Wasp is trying to find out who leaked it. That information about the latest body? It's just between you and me for the moment.'

Reggie reassured him with a smile. 'Sorry, Clary. Won't happen again. Ethics before self-interest. That's my motto.'

A couple of drinkers started arguing and shoving each other. Clary took one look and decided it was time to leave. He was off duty and wanted to get home. He slid off the stool and staggered out the door before the reporter could finish his beer.

Reggie da Costa sat on for a while, ignoring the fracas happening near him. He was preoccupied with what Clary Blain had just told him. Another body found. Another victim of the Death Mask Murderer. Would he print that? Not yet. He'd toe the line and say the crime was unrelated. Reggie needed to maintain his sources and Clary was one of his best. He couldn't afford to lose him; he was too useful.

From what Blain had told him, it was clear that Wasp was ignoring the link with the other murders because it suited him. The prosecution of Max Rushforth would be a feather in his cap; jailing him would enhance his reputation with the public and his bosses. And although Reggie didn't like to admit that he was wrong, it appeared that Max Rushforth was languishing in the City Watch House while the real killer was still on the loose.

The barman ejected the two brawlers. Reggie drained the last of his beer, slapped a ten-shilling note down on the bar, and waited for his change. This case was getting very complicated. Usually the crimes were clear-cut, and the motivation straightforward, but this one eluded him. Even with his depth of experience and insightful mind, Reginald da Costa was finding it hard to see the forest from the trees.

Chapter Twenty-Nine

As the months passed, Emma's relationship with her great-aunt had improved considerably. Although the bickering continued, it was more good-natured than before. Emma joined in with Aunt Florence's knitting group and found time passed quickly chatting to the Brighton matrons about the War and local gossip. She went into Melbourne on Thursdays and donned the Red Cross apron, prepared to do her bit for the war effort. It gave her a sense of purpose.

Although more than forty years separated them in age, Aunt Florence and Emma's shared concern for Max's welfare brought them closer together. The old lady enjoyed Emma's company and, despite herself, felt invigorated by involving herself in a new cause: proving Max innocent and freeing Christian Reason.

At Mrs Darrow's suggestion, Emma invited Sophie Fitzgibbon to stay at Seymour Grove for a few days. It would be therapeutic for Emma, thought Aunt Florence, and would provide a distraction from the worrying news of Max's arrest.

The weather had turned wintry and frequent showers kept Emma and Sophie inside. They spent the time chatting, laughing, confessing, and confiding, restoring a relationship that had been fractured by events in the past. Sophie had commenced at the Melba Memorial Conservatorium of Music and had been persuaded by her tutors to try her hand at the piano. Her injured finger had a minimal effect on her playing ability, and she was becoming a confident and proficient pianist. Success had a remarkable effect on her personality. Losing the ability to play the violin had hit her hard, for not only did she love listening to music, but she delighted in expressing herself through it. Consequently, when she saw Mrs Darrow's baby grand piano lying idle, she jumped at the chance to practise each day, and Emma and her great-aunt made for an enthusiastic audience.

It was a Tuesday in early May. John Upjohn would be visiting Mrs Darrow that afternoon to update the ladies on the case. That morning, there was a break in the weather and the two young women ventured out, wrapping themselves up warmly against the cold. They strolled down South Road and crossed The Esplanade to the pier. There were few people around, except for the occasional person walking his dog or sitting on the sand looking out to sea.

Some heavy rain-bearing clouds hung in the sky, reminding Emma of the day of the storm. She described to Sophie what the squall had looked like from afar: the charcoal grey of the clouds, the velvet sky reminiscent of slate, and the flat, leaden tone of the water. And how she had been simultaneously frightened and exhilarated by its violence when it struck Brighton Beach.

Sophie looked out over the bay. 'This is such a contrast to Donald. No doubt you come down here often to sketch?'

'Not as often as I used to. Aunt Florence says that I'm to come home if there's no one around. She says it isn't safe.'

Sophie nodded in agreement. 'You should take note of what she says.'

Emma grimaced. 'I suppose I should. And what about you? Are you enjoying the Conservatorium?'

Sophie nodded. 'Life's much better now. When the doctor told me that I'd lose some feeling in my finger, I was devastated at the thought that I wouldn't be able to play the violin again. And then he said something that resonated with me.'

'What was it?'

'He quoted Ralph Waldo Emerson. "When it is dark enough, you can see the stars." I didn't understand what he meant at first, but now I do.'

'There's wisdom in that,' agreed Emma. 'I wish I could.'

She took out her sketchpad and started to draw her friend. Sophie was seated on the steps of the pier, looking back towards The Esplanade.

'That man's watching you.' Sophie pointed down the beach at a man in a black coat and hat, who was staring in their direction.

Emma looked back over her shoulder and waved. 'Don't worry about him. That's Lewis. He's down here quite a lot. We often stop to chat.'

The man approached them. 'Good morning, miss. Drawing again, I see.' He raised his hat to Sophie. 'I'll let you two have a natter. See you again soon.'

He wandered off down the beach, glancing back occasionally in their direction.

'I don't like the way he looked at you. He gives me the creeps,' said Sophie. 'Like a big, black beetle.' She made a point of glaring at him, at which stage he turned away. 'That will teach him.'

'You have an overactive imagination. He's harmless.' Emma looked at her watch. 'We'd better go. Mr Upjohn is due soon and I want some lunch before he arrives.'

She put her drawing tools in her bag, slung it over her shoulder, and headed up towards the road. Sophie followed, occasionally glancing at the figure in black as he disappeared into the scrub above the beach.

* * *

John Upjohn was one of the new breed of solicitors, those who couldn't afford the mahogany desks, brass plaques, and expensive offices of the William Street legal fraternity. His suit was unpretentious and his manner unassuming. What Upjohn lacked in terms of the trappings of success, he more than made up for in his enthusiasm and commitment to do his best by his clients. And he had built a reputation and a respectable practice through word of mouth with the assistance of people such as Mrs Darrow, in whose hallway he now stood. It was a measure of his regard for her that he was prepared to come to her home, rather than meet her in his offices. She had brought much business his way and he appreciated it.

He was shown into the parlour, where he was greeted by his client and introduced to Emma Hart and Sophie Fitzgibbon. After tea was served, he got down to business.

'Max was remanded in custody. He's been charged with being an accessory to murder. There will be a Directions Hearing in the Supreme Court. Once various issues have been worked out, the date of his trial will be set.'

'When do you think that will be?' asked Mrs Darrow.

'Possibly two months. I'll let you know.'

'How are his chances?'

'Not good. There's a lot of circumstantial evidence.

'On the other hand, I've gone over his interrogation with Detective Inspector Wasp and I believe Max handled it fairly well. He didn't say too much, which was good. I only wish he'd insisted on having a legal representative present. It's naïve to think that telling the truth will suffice. I've seen innocent men found guilty on purely circumstantial evidence.'

'Where is he being held?'

'Melbourne Jail. I visited him there this morning.'

'How is he?' asked Emma.

'Surprisingly good. The food is terrible and the conditions harsh, but I believe he is dealing with it. He seems more positive. I think knowing that he has people working for him has made a difference.'

'Do you have any information regarding the prosecution's case, Mr Upjohn?' asked Mrs Darrow.

'The locket and hair have been excluded. We have photographs of Max's mother wearing it. Dr Bacon has also given a sworn declaration stating that he has never instructed Max in the making of death masks. He's willing to testify to that.'

'That's good.'

'And we were contacted by one of Rushforth's old Army mates, Jackie Jones. He'll be a character witness. He lost his legs in battle. Apparently, Max saved him. He says Max couldn't be the Death Mask Murderer. Doesn't have it in him. He says Max visits him every week. Takes him out to give the wife a break. Without sounding too calculating, it will make the jury more sympathetic towards Max. The fact is he needs all the help he can get.

'We do have one problem. Max won't tell me what he was doing in South

Road on the day of the storm. His alibi was false. His cousins don't live in South Road anymore.'

Emma threw her hands into the air. 'Why are they suggesting that Max was planning to kill me? Max is no murderer. He saved my life.'

Upjohn shrugged his shoulders. 'Wasp is building a profile of a psychologically damaged man whose behaviour is violent and erratic. It will come out in the trial that he assaulted a senior officer and one of the nurses at the field hospital.'

'He assaulted a nurse?' Emma's voice wavered.

'I'm afraid so.'

'Was she hurt?'

'Badly bruised cheek and a black eye, according to the records.'

Emma's shoulders slumped. Sophie and Mrs Darrow exchanged glances.

'I've spoken to Max about it,' Upjohn continued. 'He said that he panicked and hit out at her. He's deeply remorseful and doesn't like to be reminded of what he did.

'The prosecution will argue that Max has a history of violence against women. All I can offer in rebuttal was that it was the effects of shell shock.'

'What about that woman killed last week? Max couldn't have done it. He was still in the Watch House.'

'Detective Inspector Wasp claims it's unrelated. A crime of passion. Likely to have been murdered by someone close to her, not the Death Mask Murderer.'

Emma looked downcast. 'This isn't going very well, is it?'

'It's too early to judge. The only case that they can conclusively link Max with is the murder of Agnes Reason, based on the fact that he may have associated with Christian Reason on the ship coming home.'

'What's the penalty for accessory to murder?' asked Mrs Darrow, raising her pince-nez and eyeing Upjohn.

'Life imprisonment.'

It was like the air had been sucked out of the room. Emma plucked at her skirt and then brushed a tear from her eye. Aunt Florence lowered her pince-nez and pursed her lips. Sophie took in the defeated expressions of the two women and excused herself, closing the door behind her.

John Upjohn broke the silence. 'I'm sorry to bring such bad news. However, I have managed to find out that piece of information that you wanted: the name of the solicitors acting for the Crabtree estate. They're Alexander and Smythe, in William Street.'

* * *

After Upjohn had gone, Emma found Sophie in the library, thumbing through one of Mrs Darrow's volumes on music.

'Upjohn's unusual,' said Sophie, looking up at her friend. 'He actually seems to care about what happens to Max. It doesn't sound positive, though. Are you sure that you should be so involved, Emma?'

'It's time I took responsibility for my actions. It wasn't intentional, but I've made Max a suspect in the murders.'

'You can't blame yourself for his arrest?'

'Just like I didn't want to blame myself for Clive's enlistment. And his death.'

'What about your reputation?'

'You mean associating with a man accused of being accessory to murder? I have to stop putting myself first. Max needs people to stand by him, and I'm going to do that. I do like him and perhaps I am starting to fall in love with him. But this time I'm not starry-eyed. This is real life. I know that Max is fragile. I know he has problems. But I also know that he wouldn't willingly hurt anyone.'

'What about the nurse?'

Emma's clear blue eyes glistened with tears. 'I don't know what to think about that. It's awful. I find it hard to reconcile that with the man I know.'

'Maybe you don't know him as well as you think you do?'

She sighed. 'Maybe I don't.'

Sophie hesitated, considering her next words. 'You're sure that he has nothing to do with these murders?'

'I'm sure.'

'Then I'll give you some advice.' Sophie paused. 'I've always been honest with you. Don't rush into a relationship if Max is found not guilty. He's suffered in the War. He needs help.'

'I understand what you're saying.'

'What about Clive? Do you think about him much?'

'I'll always remember him fondly. I decided to take a step towards healing the rift between his mother and me. I wrote to her two weeks ago. I thought it was time. I apologised for encouraging Clive to go to war. All that patriotic rubbish that I believed in. Dying for king and country. Funny that I can see through it now. I asked her to forgive me.'

'And did she reply?'

'Not so far.

'This war has damaged so many people,' Emma continued. 'Clive's mother is just one of many. Along with me. And poor Clive paid the ultimate price. But the real problem is soldiers like Max and Christian Reason who witnessed things on the battlefield that no one should ever see. They come home and we expect them to take up where they left off. Go back to work. Be a husband, a brother, a son, a father again.'

Sophie took her friend's hand. 'Be careful. To tell you the truth, I'm afraid for you. Those drawings of death masks in the newspaper? Your name was mentioned. And this case gets worse and worse.'

'Don't worry about me,' Emma assured her. 'For the first time in my life, I'm not afraid. Max needs my help and that's the only thing that matters.'

Chapter Thirty

A week after Upjohn's visit, Emma Hart and Aunt Florence motored down Point Nepean Road to the offices of Alexander and Smythe, Solicitors. With George at the wheel, the Ford purred along, giving the two women the opportunity to have a good chat before the appointed time of their meeting with the Crabtree estate solicitors. Armed with the information provided by Upjohn, Mrs Darrow had made an appointment with Edward Smythe, one of the senior partners, on the pretext of requiring legal advice on a family matter.

Aunt Florence was invigorated by the novelty of travelling into the city. It was rare that she ventured outside Brighton, and she relished the sights and smells of the journey. The weather; the traffic on the streets; the grimy factories of Richmond; the working-class terrace houses; the outfits worn by cyclists; the garb of women walking along the footpaths; people boating on the Yarra River. Nothing was too trivial a subject for the elderly lady as they drove towards Melbourne. Emma smiled to herself, enjoying her great-aunt's good mood and the never-ending stream of conversation.

As they turned into Flinders Street, Mrs Darrow leaned in towards Emma. 'Do you have feelings for Max Rushforth?'

Emma took a moment to answer. 'When I first met him, I was grateful to him. He saved my life. I felt an affinity with him because we've both been affected by the War.'

'You're serious about him, though?'

'I confess I feel something for him. I thought he felt the same way about me. Then he was arrested and everything changed. But I still want to help him.' She studied her great-aunt. 'Living with you has changed me, Aunt Florence. You don't sit on your hands. You do something and I want to be like you.'

Mrs Darrow beamed. 'Thank you, Emma.'

'One thing hasn't changed though. You still irritate me sometimes.'

Aunt Florence burst out laughing. 'You can be quite challenging too, my girl.'

Emma shook her head. 'I was terrible when I came here. Moody. Self-indulgent. That's what you called me. You were right.'

'A gentle prod, that's all you needed. But you still need to determine what you want from your life.' Mrs Darrow looked out the window. 'We're here. Time to extract some information from Messrs Alexander and Smythe.'

The car pulled into the curb next to an impressive stone building dating from the 1880s. A brass plaque announced that they had reached their destination: the offices of the solicitors entrusted with representing the interests of Thomas Crabtree in the absence of a will.

Emma walked up the steps leading into the building. She wore a smart honey-coloured and cream-checked skirt and matching jacket, button-up boots in brown leather, and a fur hat with a small brim. Aunt Florence was also dressed to the nines, in an elegant black satin suit, frilly lace blouse, and large brimmed hat complete with feather. A fox fur was draped around her shoulders.

'We have to impress these men,' Aunt Florence had stressed earlier that day.

A clerk showed them into the office of Edward Smythe, senior partner. The room was musty, a combination of cigars and old money. Smythe emerged from behind his large mahogany desk, appraising the appearance of the two women to whom he had just been introduced. They were the sort of clients that Alexander and Smythe, Solicitors, would welcome. He was a man in his late fifties, wearing the usual garb favoured by the legal profession: winged collar, navy blue tie, silk waistcoat, and dark suit. Antiquated but professional. Behind him was an impressive collection of legal tomes, bound in red leather, which lined one wall of the office. The introductions completed; they took their seats.

'How may I be of service, Mrs Darrow?'

'A family matter, Mr Smythe.'

'An errant son perhaps or,' he suggested, glancing at Emma Hart, 'a matter of breach of promise?'

'No, nothing so exciting,' replied Aunt Florence, waving her hand as if swatting away a fly. 'I am considering changing my will. I'd like young Emma to be a beneficiary. Perhaps an allowance too, before my death.'

Emma looked startled. 'Aunt Florence, we need to talk about this. I don't need—'

Mrs Darrow raised an eyebrow at her great-niece, silencing her immediately. She turned back to the solicitor. 'But I need legal advice from someone well-versed in wills. Do you know of anyone?'

The solicitor flushed. 'I would be honoured to assist you in your legal affairs.'

'How do these things work, Mr Smythe?'

The solicitor explained the legal and financial arrangements that Mrs Darrow would have to put in place, if Emma were to receive an allowance or become a beneficiary of her will. He suggested that she give some thought to the amounts involved, and to consider the tax advantages of different approaches. Finally, he suggested that once she had made such decisions, she could return and they would draw up the necessary documents.

'How did you hear of us, may I ask?'

'A lady associated with one of my charities mentioned that you were administering the Crabtree estate. I knew Matilda and Thomas in the past. I heard that you are doing a sterling job sorting out their estate. I want the same for myself.'

'The Crabtree estate. It's the bane of my existence.' Mr Smythe mopped his brow with a handkerchief. 'So many relatives joining the queue of those contesting the estate. There won't be a penny left to distribute soon. Poor Mr Crabtree would turn in his grave if he saw what's happening.'

'It must be very difficult for you.'

Smythe put his handkerchief away. 'Indeed, it is.' He paused, noting her questioning look. 'Of course, as you say, we at Alexander and Smythe are well-equipped to deal with such situations.'

Mrs Darrow raised her pince-nez and studied the solicitor before speaking. 'It was such a sad business. The tragedy in the Crabtree family.'

'You are right. The story is a sad one.'

Aunt Florence nodded at Emma, who took her cue. 'Pardon, Mr Smythe. I'm not familiar with the story. Could you enlighten me please?'

'An unfortunate state of affairs. I'm not divulging anything confidential by telling you what is available in the public domain.'

'I would never expect you to.'

'Our company represented the Crabtree family for many years. The events of which you speak occurred in the time of my father, Edward Smythe, Senior. Thomas and Matilda Crabtree had two sons, Frederick and Henry. Tragically, the younger one died, and shortly after, Matilda Crabtree took her own life.'

'How did the boy die?'

'Henry drowned in the fishpond. He slipped and fell in.'

'How sad. And the elder Master Crabtree? Did he stay with his father?'

Edward Smythe sat back in his chair, frowning. 'As far as I know, he was sent to boarding school.'

'How tragic. Sent away after his mother's death.' She paused, her brows knitted in mock concern. 'So sad. Is Frederick Crabtree contesting the estate too?'

'Mr Frederick Crabtree was provided for while his father was alive. He receives an annuity, which is separate to the estate.'

'Just as Emma will,' said Mrs Darrow, smiling indulgently at her great-niece. 'And how does he collect it?'

The solicitor was looking distinctly uncomfortable. 'That too was organised in the time of my father. It is administered by the State Trustees.' Edward Smythe smiled uneasily. 'Perhaps I have said too much. Suffice it to say, the annuity is not part of our purview.'

'And where does Mr Crabtree live now?'

Edward Smythe came out from behind his desk. 'Thank you so much for coming, Mrs Darrow and Miss Hart. If I can be of service in the future in regard to the allowance or change of will, do not hesitate to contact me.'

The meeting was over and the two ladies were shown to the door. As they descended the steps outside the building, Aunt Florence patted Emma's shoulder. 'Well done, my dear. We nearly had him.'

'He knows more than he is letting on. State Trustees? Isn't that rather odd?'

Aunt Florence paused and looked back at the doorway through which they had come. 'Curiouser and curiouser. The plot thickens.'

Chapter Thirty-One

It was Empire Day. Emma Hart was in the parlour, listening to the gramophone. Billy Murray was singing 'Over there' and she sang along, hoping indeed that the Yanks would help finish off the War soon. A pot of tea was on the side table next to her. With Aunt Florence out visiting a sick friend, Emma had the house to herself. On her lap were two letters, one from her mother and the other from Silas Bacon.

Jenny Hart wrote regularly to her daughter. She spoke of life on the farm and the latest gossip in Donald. She told her of babies born and marriages blighted by death in the War. And she confessed how much she missed her only daughter, her beloved Emma, and hoped that she was happy in her new home. Perhaps, she suggested, Emma might visit sometime soon?

She put her mother's letter aside and promised herself that she would make the long train trip up to Donald, as soon as Max was freed and the real culprit was behind bars.

Emma picked up the letter that Silas Bacon had written the week before. It was more personal in nature than she would have expected of him. In the letter, Silas confessed that he was deeply troubled by the events of the past two months: the murder of his former colleague, Walter Eames, and the arrest of Max Rushforth.

He wrote of his friendship with Max's family, which went back some twenty-five years. He described how Max, as a child, had been kind and gentle, unwilling to engage in arguments or fights. The sudden death of his parents in a boating accident had certainly had an effect on him and made him solitary and withdrawn for a time. But, with the support and care of

163

his older sister and family friends, he had weathered the storm and finished his education, attaining a degree in engineering.

War had been a setback for him. From their recent meeting, Silas had noted the changes in Max. He could see that his friend had suffered psychologically as well as physically but, with time and support, he believed that these problems could be overcome too.

Nothing could change his mind about Max's innate goodness and strong sense of morality. In Silas's view, Max was incapable of such a crime. He believed that it would be a miscarriage of justice if Max were to be found guilty of accessory to murder.

And, in conclusion, Silas asked that if there were to be another meeting of those interested in solving the mystery of the Death Mask Murders, he would like to be included. He wanted Max freed and the real culprit incarcerated.

By return mail, Emma had invited him to join Aunt Florence, Reggie da Costa, and herself at the offices of John Upjohn on the 27th of May.

She frowned at the thought of seeing Reggie again. *The Argus*'s top crime reporter, as he styled himself, was nothing more than a study in self-interest, in her view. His attentiveness towards her was based on his assumption that she would inherit Mrs Darrow's millions. Despite what had been said in the offices of Alexander and Smythe, Emma believed that her great-aunt intended to leave the bulk of her estate to her philanthropic causes. Her question about making Emma her main beneficiary was nothing more than a clever ruse to extract information from Edward Smythe.

Emma took a sip of tea and picked up *The Argus*, which Mrs Williams had brought in for her. She read some of the main articles: the Victoria Cross would be awarded to seven soldiers of the British forces, the RAF had bombed Cologne and the Acting Prime Minister had suggested that the minimum age for enlistment be reduced to nineteen years for youths, without the need for parental consent. She was tired of war: tired of hearing about young men who had died in active service; tired of watching the government scramble to replace them with more reinforcements; tired of reading about airstrikes and battles.

Emma laid aside the newspaper and took up her sketchpad. She flipped through the drawings she had made over the last few months, some from life, some from memory. Aunt Florence, feisty and determined, her eyes full of defiance and her chin jutting forward; obstinate. Reggie da Costa, show-pony, with his thick expressive eyebrows and luxuriant black hair, impeccably groomed, as usual, a smug expression on his face. Silas Bacon, a mass of contradictions, with long effeminate fingers and broad brow, unsettling in appearance yet with kind eyes. And Max Rushforth, pale eyelashes, untidy hair, preoccupied, staring into the distance. Each one was well-defined and recognisable, showing the stuff of their personalities. She had captured the essence of those she had drawn.

And on the last page was a self-portrait. She stared at it for a while. Anyone would know it was her. But try as she might, it was hard to see the truth of her in the charcoal lines that framed her face. The other sketches indicated a strong sense of their subjects, but hers did not. It was as if she were a blank outline, to be filled in at a later date. Aunt Florence was right. She needed to believe in something. She needed to make plans. She felt in limbo, trapped, albeit willingly, by Max's plight. Until that was resolved, there could be no thoughts about the future.

Chapter Thirty-Two

Reggie da Costa was in a quandary, caught between the need to keep Mrs Darrow happy and his calling as a crime reporter. One of the biggest stories of his working life was at his fingertips and he could not publish it. Although he now believed Max to be innocent, Reggie would not have hesitated to implicate Max Rushforth in the Death Mask Murders case if it meant furthering his own career.

The problem was that Emma's great-aunt was supporting the ex-soldier in a quest to prove his innocence. If Reggie were to woo Emma Hart, he needed the old lady's approval. She could be cantankerous and obstinate if crossed. He had experienced that personally when he had published his first article on the discovery of the death masks. His mother had also made it abundantly clear that her happiness depended on Mrs Darrow's goodwill. He was in a bind.

Marriage to Emma Hart, heiress to the Seymour Grove mansion and Mrs Darrow's wealth, would give Reggie the lifestyle he craved. All the trappings of success would be his. Emma's money would provide him with the best of everything: fashionable suits, the latest automobile, servants, good food, and wine. His mother would be restored to her rightful place in society, repairing the damage done by his wastrel of a father. And Emma and he would preside over dinner parties with the cream of society, and travel to Europe once this wretched war was over.

Emma Hart. She was beautiful and talented, that was true, but she was also opinionated. In a marriage, there was only room for one such person. And that was he. It would be necessary to educate her as to the superiority of the male mind once they were married.

He frowned. Emma was far too interested in Max Rushforth. Couldn't she see that aligning herself with the da Costas was preferable to associating with a man who, quite plainly, was her social inferior? When would she come to her senses?

He studied his unpublished story, fresh from his typewriter:

DEATH MASK MURDERS
MAX RUSHFORTH ACCESSORY TO MURDER
Profile of a killer
By REGGIE DA COSTA, Senior Crime Reporter

Mr Maxwell Clifford Rushforth, aged twenty-nine, has been charged with being accessory to the murder of Mrs Agnes Mary Reason. He will be tried in criminal court as an accomplice to Mr Christian William Reason, who was convicted of his wife's murder in 1917.

His personal history is peppered with violence and psychological trauma. As a child, his parents drowned in a boating accident, leaving him to be raised by his older sister.

Unpredictable and violent

While a soldier on the Western Front, Private Rushforth saw active service at Fromelles. After showing considerable bravery in rescuing one of his mates in the heat of battle, Rushforth inexplicably assaulted a senior officer, breaking his jaw. He managed to escape a court-martial due to his fragile mental state.

Private Rushforth was diagnosed with war neurosis and was sent to a field hospital. It was there that he attacked a nurse, a woman who was ministering to wounded patients. She was hospitalised for a short period of time. His action shocked and appalled medical staff. If not for the intervention of the nurse, who selflessly spoke on his behalf, Rush-

forth would have been incarcerated in a military prison.

Unfit for duty

So dire was his condition that he underwent intensive treatment, which included electroshock therapy. Mr Rushforth was declared unfit for duty and was sent home in 1917. He took up a position as a part-time clerical officer at the St Kilda Road Barracks.

Withdrawn and anti-social

Mr Rushforth lives alone. His sister resides in Queensland and has not been in contact with her brother since his return from the War. It appears that he has few friends. Work colleagues at the St Kilda Barracks describe him as withdrawn and anti-social. They state that he has been known to react aggressively when under pressure. At a recent garden party, he collapsed.

However, according to Detective Inspector Wasp of the Criminal Investigation Branch, his sanity is not in question:

'There is no doubt that Mr Rushforth is of sound mind and body, and should stand trial as an accessory to the murder of Mrs Agnes Reason. He has a history of violent and unpredictable behaviour. We can only guess at his motivation in committing this crime. His friendship with Dr Silas Bacon, former employee at Kreitmayer's Wax Museum, has given him intimate knowledge of the means of producing death masks. What they symbolise to him is beyond my understanding. What I am sure of is that Mr Rushforth, cold-bloodedly and with prior intent, assisted in the murder of Mrs Agnes Reason and created her death mask for his own gratification. We know that he was acquainted with the deceased's husband, because they were repatriated back to Melbourne on the same ship.

'The women of Brighton will sleep more soundly when

this dangerous man is off the streets and in a prison cell where he belongs.'

Reggie took one last look at the story.

'Damn. If only—'

He screwed it up and threw it in the bin.

For the next hour, he sat at his desk in the newsroom, checking through the archives of *The Argus*, looking for a woman who had either gone missing or died in mysterious circumstances in the last eighteen months. He had committed Emma's first sketch of the death masks to memory, but he was no closer to finding a match.

He cursed under his breath and made ready to go home. On Monday, he would meet again with the delicious Miss Hart, her feisty great-aunt, and Dr Silas Bacon. Now that was a strange man! Those long thin delicate fingers and large ears, thought Reggie.

'If I had to pick a killer, it would be Bacon, not Rushforth.' He chuckled despite his sour mood.

He took the crumpled piece of paper out of the bin and smoothed it out on his desk.

'Brilliant writing, Reggie,' he told himself. 'Such a pity you can't use it.'

Chapter Thirty-Three

The next meeting of Reggie, Silas, Aunt Florence, and Emma was convened in the offices of John Upjohn, which were situated in a nondescript laneway off King Street. They sat around a large rosewood table in an interview room, helping themselves to the sandwiches provided by Mrs Darrow's cook.

As they partook of an early lunch, they listened to the solicitor, as he updated them on the progress of the case.

'I've instructed Mr Alfred Whitehead to act as Max's barrister. He's very competent.'

'Can't you do it?' asked Emma. 'I'm sure that Max would prefer you.'

'It's not how it works, Miss Hart. I am a solicitor. I do not usually represent a client in a courtroom.'

He referred to his notes. 'The case against Max hinges on the following: his unstable personality, as evidenced by his shell shock and the attack on a senior officer and nurse; the argument that he was intending to kidnap Miss Hart; his familiarity with the Crabtree mansion; his alleged expertise in making death masks, courtesy of Dr Bacon; his alleged association with Christian Reason on the *Wiltshire*.'

'What can the defence offer?' asked Mrs Darrow.

'We have to suggest a viable alternative to Max. A killer who has eluded the police. A man who visited Walter Eames and Harriett Kreitmayer in his quest to learn the art of making death masks. A man responsible for the death of Walter Eames. Unfortunately, Wasp has ruled out the family members who are haggling over the Crabtree estate. He says they have neither motivation nor opportunity.'

He referred to his notes again. 'We have four confirmed victims. Agnes Reason, died August 1917. Lillian Broderick, disappeared November 1917. Bessie Cartwright, died February this year. Rosalind Baker, died in April.'

Reggie interrupted. 'And we shouldn't forget the attempted abduction of Helen Dunphy in January 1918.'

'She escaped him? Is that right?' Upjohn scribbled down a note to that effect.

'It's clear to me that there's no evidence tying Mr Rushforth to any death apart from that of Agnes Reason,' said Mrs Darrow.

Upjohn nodded in agreement. 'That's true unless you accept the prosecution's argument that Max made Lillian Broderick's death mask.'

'I refute any suggestion that I schooled Max in the making of them,' declared Silas. 'I have furnished the police with a statement to that effect.'

'Good for you,' said Aunt Florence. She raised her pince-nez and tapped at a newspaper on her lap. 'This latest death. Surely there's a link to the Death Mask Murders?'

Reggie frowned. 'Miss Clara McSweeney. Twenty-six years old. Slashed so badly that identification took time. Detective Inspector Wasp insists it's the work of a different criminal.'

'Do you believe that?'

Reggie shook his head. 'She fits his type. And her head was partially shaved.'

'It's a bad business,' said Upjohn. 'And there's a real problem. Max won't tell me what he was doing in Brighton on the day of the storm. It looks suspicious, as if he were waiting around for his next victim. They also found newspaper articles about Agnes Reason, Bessie Cartwright, and Lillian Broderick at his house.'

'He was probably doing some research before he met with Agnes's husband,' suggested Emma.

'That's hard to prove.' John Upjohn stood. 'Unfortunately, I must leave you. I'm due in court. Max needs your help. The odds are stacked against him.'

* * *

When he had gone, Emma turned to Reggie. 'You're a crime reporter. Can't you write something to support Max's cause?'

Reggie was offended. 'I don't do opinion pieces. I report crime.'

'Fiddlesticks,' said Aunt Florence. 'I'm sure that you could help sway public opinion in his favour.'

Reggie looked uncomfortable. 'I can't promise anything.'

'Detective Inspector Wasp isn't the only one looking into the Crabtree family,' said Emma. 'I interviewed their former housekeeper and found out a few interesting facts. Matilda and Thomas had two children: Frederick, who was adopted, and a younger brother, Henry. The little boy drowned in the fishpond. Mrs Crabtree committed suicide after his death, then Frederick was sent away to boarding school. He's not been seen since. She also suggested that Frederick may have had a hand in his brother's death, but there's no proof of that at the moment.'

'Fancy sending a seven-year-old away after his mother had died.' Aunt Florence tut-tutted.

Silas stood and moved to the fireplace; his arms folded.

'Perhaps I'm missing something,' said Reggie. 'What does Frederick Crabtree have to do with the Death Mask Murders?'

'I feel there's a connection,' replied Emma. 'He's a man who knows the place, knows about the cellar.'

'So did Max. So, most probably, did many others.'

'That's true, but I'd like to know where Frederick went in 1882.'

Silas looked startled. '1882?'

'That's right. Why do you ask?'

'No reason. Just interested.'

Emma went on to explain about the annuity that was being paid to Frederick. 'Where is he now? He might have some connection with these murders.'

'Really, Emma,' smirked Reggie. 'You're letting your imagination run away with you.'

172

Emma flushed. 'It would help if we knew where he collects his allowance, but Edward Smythe is hardly going to tell us anything more.'

'We'll see,' said Aunt Florence.

Reggie shook his head. 'I really think we're wasting our time on Frederick Crabtree. Unless he developed an obsession with phrenology and death masks!' He guffawed at his joke. 'Now, Dr Bacon, you've been very quiet. What can you offer us?'

Silas Bacon looked up, distracted. He shook his head. 'I can offer nothing, I'm afraid.'

'You mustn't worry about Max,' Emma assured him. 'We'll free him.'

Silas smiled bleakly. 'Thank you. I hope you're right.'

Aunt Florence stood and surveyed the group. 'If there's nothing more, I must go. Would everyone be willing to meet again, closer to the trial date?' Reggie and Silas nodded in agreement. 'Thank you, gentlemen. Emma, do you want to come to the Red Cross or will we drop you at Spencer Street station?'

'I'll catch the train.'

Reggie stepped forward. 'I'm going back to Brighton. I could take you to Seymour Grove.'

'Are you sure? I don't want to inconvenience you.'

'I think that's an excellent idea,' said Mrs Darrow, looking at Emma through her pince-nez. She picked up her handbag and kissed her great-niece goodbye.

Reggie hovered near Emma, impatient to leave. 'Are you ready, Emma?'

'Can you give us a moment, please? I'd like to speak to Silas.'

He raised an eyebrow. 'I'll be at the car.' He turned on his heel and left.

'Silas, what is it? Something's bothering you.'

'You are very perceptive, Emma. Something was mentioned today that reminded me of the past.'

'What was it?'

'It would be premature of me to say.' He checked his watch. 'I am late. I must get back to work.'

He doffed his hat. 'It's probably nothing.'

* * *

Out on the street, Reggie da Costa was leaning against his immaculate black Dodge Roadster, tapping his foot restlessly. Emma emerged from Upjohn's offices then climbed into the passenger seat. Her shapely ankles caught Reggie's attention. He turned the crank handle and the engine responded immediately. With the car in second gear, he released the brake and revved the engine. The Dodge Roadster surged forward. Reggie smiled broadly and sat back in the driver's seat as he steered the car south.

It was hard to make conversation above the roar of the automobile. They headed out of the city and were soon making their way along St Kilda Road, past the roller-skating rink of Wirth Brothers' Circus at the Hippodrome.

Fifty minutes later they pulled up outside Mrs Darrow's house, the Dodge's engine idling noisily.

'It's always a pleasure to see you,' said Reggie, leaning in towards her and running his fingers through his hair. He smiled, winningly. 'You have it all, Emma. Beauty, artistic talent *and* intelligence. We'd make a great couple.'

'I don't think so, Reggie.'

He tried to take her hand but she pulled away.

'Admit it, Emma. You can hardly fail to notice that I have all the attributes of a most suitable husband. Look at me. I'm well-groomed, I have excellent taste and I'm on my way up in the world.'

'I thought you were a socialist? Aren't you supposed to be above all that?'

'I'm a pragmatist too.'

Emma sighed. 'Your timing is poor. Max has to be my top priority.'

Reggie frowned. 'A woman's reputation can be lost, just like that.' He snapped his fingers. 'You need a man to guide you. I am that man.'

Emma rolled her eyes. 'I don't want a guide. And, at this stage, I don't want a husband.'

Reggie was not impressed 'You'll regret turning me down. You may not have many offers after this business with Rushforth is over.'

She ignored his jibe and got out of the car. 'Thank you for bringing me home.' She smiled sweetly.

'My pleasure,' he replied. Reggie revved the engine and drove off, his mouth set in a grim line.

Chapter Thirty-Four

Silas Bacon stared out at the landscape from his carriage window as the steam train wound its way from Ballarat onto Ararat, 130 miles north-west of Melbourne. It had been thirty-one years since he had seen the town that he first called home in 1882. With a population of over 3,000 people, wine-making and mining industries, and a vibrant town life comprising numerous hotels, churches, a library, and a mechanics institute, the Ararat of the 1880s had offered the young Silas an active social life apart from his working existence. But Silas had been a serious young man, single-minded and disinterested in frivolous activities or the opposite sex.

After the meeting at Mrs Darrow's house in Seymour Grove, Silas had spent the evening at home contemplating whether his past had converged with the present, and what he intended to do about it, if it were true. There seemed no other choice but to request leave from his boss at the Melbourne Museum. It was granted without question, given that Silas had never taken holidays in the years that he had worked there. And so it was that Silas boarded the train that would force him to revisit his past.

The passing parade of farmhouses, gum trees, livestock, and ploughed fields was lost on Silas. Even his hobby of counting the different types of eucalypts growing in the fields did not alleviate his anxiety. The fate of his friend, Max Rushforth, and the victims of the Death Mask Murderer, were on his mind.

He was sharing the compartment with two women and a young child. The little boy was intrigued by the strange-looking man with the big ears and large forehead sitting opposite him. He slipped off his seat and rested his hands upon Silas's knees, staring up into his face.

'Hello, mister.'

Silas smiled, patting the boy on the head.

'Charlie. Come away. Leave the man alone.'

It was always the same, thought Silas. He scared people. If it weren't his strange and unsettling appearance, it was his analytical and detached demeanour, and his dedication to scientific pursuits, that excluded him from relationships. But Silas was comfortable with what he was. He had learned to live with the type of response that he had just evoked.

The train pulled into Ararat railway station. Collecting his bag from the overhead rack, Silas exited the platform and walked up Barkly Street to the Turf Hotel, where he checked in for three nights. His room was basic: a simple iron bedstead, washbowl on a stand, and a wardrobe. He unpacked his things, placed his books on the side table next to the bed, and proceeded down the corridor to the bathroom, where he washed and shaved. Dinner was simple but plentiful and, after downing a beer, Silas climbed the stairs, undressed, and settled into bed, drawing the blankets up around his ears. Tomorrow would be unpleasant, to say the least, and a good night's sleep would help him prepare for the emotional toll it would take on him.

It was around nine o'clock the next morning when Silas set off along Barkly Street again. He passed the impressive Classical Revival town hall, built in 1898. Its symmetrical facade was pleasing to him, with its central clock tower flanked by two bays with columns and pediments. He was tempted to linger there for a while, but his true destination was still two miles away. Reluctantly, he moved on.

The road stretched before him as he passed through the town and on to the outskirts of Ararat. How things had changed in thirty-one years, just as he had. No longer was he the newly qualified doctor fresh out of medical school, full of naïve enthusiasm. Every step along the road was a step into the past, when his beliefs and values had been so markedly different. He still believed in science, but not in the theories that he had embraced so fervently all those years ago.

Silas came to a fork in the road, one leading to Ballarat and the other leading to a place that he had put out of his mind for so long. If he had a choice, he would have gone back in time to the year 1882 and taken the road to Ballarat. But the past could not be altered. He knew that he would have to deal with the ramifications of the decision he had made when he was twenty-one years old.

The hill was steep and he trudged up the dirt road, knowing that when he looked up to the left, he would see the familiar sight of the Ararat Lunatic Asylum on the rise. And there it was: a complex of elaborate Italianate buildings dating from the 1860s. It had been extended since then to house a conglomeration of psychotics, alcoholics, drug addicts, the intellectually and physically disabled, and those whose relatives had managed to procure two signatures from doctors to commit them to its confines. On each side of the central building was a two-storeyed wing, one for each sex. Iron-columned verandahs lined the surrounding courtyards.

The asylum was a town within a town, self-sufficient with its own market gardens, orchard, and livestock. The 600 acres of grounds were surrounded by walls that consisted of a trench, one side of which was vertical and faced with bricks, the other side sloped and grassy. From the inside, the high walls prevented the inmates from escaping, while from the outside the walls looked low so as not to suggest imprisonment. He thought grimly that the Ararat residents were similarly misled by the elaborate design of the buildings. Unless one experienced what occurred within those walls, one would believe that the inmates lived comfortably.

As a gullible and unsophisticated young man, he had taken up a position as a doctor, living and practising within the asylum, believing that he could help cure the patients. But five years working in that profession shattered his idealism. Neglect and maltreatment were the norm. And what made it worse was that he, Silas Bacon, had been party to the mistreatment of the sad souls who lived and died there.

His heart was heavy as he walked up the driveway to the main gate. Above him, looking down through the stained-glass window of the main office on the first floor, was a man dressed in a white coat. Silas knew that it was most likely the asylum's superintendent. This was the man to whom he had addressed his request for a visit, mentioning his previous employment as a doctor there many years before. He had expressed a wish to study new methods of psychiatric treatment, which would give him a credible reason to gain access to the asylum. If the superintendent knew his true purpose, he would not have admitted him.

He showed the telegram that he had received from Dr Stone to the guards on the gate. After he had been issued with a visitor's pass, which he clipped onto his jacket pocket, he was admitted to the main courtyard, where he was told to wait.

A white-coated doctor emerged from a doorway and walked forward, extending his hand.

'Dr Bacon. So pleased to meet you. I'm Dr Stone's assistant, Paul Plunkett. The superintendent has asked me to show you around.' They shook hands. 'Afterwards he would be pleased if you could join him for tea in his office, before you depart.'

'Dr Stone is very kind.'

Plunkett took Silas on a tour of the institution, showing him the ornate hall, dormitories, men's hospital, kitchens, and bathrooms. He bypassed the corridors that housed those in solitary confinement. Outside, inmates huddled under large outdoor shelters, shading themselves from the sun. From experience, Silas knew that some medications could make people sensitive to sunlight.

Despite Dr Plunkett's best efforts, nothing could protect Silas from seeing the disturbing side of life at the Ararat Lunatic Asylum. They would come across patients who would stare at them blankly, the result of being medicated. An inmate wandered past, talking to himself and giggling. From afar, Silas heard the cries of mental anguish, tuneless singing, hysterical laughter, and the babbling of voices. At times, Plunkett steered Silas away from some parts of the complex, but the smell of disinfectant, faeces, and urine could not be hidden.

'Some of our inmates are difficult,' Plunkett muttered by way of explanation, 'but you would know that.'

It was what he had not seen that bothered him most. He suspected that little had changed in thirty years. He had been shown a fraction of the inmates and those he had seen were relatively well-cared for and well-behaved.

But what of the others? Where were they? Most likely they were the victims of rude and vulgar attendants, who were poorly trained and ignorant of psychiatric disorders, concerned only with stifling the ravings and torment of the patients. It was not hard to understand why a relatively normal person would become a lunatic, he thought. Filthy baths, poor quality food, uncomfortable beds, nights disturbed by the ranting and screams of one's neighbours, with nothing to occupy one's mind except the desire for freedom or death.

And he recalled the tipping point that had made him pack up and leave the Ararat Lunatic Asylum over thirty years ago: the sight of body parts in jars, the results of autopsies on some of the poor devils who died there. It epitomised the objectification and dehumanisation of the patients. They were little more than laboratory rats to be used in experiments. And he, Dr Silas Bacon, was as guilty as the rest of them.

Silas shivered. Someone walking over my grave, he thought.

'Can I visit the treatment areas?' he asked.

'Dr Stone would prefer that you stay within the main buildings. Even with your experience here, you may find some things disturbing. The inmates suffer from a range of mental problems, and we endeavour to treat them appropriately.'

'How many patients do you house these days?'

'Over five hundred.'

'Impressive.'

At the end of one of the buildings was a doctor's office. It was occupied by a secretary who waved to Dr Plunkett. Silas stopped as they greeted each other. As he waited, he glanced past the woman into the inner office. Something caught his eye. Underneath a window, stored in a glass display case, was a death mask. It was of a man, his shiny bald head catching the light. It stared back at him through sightless eyes, the lids half-closed.

Silas felt a surge of excitement go through him. As he followed Dr Plunkett out into a courtyard, Silas looked back and noted the number on the side of the building: 8B.

The superintendent's assistant took him gently by the arm. 'Now, if you don't mind, we will finish the tour. I will take you to Dr Stone's office in the administration building.'

Silas followed Plunkett up the staircase to the landing, and waited while he was announced to the superintendent. He studied the magnificence of his immediate surroundings, and compared them with the starkly clinical nature of the buildings housing the inmates.

Silas was shown into the office of Dr Stone. He was sitting behind an impressive mahogany desk. His academic qualifications from universities, along with his psychiatric credentials, were displayed on one wall. A large painting of the asylum adorned the opposite wall. The artist had depicted it in the Romantic style, its elaborate Italianate buildings rising above the landscape, bathed in an ethereal light.

The doctor himself was lean and angular, with sharp features and a long nose, accentuated by the fact that he was afflicted with curvature of the spine, so that he appeared to be leaning forward. Silas was reminded of a praying mantis. He recognised him as the same man he had seen on arrival.

'Please, take a seat. It is a pleasure to meet one of our former employees. Tea?' Silas nodded and watched as Stone poured from a white porcelain teapot. 'Remind me, when were you with us?'

'Five years. From 1882. I was hoping to specialise in psychiatric disorders. Unfortunately, it was not my calling.'

'A lunatic asylum is a challenging environment.'

'That is true. However, I have not lost my interest in psychiatry. I was hoping you could enlighten me as to the most recent methods of treatment.'

Silas allowed the superintendent to take the lead in the conversation and listened as he warmed to his subject.

'We are still reliant on some of the old techniques that were used in your time: straitjackets and restraint, ice baths, isolation, and sedative drugs such as bromides. Of course, these are only used on unruly patients.'

'Of course. Any newer treatments?'

'One of my doctors has been experimenting with lobotomies. Quite fascinating!' He smiled indulgently at Silas. 'If I may explain. About twenty years ago a Swiss physician, Gottlieb Burkhardt, removed parts of the cortex from the brains of patients with severe mental illness. He noted that it made them calm. It involves severing connections in the prefrontal lobe. Results have been inconsistent so far, I'm afraid.'

'I'm sure that you'll make progress in that area.'

'We hope so. I am, of course, deeply interested in new approaches to psychology. In fact, I have been immersing myself in the theories postulated by Freud and Jung. Have you heard of analytical psychology and psychoanalysis?'

'My knowledge would be insignificant next to yours.'

Dr Stone glowed with pleasure. 'My dear Dr Bacon, you are too kind.'

He went on to describe how psychotherapy could be used to assist the patient in re-establishing a healthy relationship with the unconscious mind.

'But I digress. Is there anything more that I can do for you?'

'As a matter of fact, I was only thinking the other day about a patient that I worked with, all those years ago. He was a mere child, but he had been committed to the asylum for an unspeakable act, the crime of fratricide. Would you be able to enlighten me as to whether he recovered and has resumed his place in society?'

'Do you recall his name?'

'Frederick. I cannot recall his surname.'

'That's because you never knew it. We only ever refer to patients by their Christian names. In this way, we respect their privacy. However, as you are a medical practitioner and former employee, I will make an exception.'

Dr Stone indicated a large set of wooden filing cabinets, which were situated behind his desk.

'I glanced at your file before you came here today. It details the patients you worked with and the research that you carried out in your time here.'

He swivelled his chair around and pulled open the top drawer, then thumbed through the files. 'Here's the B's. Babbich. Bach. Ah, Bacon.'

He swivelled back towards his desk and opened the folder, taking from it about a dozen documents.

'It appears that you were an advocate for phrenology.'

'That was short-lived,' Silas said, his mouth set in a thin line. 'I was taken with the scientific possibilities of predicting behaviour, until I realised the ridiculousness of the premise on which phrenology was based.'

'We must be open to new theories as practitioners of psychiatry, psychology, and medicine.'

'But not at the expense of our patients.'

'Granted, that is true.'

Stone jabbed a skinny finger at a name on the third page.

'Here's Frederick. My goodness me. You will be pleased. I know him well. I took a personal interest in him after I arrived here. He was one of our success stories, released back into society only recently. May 1917, in fact. He came to repent of the murder of his brother and to acknowledge the wrong he had done. It took many years, but I believe he benefitted from the care and treatment he received here.'

Silas sat forward. 'And his name?'

'Frederick Crabtree.'

Silas Bacon blanched and gripped the arm of his chair.

'Is something wrong?'

'A little dizzy. It's nothing. Could you remind me of the details of the case?'

Stone referred to his files. 'Frederick was adopted. His parents then had a child of their own. The boy was filled with jealousy and resented the attention that his mother bestowed on her biological son. Frederick drowned his brother in a fishpond and tried to make it look accidental, but one of the maids saw him from a window in the house.

'A seven-year-old is a slave to his feelings and drives. He does not have the power of reasoning, but acts on impulse.'

'How did the parents react?'

'At first, they tried to cover up the crime. Apparently, the resulting suicide of the mother made the way clear. Frederick was sent to this asylum with instructions that he should remain with us for as long as necessary.'

'Did he ever see his father again?'

'Unfortunately, he did not. I believe Mr Crabtree has passed on. It's a shame that he is not alive to witness his son's recovery.'

'Did Frederick develop any relationships with other inmates in his time here?'

'Inmates, no. But I believe that one of the female nurses spent a lot of time with Frederick. There was nothing inappropriate in that relationship, I might add. Apart from her, he only had contact with his doctor.'

'Did the nurse ever have any concerns about Crabtree?'

'At one stage she asked to be moved to another patient. When I asked her why, she said that Frederick was becoming a bit too dependent on her.'

'What did you do? Did you move her?'

'I felt that routine and certainty were important to Frederick, so I refused.'

'How did she deal with the problem?'

'It never went further. She left shortly after. She was expecting a baby. Sadly, she died a year ago. Shocking business. She drowned in a dam.'

'What was her name?'

'Alexandra James. She was such a lovely young woman, if a little naïve.'

'This might sound odd, but what did she look like?'

'Alexandra was very attractive, blonde with a pale complexion.' Dr Stone leaned forward in his chair. 'Why are you asking these questions? They have nothing to do with the reasons you gave for your visit.'

Silas rested his elbows on the edge of the desk, steepling his fingers. 'You may come to regret what you have done.'

'I don't understand,' said the doctor, recoiling. 'Are you accusing me of negligence?'

'Indeed I am. I believe that you have been played by a mind superior to your own. It may have taken him years, but Frederick Crabtree succeeded in escaping this place. And now he is seeking revenge on the society that locked him away in this hellhole.'

Dr Stone turned on him, his body arching forward. 'You're saying that Frederick has done something illegal?'

CHAPTER THIRTY-FOUR

'I am.'

'If I'm not wrong, your advocacy of phrenology would have determined that Crabtree was inherently criminal in nature?'

'That may be.'

He wagged a thin sheaf of papers at Silas. 'This is a journal article, written by you. You claimed that phrenology is an accurate indicator of personality. You used Frederick Crabtree as a case study. In this article, you claim that he was not morally responsible for his actions. Am I wrong?'

'No, but—'

'You worked with Frederick for five years. You gave this boy the belief that he was incapable of changing his nature. You would have told him that he was born that way.'

'That may be so—'

'And you have the temerity to suggest that it is *my* fault that he is engaged in criminal activity?'

'He was young. You can't blame me.'

'We both know, *Doctor*,' he said, 'that childhood is a vital time in forming personality. If anyone's at fault, it's *you*.'

Silas was incensed. 'You let him out, not me! You gave him his freedom. No doubt you will read about Frederick Crabtree's exploits.' He pointed a long, skinny finger at the superintendent. 'There will be repercussions.' Silas rose from his chair. 'I must go. Time is of the essence.'

Dr Stone flushed with anger. 'You don't understand the work that we are doing here.'

Silas studied the superintendent. 'Unfortunately, I do.'

'Dr Plunkett will show you out.' He rang the bell.

Silas followed the assistant down the stairs and out into the courtyard. He was angry with himself for allowing emotion to cloud his judgment. He had lost the opportunity to view the death mask in the doctor's office, which might have gone some way to explaining Frederick Crabtree's obsession.

Their farewells were interrupted by a male nurse. 'Dr Plunkett. We have a situation in 4G. Can you come?'

Plunkett turned to Silas and made his apologies. 'You know the way out?'

And with that, he was gone.

Silas lingered for a moment, battling with his conscience as to what he should do next. It did not take him long. Frederick Crabtree was his problem. He headed back to Building 8B.

The doctor's secretary looked up and smiled at him. She had rosy cheeks and fluffy, white hair, the epitome of a quintessential grandmother.

Silas favoured her with a smile. 'I'm Dr Bacon.'

She glanced at his visitor's pass. 'You were with Dr Plunkett. I'm Dr Foss's secretary, Mrs Culpepper. How can I help you?'

'I'm here to research the Ararat Lunatic Asylum's "success" stories, for want of a better word.'

'Dr Plunkett was giving you a tour?'

'He was. And then I spoke with Dr Stone. He suggested that I talk to some of the staff here.'

She registered surprise. 'He recommended me?'

Silas dug deep, trying to charm the woman. 'You would know so much of what goes on here, from a practical rather than a theoretical point of view.'

Mrs Culpepper glowed with pleasure. 'What would you like to know?'

'I heard about a patient who was released about a year ago. Frederick?'

The woman's face fell. 'Frederick. Oh yes, I remember him. He came by regularly.'

'He obviously enjoyed your company.'

'Not mine.' She gestured towards the doctor's office. 'Our mutual friend.'

'Dr Foss?'

She lowered her voice conspiratorially. 'Our mutual friend in the glass case.'

Silas raised his eyebrows. 'Do tell.'

She told Silas about the day a box had arrived eight years before. Its contents had been wrapped in linen and enclosed in a wooden frame. Frederick had been walking past and she had asked him to assist her. He had unpacked it and carried it over to the glass display case, gently placing it into position. For a few minutes, he had studied it intently.

'What's it for?' he had asked. 'Is it an ornament?'

'I told him it was the plaster cast of a man who was hanged. You should have seen his reaction. It was as if he were stung by a bee.'

She had told him that he could touch it, and he had run his hands tentatively over the smooth, cool surface.

'I should have stopped it there, but foolishly I chatted on, not realising that he was completely taken by the mask.

'I told him to look at the face, that you'd never imagine that this was an evil person.'

'And what did he say?' asked Silas.

'Not much. The fact was that he was making me nervous. When I'm like that, I talk too much. Stupidly, I told him that the man had been hanged for killing his brother. I didn't know at the time that Frederick had been guilty of doing the same thing.'

'And Frederick came back again?'

'Whenever Dr Foss wasn't there. I let him in to look at the mask. To be honest, there was one time when I told him "no," and the look on his face scared me. I didn't have the courage to refuse him after that.'

'Did you tell Dr Foss?'

'I couldn't. If he knew that I had invited a patient into his office, I would have lost my job. Promise me that you won't mention this to Dr Stone.'

'You have my word. Did Frederick ever say anything to you about the death mask? Anything that you thought unusual?'

'He was creepy. He'd tell me that the face was watching everything I did. He even said that it would be wonderful to have death masks made of your loved ones. Then they'd never die. They'd stay with you forever.' She glanced back at the death mask and shivered. 'What an idea.'

'One more thing, Mrs Culpepper. Did you think Frederick was ready for the world when they released him?'

She glanced nervously at Silas Bacon. 'I wouldn't want to meet him in a dark alley. Of course, that's just my opinion.'

Silas glanced over his shoulder. 'I must go. Thank you for your candour. Perhaps this conversation should remain between the two of us?'

Mrs Culpepper nodded. 'Just between the two of us.' She hesitated. 'Tell me, Dr Bacon, do you think a man can be born evil?'

* * *

The walk back to town was even more of an effort than the one to the asylum, now that Silas felt the responsibility for Frederick Crabtree's crimes weighing heavily on his shoulders. Logically, he reasoned, he had only contributed towards the killer's preoccupations and obsessions for five years, but as Dr Stone had argued so forcefully, childhood was a formative time. As such, Silas couldn't absolve himself of blame.

When he had first met the seven-year-old, Silas was surprised by how agitated and temperamental the boy was. He knew the circumstances that had brought the child to the asylum and had been initially critical of placing him there. But it became clear that Frederick was disturbed. His moods would swing from happy to sad, from angry to relaxed, for no apparent reason. His sleep was often unsettled and his temper could be ferocious, even for a seven-year-old. The suicide of his mother and his father's rejection were bound to have affected him, but it was the wilful murder of his brother that interested Silas most.

His first interaction with young Crabtree was not promising. The boy lashed out at him, tears pouring down his face, when mention was made of his mother. Silas had been shocked by the vehemence of his emotions, but he was also intrigued by the prospect that here was a case study to test the veracity of phrenology. Was the boy's action in killing his brother a sign that he had been born with criminal tendencies? It would be instructive to examine the boy in that light and to monitor his development on a regular basis.

If he were to determine which aspects of the boy's brain were dominant and which were inferior, it would be necessary to shave Frederick's head. Inadvertently, he found that this was helpful in moderating the boy's emotions.

And so it began, a practice that lasted for the five years of Silas Bacon's residency at the Ararat Lunatic Asylum. Every fortnight, in the privacy of his office, he had performed a ritual, incorporating certain phrases and actions, the repetition of which was designed to soothe and calm the boy.

A leather strop was fixed to the wall. Silas would take a razor from his bag and pull the strop tight till it was horizontal. Slowly and methodically, he would rotate the blade's edge backwards and forwards as he stroked it against the leather, polishing it until it gleamed. Silas would hold the razor up to the light and look at his reflection in the blade.

'Like a mirror,' he would intone.

'A razor must be straight.

A razor must be polished.

A razor must be sharp.'

He would touch Frederick's cheek, aware of the boy's response, almost like that of a puppy seeking affection.

'Such beautiful skin.

So smooth.'

Silas would place the razor on the table then take up a stick of shaving soap. He would drop it into the bottom of a mug and then soak the brush in a bowl of water, flicking off the excess liquid. Stirring and rubbing the brush against the soap, he'd watch the lather thicken.

'Just right.'

He'd apply the lather to Frederick's head using the brush, working it through his hair until there was an even cover of thick creamy bubbles. Next, he would massage the boy's head with his fingers. Then, with great solemnity, he would take up the razor.

He would place his left hand across the boy's forehead, holding the head steady. Using his right hand, Silas would guide the razor as it scraped through soapy hair, leaving the skull exposed.

'Above the ears.'

The blade skimmed past Frederick's left ear then his right, hair dropping to the floor. Soon he was clean-shaven.

Silas rubbed Frederick's skull with a fresh towel, removing any vestiges of soap or hair. The boy's head shone in the artificial light. Silas would step back, admiring his handiwork.

'Not a cut. Not a drop of blood. Aren't you happy?'

The effect of this intimate act bordered on the hypnotic. Frederick Crabtree would relax as they moved on to the next stage of the ritual. Taking his measuring tape and craniometer from a velvet-lined mahogany box, Silas would measure the indentations and bumps of the boy's skull, making notes and comparing his calculations with those of the previous examination. Throughout the process he would whisper words of encouragement, comfort, and assurance.

The gist of Silas's commentary never varied. 'You are not responsible for your actions, my boy. Violence is part of your personality. You were born this way.'

On the wall of his office was a phrenology chart illustrating the different parts of the brain. He used the diagram to explain his findings.

'The brain is not a single organ but is composed of many parts. Each is governed by particular mental and emotional functions. Moral values, characteristics, feelings, and actions are controlled by different sections of the brain. If you use one of these parts more than another, it will enlarge. Alternatively, others will shrink in size if you do not exhibit that behaviour. In short, the shape of your head reveals your character.

'Destructiveness is the organ above your ears. In your case, it is well-developed. It will continue to lead you on the road to cruelty and murder. You experience rage where others do not. You lack control. Conscientiousness, veneration, and benevolence are organs that you rarely use and these have atrophied or reduced in size.'

The boy cocked his head to one side, his brow furrowed. 'I don't understand.'

'I'll put it simply, Frederick. You have no choice. You were born evil.'

In the early days, the boy was too young to grasp the meaning of Silas's pronouncement but, as time passed, he came to comprehend and accept the doctor's verdict. Frederick would gaze up at him, absorbing the truth of Silas's words.

'I have no choice,' repeated the boy. 'I was born evil.'

There was no avoiding his complicity in Frederick's crimes. Silas had sown the seeds of the man Frederick had become: one who would not and could not take moral responsibility for his actions. And who had given him that conviction? Silas Bacon.

In time, Silas realised that he had been mistaken about the 'science' of phrenology. This was no diagnostic tool. The skull did not conform to the shape of the brain, he knew that now. One could no more predict criminality by the pattern of bumps on a skull than diagnose diseases and injuries by examining the iris of an eye.

And when Silas turned his back on the Ararat Lunatic Asylum, he also chose to forget about his patients there and what effect, if any, his practice of phrenology might have had on them. But the damage had been done. His case study in phrenology, young Frederick Crabtree, had followed the path that Silas had laid out for him. He had become a killer: amoral, self-absorbed, and narcissistic.

In returning to Ararat, Silas had come full circle. His obsession with phrenology had been brief but the repercussions had been long-lasting. He was forced to face the fact that he, Silas Bacon, was not unlike Dr Frankenstein, creating a monster in the form of Frederick Crabtree.

Chapter Thirty-Five

Emma was sitting in the summer house at Seymour Grove, a rug draped over her legs. She was tired of the winter; of the chill in the air and the frost on the ground; of the malaise that seemed to spread over the garden as it waited for spring to come again. She missed the chirping of the birds and the smell of gardenias, jasmine, and roses. She missed the warmth of the sun on her face and the opportunity to sketch at the beach whenever she wanted. And, most of all, she missed Max.

While she could anticipate the thrill of seeing the garden awake from its hiatus, Max was faced with the possibility that spring would only be visible through the bars of his prison window.

Emma shivered inadvertently at the thought of Max in the Melbourne Jail. She had stood outside that dark and forbidding exterior two days before, staring up at the small barred windows and wondering which cell held the enigmatic man who had captured her heart. If she felt the cold, how much worse for him? Bluestone and slate.

She had waited for what seemed hours as the prison officers deliberated whether to let her in. Their answer had hit her like a gust of cold wind bouncing off those cold grey walls: Max Rushforth was not allowed visitors, apart from his legal representatives. She had proffered a letter in case she was refused entry. Could this not be placed in Max's hands, she had asked? Surprisingly, the prison officer had acquiesced, taken by the sweetness of her face and her gentle request. And so, after one last look at the grim bluestone walls, she dawdled down Russell Street towards Flinders Street station, her long journey all for nothing.

On her way back she had attempted to drop in on Silas at the museum, only to discover that he had gone on holiday. How could he even consider such a thing when Max's fate hung in the balance? And Reggie had almost disappeared from view, most probably frustrated by her refusal to accept him as a suitor. Even Aunt Florence had seemed distracted that morning, before she was driven away by George on what she had cryptically referred to as an 'errand.' It seemed, to Emma, that everyone had lost their focus.

Emma looked at her watch. Her great-aunt had been gone two and a half hours. She yawned and picked up her book, trying to recall what she had read an hour ago.

The back door slammed. Aunt Florence swept down the path to the summer house, not unlike a willy-willy in the desert.

'I have experienced success!' she cried, her cheeks flushed. 'Mr Edward Smythe was like putty in my hands. I now know where Frederick Crabtree collects his allowance.'

'You really are formidable,' said Emma. 'How did you do it?'

'Greed. It works every time. Dangle a carrot in front of a donkey and he'll follow it where it leads.'

'What do you mean?'

'I put some of my financial affairs in the hands of Alexander and Smythe and, in return, the silly man gave me the information I required.'

'Doesn't Mr Upjohn look after your affairs?'

'In the main, yes.' She took Emma's hand. 'You may as well know now that I'm setting up an annuity for you. Just a small one, mind you.'

Aunt Florence sat back, looking pleased with herself, but her great-niece's reaction took her by surprise.

'I don't want your money.'

'We're not talking vast sums, Emma. Most of my estate will go to my various philanthropic causes. This money will give you a degree of independence, not wealth. There will be no fine silk dresses and furs for you with this annuity.'

'I don't want fine silk dresses. You have given me enough already.'

Mrs Darrow continued, exasperated. 'Don't look a gift horse in the mouth.

It'll be enough to pay your board and lodging in a proper establishment when I'm dead. And if you find yourself a husband, you'll still have your own money.'

Emma's mouth set in an angry line. 'You should have asked me first.'

'Your naïvety is breathtaking.'

'You don't understand. People will say I was after your money.'

Aunt Florence shook her head. 'You shouldn't worry about what people think. They will talk about you no matter what you do. I'm giving you an opportunity that many never get.' She raised her voice in anger. 'I'm offering you independence, my girl, something I never had at your age.'

Emma and Aunt Florence eyed one another across the table in the summer house.

'Let me help you, my dear. I know you're not after my money. I've never thought that. Just for once, be gracious and accept what I offer you.'

Finally, the younger woman's face softened.

'I'm sorry,' she said. 'You mean well and you've been more than generous. The trouble is that I do care what people say.'

'That's not necessarily true. I'm impressed by your desire to help Max, despite the threat to your reputation. You stand by your principles and I admire you for it. But at times you can be so stubborn. Perhaps there's something of me in you, after all.'

'God help me,' said Emma, laughing despite herself.

Aunt Florence was taken aback and then a smile lit up her face. 'Emma Hart. What am I going to do with you?'

Emma shook her head. 'There's no hope, I'm afraid.' She reached over and took her great-aunt's hand. 'Tell me everything.'

Aunt Florence recounted her conversation with Edward Smythe and how he had succumbed to self-interest over principles. Afraid of losing her business, he had divulged a crucial piece of information that could lead to the discovery of Frederick Crabtree's whereabouts.

'Crabtree's allowance is paid into an account at the ES&A Bank in Bay Street, Brighton, on the third Friday of every month.'

'How wonderful,' said Emma. She clapped her hands together with glee.

CHAPTER THIRTY-FIVE

'We can track him and find out where he lives.'

* * *

Later in the day, after Aunt Florence had settled into a comfortable armchair in the parlour, she looked up at the portrait of her father above the mantelpiece.

'What have I done, Daddy?' she asked. 'If Frederick Crabtree is involved in this, I'm putting us in danger. If ever a man embodied evil, it is the Death Mask Murderer.'

Eoin Brown looked off into the distance, somewhere above her head. It may have been a trick of the light or a projection of her misgivings, but it seemed to Florence that his expression was troubled.

Chapter Thirty-Six

It was Dr Silas Bacon's last day in Ararat. Sleep had not come easily after his visit to the asylum, and he was troubled and conscience-stricken. He pushed his breakfast plate away, untouched, and sipped from a cup of tepid tea. There was one more task for him to perform before he left town.

The publishing house of *The Ararat Advertiser* was not hard to find, situated as it was in a single-storey brick and render building with its name emblazoned across its façade. Silas stepped into the shop, which was dominated by a large counter. Behind it could be heard the sounds of the heavy printing press. Silas rang the bell and a small man appeared, his head only just visible above the counter. He peered at Silas through thick round glasses.

'Can I help you, sir?' he asked, above the clatter.

'I would like to examine some back issues of your newspaper. June 1917 to be exact.'

'Is there something in particular that you're looking for?'

'I'm interested in a death that occurred here twelve months ago. A young woman.'

'Just one minute.' The man disappeared from view. The printing press went quiet.

'That's better,' he said, coming out from behind the counter. He was a spry man, in his fifties, wearing a white shirt with sleeves wound back and fastened with clips above his elbows.

'You're looking into the murder of Alexandra James, I assume?' He registered the look of surprise on Silas's face.

'She was *murdered*?'

'Unfortunately, she was. Can I ask your name please?'

'Dr Silas Bacon.'

'I'm Garfield Flynn, owner, editor, printer, publisher, reporter, and general dogsbody of *The Ararat Advertiser*.' He extended an ink-stained hand and said, apologetically, 'It's alright: the ink's dry. Occupational hazard.' They shook hands. 'I am—was—Alexandra James's uncle. This is a small town in many ways, as you can see. May I enquire as to the reason for your interest in my niece's death?'

'I'm looking for a connection with a series of deaths in Melbourne.'

'Do you mean the Death Mask Murders?'

'You've heard of them?'

'What person hasn't? Are you saying there's a connection with Alex's death?'

'I can't say, at this stage.'

'As you wish.' Garfield Flynn nodded his head sadly. 'Terrible business. Alex's body was found on the 4th of June, 1917. About a year ago today.'

'I believe she worked up at the asylum.'

'She liked it for the first year, but the strain of dealing with difficult patients eventually became too much for her.'

'Did she talk about it to anyone? For example, Dr Stone?'

'You wouldn't get much help from him. That place is a law unto itself.'

'Alexandra left the asylum?'

'Five months before her death. When she was expecting a second child.'

'How did she die? Dr Stone said she drowned.'

'That's not right. She was strangled. The police arrested a farmhand but he had an alibi. Even Alex's husband was under suspicion, but no one could believe that Davy was responsible. She was eight months pregnant. Davy was over the moon. He was so happy that he was going to be a father again.' Flynn blinked rapidly and wiped away a tear.

'You said that she already had a child?'

'That's right. Little Alfie was seven when she died.' Garfield Flynn nodded sadly. 'Too young to lose a mother.'

'Tell me about her death.'

'It was a hot day when Alex went missing. Her body was found in the dam so the assumption was that she had drowned. But Alex was afraid of water so I didn't believe it for a minute.'

'You said she was strangled.'

'That's what the coroner found.'

'Was there anything out of the ordinary apart from that?'

'She'd shaved her head.' Flynn sighed deeply. 'Why would she do that? Her hair was her crowning glory.'

Silas blanched. 'Her head was shaved?'

'The local copper did his best, but the case remains unsolved. Such a shame, just when it seemed her life was back on track, what with another baby and all that.' Flynn shook his head. 'Bewildering. That's what it is.'

'Was her murder reported in the Melbourne newspapers?'

'I would doubt it. Country news is of little interest in the Big Smoke.'

Silas shrugged his shoulders. 'Do you have a picture of Mrs James?'

Garfield Flynn took a photograph from his wallet and handed it to Silas. 'She's beautiful, isn't she? Only twenty-seven years old. Too young to die.'

Silas stared at the image of a fresh-faced country beauty, with long blonde hair, a happy unaffected smile, thick full lips, and slightly upturned nose. His shoulders slumped. He knew her immediately. Emma Hart had captured her well when she had sketched her death mask. He handed the photograph back to the little man.

'You know her, don't you? But how?'

'You will have to trust me. I'll do my best to solve your niece's murder. Now, could I trouble you for those newspapers? I would appreciate the opportunity to become more familiar with the circumstances of her death.'

Garfield Flynn went behind the counter and disappeared through a doorway leading to a storeroom. Shortly after, he returned, carrying half a dozen newspapers.

'Please make yourself comfortable at my desk. I have work to do out the back. Call me when you've finished.'

'Before you go, did the police check if any inmates from the asylum were involved?'

'They interviewed Dr Stone, the superintendent, but no one was released at that time. Why do you ask?'

'No reason. Thank you, Mr Flynn.'

The printing press clattered into life again. Silas settled down and thumbed through the pages detailing the disappearance of Alexandra James, the discovery of her body in the dam, her shaven head, the coroner's report, and the police investigation. It made for sad reading, especially when one took into consideration that she had been heavily pregnant when she died. Her loss was keenly felt, by her family, friends, and husband.

Silas considered the implications of what he now knew. It was clear to him that Dr Stone had deliberately hidden Frederick Crabtree's release from the police. An innocent woman and her unborn child had died because a manipulative killer had been freed. Rather than bringing Crabtree to justice, the superintendent had chosen to protect his reputation and that of the Ararat Lunatic Asylum. And now, others had died. If he, Silas Bacon, had been in denial for his part in this whole sorry business, then so had Dr Stone. He put the newspapers aside and rested his head in his hands. How was he going to make this right?

Chapter Thirty-Seven

Max leaned up against the bluestone wall in the exercise yard of the Melbourne Jail. A wintry sun was trying to break through the clouds. A couple of prisoners shuffled around in the dirt, aimlessly filling in time. In another corner was a group of men who had huddled together to try to escape the cold. Up on the walls, guards kept watch, their faces pinched in the chill wind. One was stamping his feet while another sheltered against the watchtower wall, looking distractedly at the city buildings to the south.

Max's cell was on the first floor. He regarded himself as lucky that he had the cell to himself but that, apparently, was a common occurrence. The War had depleted the number of potential criminals; some had been given the opportunity to enlist rather than serve time. There was even talk of the jail's closure, given that prison officers oftentimes outnumbered the prisoners themselves.

The gallery of the building was flanked by three tiers of bluestone cells, with heavy wooden and metal doors. The cells were cold and unlit, with high-barred windows. The floor was paved with slate flagstones and the walls were whitewashed. Soaring above was the corrugated iron roof. It featured a series of barred skylights, which were designed to filter light down to the bottom storey. One of the prisoners had compared it to the central nave of a church, but Max failed to see the likeness. He had never been in a church that was as bleak and forbidding as the Melbourne Jail.

For a few hours a day he had the run of the exercise yard, with a range of prisoners on remand, such as he, and those incarcerated for short sentences.

The labour yard no longer existed and the general tedium, of having nothing to do, meant that the prisoners were looking for a distraction, whether it be fighting or arguing. He did his best to keep to himself but, as in the case of his stint in the City Watch House, his notoriety preceded him. Fortunately, his size discouraged most from taking him on, but some of the more pugnacious inmates had not been so reluctant. Max had learned that he had to stand up for himself if he were to survive but, even so, he feared the homemade shiv whose sharp point might pierce his skin when he least expected it.

In Max's pocket was Emma's letter which he had read and re-read. The torn envelope was proof that nothing was private here; all written communication was checked for concealed contraband or messages that might suggest an escape was in the wind. Max didn't care; he was indescribably happy that she had bothered to write to him, and that her letter had been passed on to him.

It wasn't necessary to read the words anymore; he had committed them to memory. His lips moved soundlessly as he recited its contents:

'Dear Max,

   If you receive this letter it's because they wouldn't let me in to see you. I want you to know that Aunt Florence, Silas, Reggie, and I are doing whatever we can to support Mr Upjohn in the search for evidence that will prove you innocent. Not one of us believes that you are guilty of such terrible crimes.

   I sincerely hope that you are keeping well. I look forward to seeing you when you are released, and hope that it will be soon.
   Your friend
   Emma.'

It comforted him to know that he had her support and that he hadn't been forgotten. Even his sister had written to him, after Upjohn had contacted her to let her know what had happened. She promised that she would travel down from Townsville to be at the trial.

Ironically, his imprisonment had made him realise that he wasn't alone.

There were people outside the bluestone walls who cared what happened to him, and were working to free him.

Despite the debilitating effects of the War and the threat of life imprisonment, Max felt the veil of melancholy and pessimism lifting. The prosecution's case against him had made him realise that he needed to face his behaviour squarely and honestly. He now felt shame for the things he had done: the assault on his superior officer and the attack on the nurse. Neither could be justified. It had been too easy to blame everything on shell shock, which he had used as an excuse to distance himself from his actions. It was time to face the reality of what he had become and to do something about it, if he were given the chance. In the isolation of his cell, Max acknowledged that his violent behaviour needed to be addressed. He felt that he was finally emerging from the darkness into the light.

But there was one reality that he was reluctant to accept. Emma Hart would never be his. She was everything he could hope for: talented, courageous, beautiful, and feisty. Although the War had dealt her a terrible blow, she had picked herself up and faced life again. Just as he intended to do for himself, if he could extract himself from this dire situation. But he knew he was only fooling himself if he thought that their relationship had a future. She had the world at her feet, while he had a long, hard road to travel before he would ever be in a position to love and to be loved in return.

Chapter Thirty-Eight

The trip back to Melbourne took just over eight hours, the steam locomotive stopping periodically to replenish its water supply, and to collect passengers along the route from Ararat to Melbourne. The fields were expansive, with gum trees pressed against the sky. Occasionally, flocks of galahs and sulphur-crested cockatoos flew past, while sheep grazed on the lush winter grass. The steam locomotive left behind a trail of smoke as it rounded the curves of the Pentland Hills outside Ballarat on its way to Melbourne.

Silas Bacon stared out the window, oblivious to the view. He was alone in the carriage and, for once, he regretted it. There was no one to distract him from the unwanted thoughts that assailed him.

For years he had tried to put the past behind him. Dr Stone, in denying his part in the formation of Frederick's depraved character, had forced Silas to face reality. It was true that he had played a significant part in the boy's development. No matter how he looked at it, he couldn't escape the truth of Dr Stone's accusation.

With time on his hands, he gave himself a task: what circumstances contributed to the development of Frederick's personality? In short, what hypothesis would explain Crabtree's murderous rages?

The events of Frederick's childhood would have scarred the most well-adjusted child. He left the orphanage to become part of a family where he felt loved and cherished. But the arrival of Henry, the biological son of Thomas and Matilda, had supplanted his place in the family. Ultimately, he gave vent to his jealousy by killing his younger brother. The devastated

Matilda Crabtree committed suicide.

In Frederick's eyes, his mother's rejection of him was two-fold: she had favoured Henry over him and she had taken her own life, leaving him totally bereft. And then came the final blow: his distraught father had banished him to a lunatic asylum, where he spent the next thirty-six years stewing over his rejection, a ticking time bomb ready to explode.

Unfortunately, there was more in store for the young boy. As the doctor assigned to him in his formative years, Silas had neglected the boy's emotional state, treating him more as a case study than a human being. He had convinced Frederick that he was born evil, basing his opinion on the simplistic tenets of phrenology. The fact was that Frederick's future criminal behaviour ultimately fulfilled Silas's prophecy. Reflecting on his treatment of the boy, Silas believed that he was complicit in what Frederick Crabtree had become as a man.

The death mask in Dr Foss's office had fascinated Crabtree. In his perverted view of the world within the asylum walls, the adult Frederick became convinced that a death mask would substitute for a loved one who would invariably leave him. Just as his mother had. It was as if a bad seed had taken root in Frederick's mind. Through lack of exposure to healthy, normal thoughts and surroundings, it had fed on itself, festering until it became a sick and twisted obsession.

The parallels between Alexandra James and Matilda Crabtree were too close to be ignored. The psychiatric nurse had triggered Frederick's memories of his mother. She was much the same age, blonde and attractive. And she was also the mother of a seven-year-old boy, the same age that Frederick had been when his world fell apart. Alexandra was also ripe for manipulation. She had found herself drawn into a relationship with a man who was shrewd and devious. Discovering that she was pregnant, she had an excuse to leave her job.

This line of thought begged the question: What was the nature of their relationship? Did it stray from the traditional nurse-patient one? Had Alexandra become his lover, if indeed Frederick Crabtree were capable of expressing love? Was there the possibility that Alexandra James had become pregnant with Frederick's child? Silas turned these thoughts over and dismissed them. There was no point in indulging in pure speculation. The answer would never be known.

He returned to what he believed to be true. Alexandra's departure made Frederick relive his mother's abandonment all over again. It gave him the impetus to flee the asylum. Within a few months, he had duped the doctors, gaining the eight required signatures that would secure his release.

And ultimately, Alexandra James had paid with her life, becoming the model for the first death mask. Powerless to punish Matilda, Frederick had transferred his latent rage to Alexandra and exacted retribution. But the murder of one innocent woman was not enough for Frederick. The urge to kill lay dormant until he encountered another woman with similar physical characteristics to Matilda Crabtree, and the cycle began again. Silas was no psychiatrist, he admitted, but his theory provided a workable explanation for Frederick's killing spree.

The train had reached the outskirts of the city. Soon Silas would be home. But there was nothing warm and comforting about that thought now. While Frederick Crabtree was free, Silas would not sleep the sleep of the innocent.

Chapter Thirty-Nine

It was a Saturday afternoon. Aunt Florence and Emma were in the parlour, knitting socks for the troops in France. A heated discussion was taking place between them, a continuation of the argument from the night before.

'You are not going to do it, Emma. My mind is made up; it's too dangerous.'

'But you went to all that trouble to find out where Crabtree picks up his allowance. We need to find out where he lives.'

'Let the police deal with it.'

'You know that they're only interested in locking up Max. There's no one else who will do it.'

The sound of footsteps caught their attention. Mrs Williams announced the arrival of Reggie da Costa.

'Ladies,' he gushed, stepping into the room. 'I'm so glad I found you at home. Mother asked me to bring you some balaclavas that she's knitted for the boys at the Front.' He put the bag next to the door.

'How kind. Do join us,' said Mrs Darrow, indicating an armchair across from her.

'Your timing is excellent.' Emma smiled sweetly. 'I couldn't have asked for anyone better.'

Reggie glowed with pleasure. He smoothed the wrinkles from his trousers and gave the ladies his full attention.

'This business of Frederick Crabtree,' continued Emma.

Reggie's face fell. 'I don't understand your preoccupation with Crabtree, Emma.'

Aunt Florence raised her pince-nez and glared at her great-niece. 'I told you to forget it.'

'Forget what?' inquired Reggie, his curiosity piqued.

'It's quite simple,' explained Emma. 'Frederick Crabtree collects his allowance from the ES&A Bank in Bay Street, Brighton, on the third Friday of every month. Aunt Florence says it's not safe for me to follow him.'

'Mrs Darrow is quite right. It's ridiculous to even contemplate such an idea.'

'And if I can't, perhaps you will.'

'And I say that it's too dangerous for Mr da Costa, too,' reiterated Aunt Florence, staring down her great-niece.

Reggie pooh-poohed her concerns. 'I am a master of disguise. He will never guess that I'm tailing him.'

'Does that mean you'll do it?' asked Emma.

'If it's important to you, I will. But only if Mrs Darrow agrees.'

Emma clapped her hands together with glee.

'Are you sure?' asked Aunt Florence, looking doubtful.

'Of course. If it makes Emma happy. Let's see,' he said, taking out his notebook. 'That will be the 21st of June, a fortnight away. I don't see why I couldn't. It is undoubtedly a waste of time but for you ladies, nothing is too much trouble.

'I will station myself outside the bank when it opens and wait for Frederick Crabtree to appear. But how will I recognise him?'

Emma smiled knowingly. 'I've been thinking about that. What if you spin the bank teller a tale—I'm sure that you of all people can think of something—and ask him to indicate when he serves our man? Perhaps he could mop his brow with his handkerchief?'

'In the middle of winter?' Reggie guffawed. 'You are a card. But yes, I will think of something.'

Mrs Williams appeared at the door again. 'Dr Bacon to see you, Mrs Darrow.'

Silas entered the room. He paused and stood uncertainly, as he caught sight of Reggie.

'I didn't mean to disturb you. I'll come back another time.'

Emma was out of her chair in an instant and shook his hand warmly. 'Silas. Where have you been?' She studied him. 'Are you ill? You look like you've seen a ghost.'

'In a sense, I have.'

'Do come in and take a seat,' said Mrs Darrow. 'We seem to be overrun with visitors today. Not that I mind. We were just talking about Frederick Crabtree. Mr da Costa has kindly agreed to find out where he lives, now that we know where he collects his allowance.' She glanced at the crime reporter who was smirking. 'However, he doesn't think that Crabtree is involved in the Death Mask Murders. He thinks we're wasting our time.'

Reggie ran his fingers through his hair. 'I have associated with the criminal underclass for some time now, and this case will be like all the rest. Why would Frederick Crabtree be involved in these crimes? Pigs might fly.'

Silas replied wearily, 'Then prepare to see a pig with wings. I have news and it confirms that the Death Mask Murderer is none other than Frederick Crabtree.'

Reggie went quiet.

'What have you learned?' asked Emma.

Silas paused, collecting his thoughts, and then slowly recounted the details of his visit to the Ararat Lunatic Asylum. He revealed to them the painful truth of his work with Frederick Crabtree over thirty years before, and how he had contributed to the development of the boy's character. Silas omitted nothing. He spoke of Frederick's fixation with death masks. And then he told them of Alexandra James, the model for the first death mask and Crabtree's first victim.

He put his head in his hands; a picture of misery.

Reggie fixed him with a withering look. 'You're the one who set this maniac loose on the world. Perhaps you should apologise to the families of the women that Frederick Crabtree murdered.'

'Really,' said Mrs Darrow, shaking her head, 'there's nothing to be gained by this.' She turned to Silas. 'I understand that you regret the past, but this was many years ago.'

'Reggie's right.' He raised his long thin fingers and stared at them. 'I have blood on my hands.'

Emma reached out and touched his arm. 'It's not your fault, Silas. Frederick Crabtree chose to pursue a life of crime. He was a killer before you met him. You didn't murder those women. He did.'

Aunt Florence nodded her head in agreement. 'We can bring Frederick Crabtree to justice. We'll make him pay for the evil he has done, and stop him before he kills again.'

Silas squeezed Emma's hands, such was his emotion. 'Thank you, ladies. I will do everything in my power to help you. However, there's one thing I need to know.'

'What's that?'

'What colour was Matilda Crabtree's hair?'

'It was blonde,' replied Aunt Florence.

'That fits with my hypothesis.'

Silas offered them his theory about Frederick Crabtree's motivation for murder, the type of female victims he chose, their resemblance to his mother, and his obsession with death masks.

'In Frederick's twisted mind, the mask replaced the woman.'

'Sounds like psychological mumbo jumbo,' sneered Reggie.

'I disagree,' said Emma. 'Silas's explanation makes perfect sense.'

Reggie shook his head in disgust. 'Really, Emma. You are quite gullible.'

'Really, Mr da Costa?' said Mrs Darrow. 'I agree with my great-niece.'

Reggie reddened in anger. 'I can't see any evidence that Frederick Crabtree is linked to these crimes. It's all speculation.'

'Then you won't follow Frederick Crabtree after all?' asked Emma.

'I said I would.' Reggie rolled his eyes.

Aunt Florence took up her diary and consulted it. 'We should meet the day after you have discovered Crabtree's whereabouts. Saturday, the 22nd of June. I have a meeting in the morning. We're planning to campaign for a minimum wage for working women. I will be back by 2:00 p.m. at the latest. Hopefully, you will bring us news of where Frederick Crabtree lives.'

Emma accompanied the two men outside.

'Goodbye, Silas. You have a good heart.' She kissed him on the cheek. 'It takes a brave man to admit that he's made a mistake. Go home and try to put this out of your mind.'

Silas sighed heavily. As he walked away, he touched the spot where her lips had brushed his cheek.

Reggie da Costa touched Emma's arm. 'Looks like I have a rival for your affections.'

'It's called friendship,' said Emma, staring after the departing figure of Silas Bacon.

Reggie was not to be put off. He straightened his tie and checked his new winter suit, made of fine herringbone tweed. 'I hope that we can be more than just friends.'

The smile left Emma's face. 'Before you go too far with this, I think it's necessary to tell you that I have no money. I am the daughter of a farmer. I have no expectations.'

Reggie was put on the back foot. 'Your great-aunt is childless. Surely she will look after you?'

'A small allowance, that's all. Aunt Florence supports many worthy causes. I am not one of them.'

He struggled to regain his equanimity. 'I don't know what to say.'

'Then say nothing.' She looked him in the eye. 'You are an attractive man. I'm sure that there are many women out there who would be grateful for your attention, but I'm not one of them. I have no intention of marrying *anyone* in the near future.'

Reggie's mouth set in a grim line. 'I will continue to help you only because my mother values her relationship with your great-aunt.'

He paused, considering his next words. His tone was menacing. 'A word of warning, Emma. You should be wary. You fit the profile for the Death Mask Murderer. You might even be in his sights as we speak.'

Emma stared at him in disbelief. Reggie started the car and put his foot on the throttle. He drove off without a backward glance, the Dodge Roadster leaving a trail of dust in its wake.

Chapter Forty

MISSING WOMAN
Link to Death Mask Murders?

By REGGIE DA COSTA, Senior Crime Reporter

Last Thursday afternoon, Miss Drusilla Rook, aged twenty-four, disappeared on the foreshore of Hampton beach. The weather had been inclement and her parents assumed that she had sought shelter from the rain. Her father went in search of her and found her hat and handbag in a neat pile on the beach opposite the intersection of Holyrood and New Streets.

Detective Inspector Wasp, lead detective in the Death Mask Murders investigation, stated that there were no suspicious circumstances. This is despite her disappearance in the location where four women have been found dead. He issued the following statement:

'Miss Rook received news of the death of her soldier brother late last week. We have a witness who saw Miss Rook walking alone along the beach on Thursday. We believe that she swam out into deep water and drowned, given that there were no signs of violence or a struggle on the sand. To this end, local police are carrying out a search of adjacent beaches along Port Phillip Bay, in case the body is washed ashore.'

Brother's tragic death

Family members have revealed that Miss Rook's brother, Lieutenant William Rook, was rejected for active service in Melbourne in 1915. He travelled to London where he joined the King's Own Royal Lancaster Regiment and quickly gained his commission. He then saw service in France where he lost an arm in battle. After a period of rehabilitation in England, Lieutenant Rook returned to the trenches, and was fatally wounded in early June.

Link to the Death Mask Murders?

At least four women have died tragically at the hands of the notorious Death Mask Murderer, whose bizarre practice of creating death masks of his victims was first discovered in February this year. It is suspected that Miss Lillian Broderick, who went missing in November 1917, may also have been preyed upon by this vicious killer.

Miss Rook, a Hampton resident, disappeared in the region where his other victims were found. In answer to the question of whether Miss Rook fitted the profile of the Death Mask Murderer's victims, Detective Inspector Wasp was dismissive:

'We have the perpetrator in prison awaiting trial. Eventually, we will discover where he keeps his hoard of death masks and put these salacious rumours behind us. I would like to assure women that they have nothing to fear. There is no longer any Death Mask Murderer wreaking havoc in Brighton; he is behind bars in Melbourne Jail.'

Miss Rook was a teacher at Hampton Primary School. She was described by friends as a caring, considerate woman.

One friend, Mrs Iris Blakely, said it was inconceivable that Miss Rook would commit suicide. 'She was devoted to her family. She loved teaching children. I cannot believe that she would end her life this way. She was a positive, optimistic woman with a heart of gold.'

[*The Argus* June 17, 1918]

Chapter Forty-One

Melbourne was brimming with crime, Reggie was pleased to note, as he sat at his desk in the offices of *The Argus* newspaper late Thursday night. A daring daylight robbery had been carried out. Two bags were stolen from State officials outside the Government Printing Office, netting the thieves over £4,000.

And, in a further development to the robbery from Kilpatrick's jewellery store in Collins Street, where rings worth nearly £1,500 were stolen, two arrests had been made and more were expected to follow. Detective Sergeant Clary Blain had told Reggie that rival gangs from Richmond and Fitzroy were involved, one of which was Squizzy Taylor's bunch of larrikins. According to Clary, Squizzy was convinced that someone from the other gang had 'squealed' to the police. There would be violent repercussions. Things were looking up on the crime front.

He opened his file on the Death Mask Murders. The more he considered the possibility that Frederick Crabtree was behind the deaths, the more he believed that Silas Bacon and, by association, Mrs Darrow and Emma Hart, were deluded. There was no evidence linking Frederick Crabtree with this case, apart from the fact that he lived in the Brighton mansion as a child. And, even if Crabtree had been released from the asylum prior to the start of the murders, there was no physical proof that he had killed Alexandra James. Without seeing Garfield Flynn's photograph of his niece, Reggie could not be sure that it really did match Emma's drawing of the death mask in the cellar. He only had Silas's word for it. In his view, it wasn't enough to say it was *likely* that Crabtree had murdered the psychiatric nurse, there had to be hard evidence.

All that mumbo jumbo psychology nonsense that Bacon had spouted didn't fit with Reggie's understanding of the workings of the criminal mind. As if a death mask would be a substitute for a woman? Then again, they wouldn't talk back! Reggie chuckled at the thought.

Silas Bacon was possibly of unsound mind himself. How could someone be taken seriously when they had subscribed to such a harebrained theory as phrenology? Anyone who had expertise in the field of crime—whether it be investigative reporters, police, or even criminals themselves—knew that the major motivations for criminal acts came down to the fundamentals of love, hate, revenge, and greed. It was that simple. Convoluted theories of feeling rejected and killing women based on the idea that the victims resembled someone's mother were nonsense. If anyone belonged in an asylum it was Silas Bacon.

Frederick Crabtree's location was unknown. So what? That didn't mean anything. Reggie saw it all the time. Some people chose to disappear; some people chose to leave their pasts behind. If he, Reggie, God forbid, had been committed to a lunatic asylum and then released thirty years later, he would want to make a new life for himself.

One fact was incontrovertible: there *was* a murderer on the loose, but nothing pointed to him being the adopted son of Thomas Crabtree. Or to him being Max Rushforth either. Weak, damaged Max.

Reggie swore under his breath. Tomorrow would be a waste of his precious time but, at least, by the end of the day, it would be clear that Frederick Crabtree had nothing to do with the Death Mask Murders. Reggie had no choice but to do what Mrs Darrow had asked of him. Where his mother's friendship with the formidable Mrs Darrow was concerned, his opinion carried no weight. He couldn't afford to put either woman offside again. Mother wouldn't like it!

Reggie put the Death Mask Murders file away and sat lost in thought. Now that Emma Hart was out of his reach, he'd have to look elsewhere for a rich wife. What a nuisance. His mother had been less than amused when he had told her that Emma was not an heiress. She had even made the comment that her precious son had been deliberately led on because he was such a catch. Admittedly, Reggie had omitted Emma's declaration that she would never consider marrying him. It was damaging to his ego to even repeat her words. If anything, it confirmed that she was misguided and unworldly. Thank God he had not made a formal offer.

'Costa. You heard the latest?' Bluey Talbot, one of his fellow reporters, was standing in the doorway.

'What?'

'Body on Mentone Beach. Female. Mid-twenties. They've identified her as Drusilla Rook.'

'Was she bald?'

'Hard to say. It's possible. She'd been in the water for a while, if you take my meaning.'

Reggie's lip curled in satisfaction. 'I wonder how Wasp will react if the coroner says it was murder? Suicide? I don't think so. How do they know it was her?'

'Birthmark on right hip.'

'Lucky Rushforth's in jail or they'd pin that one on him too.' He raised a hand in mock salute. 'Thanks, Bluey.'

'Adiós, Costa.'

Reggie opened the Death Mask Murders file and added a note: 'Death no. 7: Drusilla Rook.'

Chapter Forty-Two

It was 9:45 a.m. on Friday, the 21st of June. The day that Frederick Crabtree was due to collect his allowance. The day that Reggie da Costa would prove to Mrs Darrow and Emma Hart that they were wrong about the identity of the Death Mask Murderer.

The Argus's senior crime reporter was standing on the footpath opposite the ES&A Bank in Brighton. Reggie was feeling glum. The weather mirrored his state of mind. The drizzle had started falling as soon as he arrived, and he had forgotten his umbrella. His clothing, carefully chosen so that he would merge in with the crowd, was putting him in a black mood. Charcoal grey trousers, ivory shirt, green cable knit jumper, and cream coat and hat. He looked ordinary, a thought that depressed him even further.

Reggie took cover under the awning of a shop and started to read the latest issue of *The Socialist* to pass the time. He guffawed at the article by Mrs Lavendar: 'Women in the Labor Party: Poodle or Packhorse?' It asserted that women in the labour movement should have an equal partnership with men.

'Bloody ridiculous,' he said, folding up the newspaper.

He pulled his coat around him and jammed his hat on his head.

'Come on. Open the damn bank,' he muttered.

He checked his watch. Ten minutes to go. A few shoppers dashed past but in the main, Bay Street was relatively empty. Any intelligent person would be inside, Reggie thought, not standing outside in this weather, wasting time.

Time ticked on. The rain was getting heavier and thick grey clouds were rolling in from the west. A train rumbled past, slowing down as it pulled into North Brighton station.

Reggie looked up and down the street. No one of interest was in sight. How senseless was this, waiting in the rain? His beloved Dodge Roadster was parked out of sight around the corner in Asling Street. It would be a five-minute drive home, to a roaring open fire and a nip of brandy. He was tempted, but the thought of his mother's disapproval made him hesitate. He turned up the collar of his coat and felt a trickle of rainwater drip down his neck. Damn, he thought.

He checked his watch. Ten o'clock.

Almost on cue, one of the tellers opened the front door of the bank and looked out into the street. Reggie crossed the road, pausing at the door to slip a card from his wallet into his pocket. It read 'James Silver: private detective.'

He entered the bank. A couple of customers pushed in ahead of him, making him crankier. At last, he reached the counter.

The teller looked up. 'Can I help you, sir?'

'I think you can.' Reggie forced a smile and passed his card to the bank teller. 'My name is James Silver. I work for Alexander and Smythe, Solicitors.'

The bank teller looked past him to the next customer. 'I'm not sure that I can help you. You might want to speak to the manager.'

'You'll do me. Alexander and Smythe are searching for a Mr Frederick Crabtree, the sole surviving son of Thomas Crabtree, who died ten years ago. We believe that he comes here each month to collect his allowance.'

'I still don't see—'

'Mr Crabtree may be eligible to inherit the bulk of his father's estate. We need to speak to him. This is the only point of contact that we have.'

The bank teller shook his head. 'We don't give out such information.'

'We were hoping that you might assist us in identifying Mr Crabtree. And to this end we are happy to give you a "finder's fee" which, of course, remains confidential and will not be disclosed to either Mr Crabtree or to your employers.' Reggie winked at the teller. He took his wallet out of his pocket and laid it on the counter.

The bored expression left the man's face. 'A finder's fee? Mr Crabtree's not in any trouble?'

'On the contrary, you'd be doing both him and us a favour. Imagine being the means of bringing happiness to one of your customers?'

The teller looked over his shoulder and then nodded. 'I know Mr Crabtree.'

Reggie passed a banknote under the grille.

The bank teller raised an eyebrow. 'Ten shillings? Is that all?'

'Let's make it a pound,' said Reggie, slipping another note across the counter.

The bank employee pocketed the money. 'He usually arrives at ten-thirty on Fridays. Very soon in fact.'

'Signal me when you serve him.'

'What do you want me to do?' The teller grinned. 'Raise my hand like this?' He put one arm up in the air.

'Perhaps a bit obvious. Why don't you blow your nose? I'll wait over there.' Reggie pointed to a seat near the bank manager's office. 'And please, no mention of this to Mr Crabtree. Understood?'

The teller leaned forward and tapped his nose. 'Just between you and me.'

Reggie grinned. 'Of course. Good man.'

Thirty-five minutes passed by. Reggie sat in a corner of the bank, to all appearances waiting for an appointment with the bank manager. He watched customers come and go, but there was no sign of Frederick Crabtree. He looked at his watch. It was 10:45 a.m. Where was he? Ten more minutes, that's all he would give him. There were better places to spend his time. But then he remembered his two ten-shilling notes in the bank teller's pocket. He sat on.

Occasionally he cast an eye in the direction of the teller, who shrugged his shoulders or shook his head in response. It was starting to look like a complete waste of time.

He looked up at the clock. It was 11:00 a.m. Enough. He stood and walked to the door, bumping into a man who was entering the bank, a man in a thick black coat, with his hat drawn down over his brow. The stranger glanced at him briefly. The bank teller took out his handkerchief and blew hard, twice. It was Frederick Crabtree. Reggie pushed the door open and exited the building.

It had started to rain heavily and Reggie was not amused. He was going to get very wet. And he looked conspicuous. He crossed the road and stared into a shop window, occasionally glancing back at the bank's entrance.

Five minutes later his quarry left the bank and headed for the railway station. Reggie followed him at a distance. Crabtree crossed the tracks and strode up the ramp towards the ticket office. An employee started to close the gates across the railway line; a train was coming.

Reggie pulled his coat around him, shoved his hat down on his head, and ran, darting across the tracks and up the ramp. A steam train pulled into the station. Frederick Crabtree stepped up into a carriage, further down the platform. Reggie needed to get on the train fast, or he would lose him. No time to buy a ticket, he thought. He dashed past the ticket office as the conductor blew his whistle, then barrelled along the platform as the train started to pull out of the station.

The passengers stared as Reggie threw open a door and leaped into the carriage. He brushed the rain off his coat and removed his hat. There was a seat available next to the window. Ignoring the protests of his fellow travellers, he lowered the window, letting in a strong gust of chill wind. Too bad, he thought. He needed to keep an eye out for when Crabtree left the train. Luckily, there were only four possibilities: Middle Brighton, Brighton Beach, Hampton, and lastly Sandringham, the end of the line.

At the first stop, he stuck his head out the window, looking for the man in the black hat and coat, but there was no sign of him.

The train pulled out of Middle Brighton station and clattered along the tracks, gathering speed. Reggie shivered as the chill penetrated his thick woollen coat. His mother had better appreciate what he was doing for her, he thought grimly. The sea came into view as the locomotive slowed down and rounded the turn, steam pouring from its stack. It ground to a halt at Brighton Beach station.

A large woman pushed back the door and stepped down onto the platform. She paused, searching for her umbrella, blocking Reggie's view in the process.

'For God's sake, move!' he yelled at her.

She looked up, shocked, and heaved her body forward. Immediately Crabtree came into view, walking down the ramp.

The station master blew his whistle. The train lurched forward. Reggie grabbed the handle and forced the door open, losing his balance as he jumped from the moving train. He fell heavily on the slippery platform, ripping the knees of his trousers. He swore loudly. A small group of women sheltering in the waiting room glared at him but he was beyond good manners.

He got to his feet and felt for his hat. Gone. Left on the train, which was now steaming towards Hampton. His £4 homburg would soon be in the hands of some opportunistic thief. He groaned and ran his fingers through his wet hair.

Damp and cold, with no umbrella, no hat, and torn trousers, Reggie da Costa shook his head, a picture of misery and woe. He looked around him and sighed. To add insult to injury, Frederick Crabtree was nowhere to be seen.

The thought of his two ten-shilling notes in the bank teller's pocket made him rally. He walked out onto South Road. Not there. A chill wind blew in from the sea. He sprinted across the railway line and gazed up and down The Esplanade. No sign of the man in the black hat and coat there either. In desperation, he returned to the Sandringham side of the railway line and slowly looked around him, trying to see some sign of the man who appeared to have disappeared off the face of the earth.

And then he noticed a grassy laneway that followed the railway line back in the direction of Middle Brighton. It was the only option left. The narrow track was edged with shrubs and trees. If Crabtree had taken this route, he had a considerable head start.

Reggie moved at a steady pace, despite the rain that stung his face and dripped down his neck. He checked the backyards and clearings that opened off the path for signs of life. Overhanging tree branches, heavy with raindrops, obstructed him, drenching his coat, while lush long grass brushed against the cuffs of his trousers, leaving them sodden. His good leather shoes would be ruined. And, to add to his displeasure, newsprint had rubbed off from *The Socialist* on to his cream coat. It would have to be professionally cleaned. Pursuing Frederick Crabtree was proving to be a costly exercise.

At last, he came to the end of the track, blocked as it was by heavy scrub and blackberry bushes. To his right was a vacant block of land. Reggie swore in disgust. He found a tree trunk and sat down heavily, before realising that it was soaking wet. It was the last straw. Crabtree was gone. As was his hat. And his two ten-shilling notes. It would be late July before he would try this again, if someone could persuade him to do it.

He ran his hand through his hair. It had stopped raining but the sky still looked threatening. How was he going to explain his failure to Mrs Darrow and Emma Hart? The whole episode had been a fiasco from start to finish.

A movement caught his eye. On the other side of the road was a derelict general store. Emerging from the back of it was Frederick Crabtree. Reggie retreated so that the bushes hid him from view. The man looked around him and then set off down the road, obviously in a hurry.

Five minutes passed. Reggie stepped out, then realised that his coat had snagged on a blackberry bush. He swore as he disengaged the prickles from the material. How much worse could this become? Reggie strode across the vacant block and crossed the road. The street was empty.

The shop, with its rear dwelling, was situated to the front of half an acre of land, bordered by thick hedges that gave it privacy from neighbouring houses. Its rendered facade was discoloured and cracked, revealing old hand-made red bricks. The large front windows were shuttered. Around the building, long grass, straggly bushes, and brambles had taken over, making the garden an uninviting wilderness. Frederick Crabtree had chosen well if he wanted to be undisturbed.

Reggie crept down the side of the shop past boarded-up windows. There was a heavy padlock on the back door of the attached dwelling. A towel was hanging from a clothesline that had been rigged up between two trees, not far from the outhouse. Near the back fence, a bag of rubbish was propped. Its contents would tell him if someone were living there. He covered his nose with his handkerchief and rummaged through it, finding empty cans, food scraps, and a couple of empty bottles of beer.

Reggie was curious to see what was inside the building. He ventured up the other side. One of the boards, which had been nailed across a window, had come loose. He found a piece of metal pipe and prised the timber away from the nail that secured it. The window itself was broken. He pushed his face up to the gap and peered inside, making sure that he didn't cut himself on the jagged edges of the glass.

His eyes slowly adjusted to the gloom. On the counter in the shopfront was a set of scales and an ornate silver cash register. Patent remedies, soaps, elixirs, and toiletries, the products of a bygone age, were lined up along the shelves to his right, which formed the back wall of the store. In the middle of the floor was a makeshift bed.

He moved his head so that he could see to his left. Jars of fruit and bags of spices and coffee beans sat on storage shelves attached to the wall, to one side of the front door. Blocking the doorway were pots and pans, crockery, and lamps, waiting to be purchased by customers who would never return. The contents of the shop were covered in a thick layer of dust, the result of neglect and the passing of the years.

A brief burst of sunshine split the clouds. He stepped back from the window, allowing the shaft of light to spread further into the interior. As he did so, he thought he saw something white gleam further to his left. Reggie put on his leather gloves and yanked at the edge of the broken glass. It fragmented. He removed the shards carefully and threw them into the undergrowth. The hole in the glass was now wide enough for him to see more of the interior of the shop. He angled his head so that he could see the counter properly.

Shock made him pull back too fast. His cheek caught on a jagged piece of glass and he yelped in pain. He shoved his handkerchief against his face to stem the bleeding, his mind in disarray as he processed what he had just witnessed.

Reggie propped the piece of timber back into position across the window. It was time to make himself scarce. As he came level with the front of the general store, Reggie checked the street. It was deserted. He looked around for a signpost and spotted one. Esplanade Avenue was the address of Frederick's new home. Only half a mile away was the Crabtree mansion in South Road. And Seymour Grove was a ten-minute walk.

Reggie retraced his steps to Brighton Beach railway station. His clothes were wet and filthy, his hat lost, his trousers torn. For the first time in his life, such things didn't matter to him. What mattered was that he, Reggie da Costa, senior crime reporter for *The Argus*, had been wrong to doubt Dr Silas Bacon. When he looked through the window of the shop, Reggie had seen a death mask from the corner of his eye, perched on the counter. It was incontrovertible proof that Frederick Crabtree *was* the Death Mask Murderer.

Chapter Forty-Three

It was Saturday afternoon. Mrs Darrow was nestled in her favourite armchair opposite Silas Bacon. A fire had been set in the parlour and Reggie da Costa stood before it, warming his hands. The grandfather clock in the hall struck two.

'I can't imagine where she's got to,' said Mrs Darrow, frowning. 'Emma is usually so punctual.'

Silas walked over to the window and stared out at the garden, while Reggie fidgeted with his hat. Mrs Darrow pursed her lips and tapped her foot.

'She said that she would be back well before you arrived.' The elderly lady shook her head. 'This is totally unacceptable.' She paused, then made her decision. 'I won't make you wait any longer. Tell us, Mr da Costa. Did you find out where Frederick Crabtree lives?'

The crime reporter smiled broadly. 'I did, Mrs Darrow. Frederick Crabtree is living in the back of an abandoned general store in Esplanade Avenue, not far from here.'

'Well done! Please tell us what happened.'

Reggie offered them an edited account, leaving out the details that would reflect poorly on *The Argus*'s senior crime reporter. The loss of his hat, the torn trousers, getting caught in the rain without an umbrella, and the serendipitous reappearance of Frederick Crabtree from the back of the shop were all a distant memory, not to be revisited.

Instead, his account was transformed into a master class in the art of detection. Not only were there his persuasive skills in convincing the bank teller to divulge the identity of Frederick Crabtree (without the need to resort

225

to bribery), but there was his uncanny ability to foresee that Crabtree would catch the train. Allied with his impeccable skills in tracking Crabtree along an almost impenetrable overgrown path, there was his instinctive realisation that the killer had taken up residence in the derelict shop. Throughout 'the chase,' as he called it, he remained metaphorically one step ahead of his quarry.

Mrs Darrow was dumbfounded. Silas looked unconvinced. It occurred to Reggie that perhaps he had embellished his account a little too much.

Silas couldn't help himself. 'I have underestimated you. Your skill as a detective is only surpassed by your ability to spin a yarn. But you still haven't told us if we were right about Crabtree's involvement in the murders.'

'Ah, that. It appears that you were right. The death mask that I saw on the counter is irrefutable proof of his guilt.'

Mrs Darrow was shocked. 'You saw them? The death masks?' Reggie nodded. She turned to Silas. 'Your theory is true, after all.'

'Let's not get carried away,' argued Reggie. 'Crabtree's motivation is probably simpler than Dr Bacon has suggested.'

Silas was affronted, but he refused to be drawn. 'What do we do now?'

'We involve Wasp,' said Reggie. 'It's too dangerous to deal with this situation ourselves. The evidence is there to convict Crabtree. And if Wasp is reluctant to act, I'll threaten him with going public. I'll reveal the ineptitude of the police in dealing with these murders.'

'Well said,' said Mrs Darrow. 'They'll have to release Max and Christian Reason.'

The grandfather clock struck the half-hour.

'Where is that great-niece of mine? She said she'd be back at one o'clock. I don't like this. Something must have happened to her.'

'What was she doing?' asked Reggie.

'Sketching at Brighton Beach.'

'Then I shall pick her up in the Dodge.'

'Would you? That would be such a relief.'

'I'll go, too,' said Silas. He picked up his hat and followed Reggie da Costa out into the hallway.

* * *

When they had gone, Florence Darrow stared up at her father's portrait, hanging above the mantelpiece.

'Emma is safe, isn't she, Daddy?'

Eoin Brown looked off into the distance somewhere above her head, but it seemed to Florence that his expression was one of concern.

* * *

Reggie da Costa leaned against the railing of the Brighton Beach pier, using the raised platform as a vantage point. A milky veil of fog hung over Port Phillip Bay. The occasional fishing boat emerged from the mist; its wake resembling trails of gossamer thread on the silver sea. The only disturbance to the eerie silence was the lapping of the waves against the pillars of the pier. Reggie rubbed his hands together and wrapped his muffler tighter around his neck. The air was icy. He looked down the beach. Silas had reached the end and was on his way back.

Silas stepped up onto the pier. 'There's no sign of Emma. Where is she?' he asked.

'I don't know,' replied Reggie. 'Maybe she's visited a friend.'

'That doesn't make sense. She would have been keen to hear your news.' He glanced past Reggie and noticed a bag lying against the railing, towards the end of the jetty.

'What's that?' He walked the length of the pier and picked it up. 'Isn't this Emma's? I remember it from when I first met her.'

Reggie joined him and watched as Silas rummaged through it, producing her sketchpad.

'Look at this,' said Silas. He was staring at the last drawing. 'She's written: June 22, 1918: Lewis on the pier. It's a picture of a man.'

'Let me look.' Reggie took the book from Silas's hands. He swore violently.

'What's wrong?'

'Bloody mongrel. He's taken her.'

'Who?'

'Frederick Crabtree. It's him. Still wearing the same coat and hat he wore to the bank. We have to find them before he kills her.'

Chapter Forty-Four

Emma Hart was tied to a chair, a gag in her mouth. She watched as Frederick Crabtree paced up and down in front of her, muttering to himself. She caught snatches of what he was saying but they made no sense. It was as if she weren't there.

She looked around her. The dwelling was a simple setup, with a small kitchen and a trough for washing. Most of the trappings of the cellar had been transplanted to this place: the basin, jug, shaving gear, a vial of oil, leather strop. Light from two lanterns bounced off the walls of the windowless room, creating eerie shadows that unnerved her. A thick layer of dust covered the floor. Occasionally she heard the scuttle of rodents and saw a skinny tail disappear behind a sack or under a piece of furniture. As a country girl, that did not frighten her. Her fear was reserved for what lay ahead of her.

Frederick stopped pacing and faced her. He came in close and sniffed her neck.

'I can smell your fear, Emma.'

She stared up at him, blinking rapidly. The man she had often chatted to on the beach, whom she knew as Lewis, had been transformed into the killer, Frederick Crabtree. Sophie had been right; she had sensed that there was something peculiar about him. And then there was the advice offered up by her great-aunt and the newspapers. Avoid talking to strangers. Be alert. Stay clear of the beach whilst the Death Mask Murderer is on the loose. How foolhardy she had been. She, of all people, should have known better.

And now the mask had slipped. Gone was the friendly smiling face. Gone was the lightness in his voice. Crabtree radiated menace as he drew himself up to his full height and loomed over her. Up close, she could see his sallow skin, his close-cropped grey hair, and the fleshiness of his neck. His deep-set eyes seemed to bore into her.

'You remind me of her. She left me, you know. But you won't.' His dark eyes glistened. 'I always enjoyed our little chats down at the beach. The truth is I've been waiting a long time to get you on your own. And now, here we are.' He cocked his head to one side. 'Will you be quiet if I take your gag off?'

She nodded. The smell from the rag in her mouth was making her retch.

He removed the gag and pulled a chair over towards her. 'That's better. We can talk now.'

She stared at him, lost for words.

'Talk, I said.'

Emma tried to speak but her throat was dry. He reached across and touched her lips.

'Poor little Emma. Cat got your tongue?'

She started to cry; her face soon wet with tears. Crabtree ran the tip of his finger across her cheek and licked it. 'Mmmm. Salty.' He closed his eyes and smiled.

'Please don't hurt me,' she whispered, recoiling from him. 'I promise I won't say anything if you let me go.'

Crabtree sighed. 'Don't waste your breath. We have a connection, you and I. You've seen my lovelies. I can tell that you appreciate their beauty.' He reached out and stroked her hair, twirling a long lock around his fingers. He tightened his grip and drew her head close to his, so that their eyes were only inches apart.

'Do you remember that day when I locked you in the cellar? I could sense that it was you. I could smell you. If only I'd come back sooner. But now, all is as it should be.' He chuckled. 'The fact is that we're destined to be together.'

He released her and stood, taking off his coat. Without it, his dirty white shirt strained to conceal his fleshy arms and his paunch. She stared up at him, her breath coming in quick bursts.

'Come with me, Emma. It's time to introduce you to the others.'

He untied her and let the rope slip to the floor. Then, with a lantern in one hand, and gripping Emma's upper arm with the other, Frederick thrust her forward into the shop.

Emma's eyes took in the general air of neglect and the detritus of a business that had long ago folded. A space had been cleared in the middle of the room for a thin mattress, over which a couple of grey woollen blankets had been thrown. A plank had been nailed across the door leading to the street, securing it to the frame.

Frederick placed the lantern on the counter, illuminating six death masks. Not three. Six.

Emma heard a whooshing in her ears, the sound of her heart pounding, which drowned out Frederick's voice. She struggled to breathe. As if from a long way away, she heard him speaking to her, calling her back.

'Emma? Emma? Pay attention. I want you to meet my lovelies.' He pointed to each death mask in turn, calling them by name. 'Alexandra. Agnes. Lillian. Bessie. Rosalind. Drusilla.'

His eyes drifted away from her, reliving the past. 'There was one other: Clara. She was mesmerising. Cupid-bow lips and long blonde hair, the colour of spun gold.

'I started to shave her.' Frederick Crabtree's chin quivered with emotion. 'It was shocking. She was disfigured.'

Emma watched in amazement as tears rolled down his cheeks, his face contorted with loathing and outrage.

'She had a scar on the back of her head. A scar!'

As quickly as the emotion had ripped him apart, it was gone. His expression became one of quiet intensity, a study in concentration, with nostrils flared and lips parted.

'She wasn't smooth.' The disgust in his tone oozed like thick treacle.

'What did you do to her?' whispered Emma.

'I killed her. She brought it on herself.' He raised his hands and stared at them. 'There was a lot of blood.'

Emma's throat went dry. She swallowed hard. 'Tell me about the others. These women.' She pointed at the death masks.

Frederick Crabtree stared at her, his face working with emotion. He bit his bottom lip, then his jaw tensed and his eyes gleamed. He made a guttural sound.

'I see what you're doing.'

He slapped her hard across the face then dragged her back into the dwelling. She screamed and kicked out but he was too strong for her. He shoved her in the chair and tied her tightly, her arms and legs pinned.

'You're a monster!' she cried defiantly.

He thrust the gag back into her mouth and then he snarled at her. 'Bitch. Whore. That's what you are. You're like all the rest.'

Emma looked up at him in horror, her bravado evaporated.

He picked up a large pair of scissors. 'Time to begin.'

Chapter Forty-Five

Silas stared at Reggie, white-faced. 'Crabtree has her? What do we do now?'

'We go after them.'

'But we don't know where they've gone.'

'I do. Come on.'

They ran across the beach to the Dodge Roadster, parked on the edge of The Esplanade. Silas turned the crank handle and jumped in. Reggie threw the car into second gear. The automobile responded with a growl and surged forward. Ignoring the cries of two cyclists, Reggie executed a U-turn in front of them, and then headed the Dodge for the railway crossing.

'Watch out! There's a train coming.' Silas's warning was lost in the roar of the engine.

The gatekeeper had shut both gates on the opposite side of the tracks and had closed one on the beach side. The Sandringham train steamed around the bend heading towards the crossing. The gatekeeper yelled a warning as he saw the Dodge Roadster coming fast.

'Bugger!' cried Reggie. 'Hold on, we're going through.'

He turned the wheel hard and threaded the Dodge through the gap. The gatekeeper screamed in fright and jumped out of the way. Reggie threw the Dodge into third gear and crossed the tracks. The train was almost upon them, the driver blowing his whistle. The car slammed into the gates on the other side of the railway, leaving splintered wooden railings in its wake.

Silas looked back. The gatekeeper had recovered in time to push the second gate out of the path of the train. The steam locomotive powered through the crossing, billowing smoke. The gatekeeper stood amongst the wreck of the gates, shaking his fist at the departing car.

'You could have killed us!' Silas yelled above the roar of the Dodge Roadster. He stared at Reggie, shocked to see the expression of exhilaration on the reporter's face. 'You're enjoying yourself,' he said in disbelief.

Reggie glanced at his companion. 'Hold on.'

The first street on the left was Esplanade Avenue. Reggie took the turn too fast. The Dodge's rear flipped out as he fought to get the steering under control. He pressed down on the accelerator and the car surged forward.

Silas stared in horror as the needle of the speedometer nudged thirty and rising. They tore along the road and then Reggie unexpectedly slammed his foot on the brake and coasted the car into the curb.

'What a ride. Did you see how well the Dodge performed?' Reggie's cheeks were flushed with excitement. He ignored the glowering look that his companion directed at him.

'Come on, Silas. This is the place.' He pointed at a boarded-up, derelict general store, some twenty yards away.

They got out of the automobile and approached the shop. Reggie raised his forefinger to his lips. They crept down the right-hand side of the building, stepping around the rubbish that was strewn against the hedge, and amongst the undergrowth that blocked their path. Reggie stopped in front of the window with the loose board. Taking great care, he levered the timber so that the gap in the glass was revealed. He peered through. The shopfront was empty.

He put his ear to the gap and listened. A voice could be heard from the back room, engaged in an earnest one-sided conversation. The tone was cajoling and soothing, much like a mother might sound as she calms an upset child. The occasional word made its way to him, and then he heard the name he dreaded: 'Emma.'

Reggie replaced the board and moved away from the window. He beckoned to Silas.

'They're in the back,' he whispered. 'I heard him talking to her.'

'She's still alive. Do you have a plan?'

'We'll drive to the police station,' said Reggie.

'You intend to leave Emma with a killer?'

'There's no choice. He's dangerous.'

Silas shook his head. 'I can't leave her. It's my fault she's in this situation. I'll find a way to stop him.'

'Are you mad?'

'No, but he is. Go. Fetch the police. Be as quick as you can.'

Reggie took a long look at his companion. 'I underestimated you, Silas. If nothing else, you've got guts. Good luck.' He gave Silas a quick salute, then disappeared down the side of the shop.

Silas went around the back. He clasped the door handle and took a deep breath. Then he turned it gently, surprised to see that it was unlocked. He pushed it open an inch or so. He could hear a male voice. Frederick Crabtree was talking to Emma. Silas opened the door a bit more and waited. Then he peered through the gap and stifled a gasp.

The light from the lanterns illuminated Emma Hart, looking pale and fragile. She was strapped to a chair, a gag stuffed in her mouth. More shockingly, her waist-length hair had been erratically cropped, hanks of it strewn on the floor. Her view of Silas was partially blocked by Frederick Crabtree, who was so engrossed in his task that he was unaware that Silas was behind him.

Frederick took up the razor. It gleamed in the light from the lanterns. He stroked the blade back and forth against the leather strop.

And then he uttered the words that Silas knew so well, the words from a ritual that Silas had created some thirty years ago at the asylum, in the days when Frederick was young and Silas was beginning his adult life as a practising doctor.

He held the blade up to the light and purred as he studied his reflection. *'Like a mirror.'*

He intoned the words of the ritual:

'A razor must be straight.

A razor must be—'

The door creaked as Silas pushed it wide open, allowing the light to flood in. Frederick Crabtree froze, the sentence unfinished, the razor poised to strike.

Silas took up the chant.

'A razor must be polished.

A razor must be sharp.'

Frederick was spellbound, but Silas could detect a slight tremor in his hand. Silas came up behind him, and reached around to touch his cheek.

'Such beautiful skin.

So smooth.'

Frederick turned, his face working with emotion. 'Doctor?'

'Yes, it's me. It's been a long time.'

Silas faced his former patient, observing the changes that more than thirty years had made to the thin, pasty-faced twelve-year-old he had left behind in 1887. Devoid of his hat and coat, the adult Frederick Crabtree looked bloated, his torso straining against his grimy white shirt and shapeless black trousers. His complexion was pallid and unhealthy, as if he had spent his whole life avoiding the sunshine. He'd traded the artificial light and clinical environment of the Ararat Lunatic Asylum for a life in the shadows of a cellar and the gloom of a boarded-up shop. And when he stepped outside into the light of day, he had hidden himself beneath a black coat and hat.

Silas took a moment to take in his surroundings. Two lanterns were placed strategically so that their light fell on Emma. A table, with a bowl of water and shaving implements on it, was situated to her left. A bag of plaster sat open beneath it.

Frederick and Silas took a long look at each other, the one-time child murderer on one side and the doctor on the other.

'You're right,' whispered Frederick Crabtree. 'It's been a long time.' His eyes glinted in the half-light.

Silas looked down at Emma, strapped into the chair. She gazed up at him, drained and defeated.

Frederick still held the razor in his right hand. 'Have you read about me, Doctor?'

'I have. You've been busy.'

CHAPTER FORTY-FIVE

'They call me "The Death Mask Murderer."' He chuckled.

'How do you feel about that?'

Frederick shrugged his shoulders. 'I'm no better or worse than the politicians that sent us to war.'

'But what about the women you killed? Did they have a choice?'

'You don't understand. I gave them immortality. Come and look.'

He put the razor down and picked up a lantern. They walked through into the shop, Silas surreptitiously patting Emma on the shoulder as he passed her, trying to instill some brief comfort from his touch.

'Aren't they beautiful?'

Frederick directed the beam of the lantern onto the death masks. Six pairs of sightless eyes returned Frederick's gaze. Silas was unnerved, realising that six women had fallen victim to the man who now stood beside him. He glanced sideways. Frederick was very still, his attention focused solely on the women.

Crabtree pointed at each woman's mask as he named them. 'Alexandra. Agnes. Lillian. Bessie. Rosalind. Drusilla.'

Silas was surprised by Frederick's reaction to him being there. There was no questioning as to how he knew where to find him, no curiosity about whether he had come alone, no interest in his motivation for being there, just a quiet acceptance that the doctor had returned to spend time with him.

'Alexandra was your first?' asked Silas. He remembered the pained look on Garfield Flynn's face as he talked about the death of his beloved niece.

'She was a nurse at the home. She reminded me of someone I once knew. We bonded immediately. I didn't realise at first that she was manipulating me. Using me. She was a whore. Then she tired of me.'

'What do you mean?'

'Women are weak. They pretend to like you.' His face darkened. 'Sometimes they claim to love you.'

'And then they leave you?' suggested Silas.

'Not for long.' The anger vanished. Frederick shook his head in wonder. 'You knew everything about me back then. And you still do.' He cocked his head to one side. 'Women leave, but these remain. Look at my lovelies.

They're beautiful, aren't they? Like works of art, captured in time.'

'You killed them.'

Frederick's expression changed again. His eyes filled with tears.

'It wasn't my fault. I didn't deserve to be rejected. She said she loved me but she lied. How could a mother treat her son that way?'

'What did she do to you?'

'She loved *him* more than *me*.' He spat out the words then took up the lantern. 'I need to get on. You can watch if you wish.'

Silas followed him back to the dwelling, his mind in turmoil as he realised the intent in Crabtree's words.

'Don't do this, Frederick. She's innocent.'

Silas's plea had no effect. With renewed vigour, Crabtree grabbed the strop and started to sharpen the razor. There was a manic quality in the way he rotated the blade's edge against the leather. He ran his finger down the razor's edge and smiled as droplets of blood appeared. He licked them away.

'Just right,' he whispered.

After working up a lather using the shaving soap, he started to massage it through Emma's cropped hair, his face a mask of concentration. Emma's shoulders sagged and she closed her eyes.

Frederick took the razor from the table and, with his left hand, jerked Emma's head back. In one swift and expert movement, he scraped the blade across her scalp, removing a clean line of hair from her forehead to the top of her head. He tapped the blade against the side of the bowl, then rinsed it in the water.

Silas was all but forgotten. He had to do something to stop Crabtree. He stepped forward and grabbed Frederick's left hand, which was pressed against Emma's forehead.

The reaction was immediate. Frederick growled and slashed at Silas's hand with the razor. The doctor recoiled, holding the back of his hand in horror as blood dripped onto the floor.

Crabtree eyed him balefully. 'Stay out of this, Doctor. I won't be so kind next time.'

Silas took his handkerchief from his pocket and tried to stem the flow of blood. He felt impotent in the face of such malevolence.

Frederick meanwhile continued to shave Emma's head, his whole focus on the task.

Silas took a deep breath. He couldn't watch while this young, kind woman was murdered in front of his eyes. He concentrated on calming the tumult of emotions that were threatening to overwhelm him. You are a rational and logical being, he told himself. You are a scientist who seeks solutions while others succumb to impulses and sentiment. Brute force won't stop him. Your strategy must buy Emma time until Reggie returns with the police.

And then a small voice seemed to speak to him. 'Draw on the times you had together at the asylum. Build his trust.'

He hesitated, then spoke haltingly. 'Frederick. May I shave you? For old times' sake?'

Crabtree stopped in midstream, the razor poised above Emma's head. He cocked his head, as if processing the question. Then he lowered the blade and turned towards the doctor. Any trace of anger or irritability was gone. His expression was genial.

'If you would?'

'I would be honoured.'

Emma had slumped in the chair, on the edge of exhaustion. Crabtree pushed her aside. She was of no interest to him now. He moved another chair into position and sat. He was eager, his eyes bright with anticipation.

Silas placed his hands upon Frederick's shoulders. 'Relax.' He modulated his voice so that it was soothing, almost hypnotic in tone. 'Are you ready?'

'Yes, Doctor.'

Silas took the stick of shaving soap and created a lather that was thick and creamy. He applied it to Frederick's head. Rich, soapy bubbles spilled between Silas's fingers as he worked the lather into his former patient's thin, grey hair. He could feel the tension leaving Frederick's body.

He picked up the razor and stroked it back and forth on the leather strop. Then he intoned the words of the ritual:

'A razor must be straight.

A razor must be polished.

A razor must be sharp.'

He placed his hand on Frederick's forehead and pulled his head back gently, lifting the razor so that it caught the light.

The blade slid smoothly from Frederick's hairline to the top of his skull. Silas tapped the edge of the razor against the bowl, and then wiped the blade with a towel that he'd hung over his left shoulder. His face was a picture of concentration.

'Above the ears.'

The razor skimmed around Frederick's left ear, short strands of hair dropping to the floor. Again and again, the blade flashed as the remainder of the stubble was shaved away, leaving him bald.

Silas lowered the razor until it hovered close to Frederick's throat. He said thickly,

'Not a cut. Not a drop of blood. Aren't you happy?'

Frederick Crabtree raised his eyes, to gaze reverentially at his mentor. He reminded Silas of the look that an innocent child gives its mother. But this was no innocent child. This was a sick killer, one who had brought extreme pain and suffering to his victims and their families. Silas edged the razor closer to Frederick's throat. One slash. That's all it would take. One slash and this would all be over. His hand trembled. But then he would be no better than the man who sat beneath him.

The moment passed. Silas put the razor down and using a fresh towel, rubbed Frederick's head until it shone.

Silas took a deep breath. 'It's been such a long time. Would you allow me to do a reading?'

'I'd love it.'

Silas Bacon placed his hands on Frederick's head. He slowly worked his fingertips over Crabtree's skull, feeling for its contours. He closed his eyes, recalling a time when the theories of phrenology had been like a religion to him; a science that offered explanations for human behaviour and could predict people's actions. After a few minutes of intense concentration, he began:

'Your brain has developed as you have grown into manhood, making you the person you are today. Below the top of your skull is the organ Benevolence. I can feel a marked indentation indicating that altruism and generosity of spirit are not part of your nature.'

Silas moved his fingers to the base of the skull. 'The organ of Spirituality is also diminished.'

He felt for the rise of bone at the top of the skull. 'There is an increase in the size of Self-Esteem, revealing a preoccupation with your own self.'

He touched the sides of Frederick's head and rotated his fingertips. 'Cautiousness and Conscientiousness are underdeveloped. There is a significant bulge in the bone above your ears. I would interpret this as an indication that you have become Secretive. The organs of Combativeness and Destructiveness have enlarged. Taken together, these confirm my original hypothesis that you have criminal tendencies.'

Frederick nodded enthusiastically. 'That is all true. Don't stop, Doctor, tell me more.'

'There is little more to say, Frederick, except that much of this is my fault. I took a naïve and trusting boy, who had committed a terrible deed, and made him a killer. Please, forgive me.'

Silas stepped away from his former patient, sadness in his eyes.

Crabtree shook his head vehemently. 'No one's at fault, neither you nor me.'

'I wish you were right. There's one thing I'd like to know. How did you manage to convince the doctors to release you?'

A knowing smile lit up Frederick's face. 'People are weak and gullible. They believe whatever you tell them. People liked me. They trusted me. They never knew what I was really thinking.'

He mimicked a conversation with Dr Stone, his voice alternating between the wheedling and insinuating tone of his seven-year-old self and that of the superintendent, sombre and serious.

'I've been a bad boy, Dr Stone. (Sob, sob.) I killed my brother.'
'This is a significant admission, Frederick. I'm impressed with your progress.'
'I couldn't do it without you, Dr Stone.'
'I am brilliant, aren't I?'

Frederick snorted in amusement. 'Stone was easy. Conceited, pompous, smug fool. All I had to do was compliment him on his enormous intellect and he was like putty in my hands. There were a couple of doctors who were unsure about me. Stone convinced them to sign my release papers.'

He giggled.

'You tricked them?'

'I tricked them all.'

Silas squatted down, eye to eye with his former patient. 'You trusted me once. Do you trust me now?'

'Of course.'

'What would you say if I suggested that the asylum is the best place for you?'

Frederick cocked his head. 'You think I should go back?'

Silas nodded slowly. 'To the home.'

A faraway look came into Frederick's eyes. 'That's right. The home. I was happy there.'

'All those good doctors ready to help you. All the staff who liked you. And still do. Like Mrs Culpepper.'

Crabtree glanced over at Emma. 'What about her?'

'It's over, Frederick. Enough.'

As he spoke, he heard the pounding of feet running down the side of the shop. Four policemen burst through the doorway, followed by Reggie da Costa.

Frederick Crabtree sat very still. He didn't acknowledge their arrival.

'He'll go quietly,' said Silas, raising Frederick from the chair and into the hands of the policemen.

Silas turned his attention to Emma. She was a terrible sight, with her beautiful blonde hair hacked and shaven.

'Look after her, Reggie. She's in shock.'

Reggie gently removed the gag from her mouth. Then he undid the ropes and wrapped his muffler around her head. Emma stood uncertainly then slumped into his arms, the blood draining from her face. Reggie, his arm wrapped protectively around her waist, supported her as they walked from the room. She paused on the threshold and looked back at Silas. A faint smile reached her eyes as she mouthed, 'Thank you.' Then she was gone.

Frederick waited silently while the policemen secured him. Handcuffs in place and with a constable on each side, he took one last look at Silas Bacon.

'Will you visit me, Doctor?'

'I will. I will come often.'

'And my lovelies?'

'They will be cared for.'

Frederick smiled beatifically as he was led away.

Silas sank down onto a chair, his head in his hands.

Reggie walked back through the door. 'Emma's safe. They're taking her to the hospital. You saved her life, Silas. I didn't think you could do it, but I was wrong.'

Silas looked up at him, his face haggard and pale. 'You timed that perfectly. I'd run out of ideas.'

'You did well.'

'What will happen to the death masks?'

'They'll be used as evidence, although I suspect that Crabtree will never go to trial. Let's go.'

Silas shook his head. 'There's something I have to do first.'

Silas walked through, into the shop. He stood silently in front of the masks of the six slain women. 'I am so sorry,' he said to them. 'If I had my time over again—'

They stared sightlessly at him, indifferent and impassive in the face of his apology. He turned on his heel and left the shop, closing the door on an episode of his life that he hoped never to revisit.

Chapter Forty-Six

DEATH MASK MURDERER ARRESTED
Argus Crime Reporter Foils Killer

By REGGIE DA COSTA, Senior Crime Reporter

Late on Saturday, police stormed the hideaway of Frederick Crabtree, the alleged Death Mask Murderer, where he was holding his latest victim, Miss Emma Hart. The discovery of his identity was the result of intensive investigations undertaken by *The Argus*'s own senior crime reporter, Reginald da Costa. His intervention was instrumental in saving the life of twenty-year-old Miss Hart, a talented artist and great-niece of Brighton widow and philanthropist, Mrs Florence Darrow.

Death was imminent

In a tale that will go down in the annals of crime, Mr da Costa led the police to Crabtree's hide-out, a derelict shop in Brighton, and assisted with disarming him as he was about to strangle the helpless woman. Miss Hart's head had been shaved in preparation for the creation of her death mask. She is now being cared for by friends and family.

The Argus can reveal that Frederick Crabtree, aged forty-four, is the adopted son of Thomas and Matilda Crabtree, both deceased, once wealthy residents of the Melbourne bayside suburb of Brighton. At the age of seven, Frederick murdered his younger brother. Tragically, his mother took her own life soon after. Consequently, Frederick was sent to the Ararat Lunatic Asylum where he spent the next thirty-six years. It is believed that Frederick's resentment festered over the years, and provided the motivation for the murders he committed after his release in May 1917.

Killing spree

Shortly after his release, Crabtree allegedly murdered Mrs Alexandra James, a former psychiatric nurse at the asylum. He used her as the model for his first death mask. By August 1917, he was living in Brighton in the derelict house of his deceased father, carrying out his sadistic activities in the cellar. Crabtree is believed to be responsible for the murder of Mrs Agnes Reason, who was found strangled at Green Point on the Brighton foreshore in September 1917. It appears that he may also be involved in the disappearance of Miss Lillian Broderick in November of the same year.

In March, *The Argus* reported on the discovery of three death masks in the former home of Thomas Crabtree in South Road, Brighton. Before the police could attend the scene, the death masks mysteriously disappeared. Proving that truth is stranger than fiction, Miss Emma Hart was one of the two people who found the death masks in the cellar. The other was Mr Maxwell Clifford Rushforth, who was charged with being accessory to the murder of Mrs Agnes Reason. He is presently being held in Melbourne Jail awaiting trial. Mr Christian William Reason, husband of the murdered woman, is serving a life sentence for her murder in Pentridge Prison.

Six death masks were found in the shop in Esplanade Avenue when Frederick Crabtree was arrested. They are now in the possession of the police, and will be used as evidence when Crabtree is sent to trial. The status of Mr Reason and Mr Rushforth will no doubt be reviewed in light of recent events.

The remaining three death masks have now been identified. The murdered women were Mrs Bessie Cartwright, whose body was found next to the Brighton Beach railway tracks in February, Mrs Rosalind Baker, who was found dead on Hampton Beach in April, and Miss Drusilla Rook, who was initially believed to have committed suicide after the death of her soldier brother. Her body was washed up on Mentone Beach earlier this month.

The women who died at Crabtree's hands bear more than a passing resemblance to his mother. This applies most closely to Mrs James, his first victim. She was blonde, in her twenties, and the mother of a seven-year-old boy (Frederick's age when he killed his sibling). She was expecting her second child when she was strangled. It is believed that her departure from the asylum sparked Frederick Crabtree's bid for freedom and his murderous rage.

The Argus approached Dr Gideon Stone, superintendent of the Ararat Lunatic Asylum, for comment on Mr Crabtree's release and his subsequent killing spree. At the time of going to press, his office has not furnished a statement.

Police incompetence?

Two lives hang in the balance at this stage, innocent victims of police incompetence. They are Mr Christian Reason and Mr Maxwell Rushforth. Detective Inspector Felix Wasp, lead investigator on the Death Mask Murders case, was asked for comment on the urgency of releasing both men, given the arrest of Frederick Crabtree. At this stage, he has declined to issue a statement.

Questions are being raised about the possibility that Miss

Clara McSweeney, who was found in scrub near Mair Street, Brighton, in early May, may have been yet another of Crabtree's victims. Although her head had been partially shaved, the authorities have characterised her death as the work of someone other than the Death Mask Murderer. We can now reveal that she had been horrifically disfigured, suggesting that her killer lost control and lashed out at her in a frenzy of madness. In the light of recent developments, we suggest that the circumstances of her murder be re-investigated.

It is evident that the identification of Frederick Crabtree as the Death Mask Murderer will lead to an examination of police procedures and performance. Similarly, the actions of the Ararat Lunatic Asylum in releasing a crazed killer must undergo scrutiny. *The Argus*, in its editorial today, calls for the Victorian Government to hold an inquiry into the case. Seven women have died. Their deaths should not be in vain.

NEXT WEEK: What is a death mask and why were they made? Dr Silas Bacon, an expert from the Melbourne Museum, gives you the answers.

[*The Argus* June 24, 1918]

Chapter Forty-Seven

The Armistice was signed and Germany had surrendered. Word came through late on Monday, the 11th of November, and the news spread like wildfire. A public holiday was declared throughout the Commonwealth.

Hordes of people surged into Melbourne on the Tuesday to join in the festivities, forming one dense mass in Collins Street between Russell and Elizabeth Streets. And, in the midst of the crowd, were Emma Hart and Reggie da Costa.

The celebrations were in full swing. Streets were filled with bunting and streamers, shops were decorated in patriotic colours and innumerable Union Jacks and the flags of Australia and France decorated flagpoles or were carried by revellers. Uplifted faces sang 'Rule Britannia,' proudly declaring that 'Britons never, never shall be slaves.' The words came in a mighty roar, that resolved into cheering. It was a riot of excitement that ignited a blaze of unrestrained heartfelt joy in Emma, that she had never experienced before.

Reggie and Emma smiled, laughed, and sang till they were hoarse, as they joined in with the sound and cacophony of jubilation: the shouts and cheers, the strains of 'The Marseillaise' and the National Anthem, and the explosions of crackers and fireworks. Bands played, using any form of improvised musical instrument, from tin whistles to kerosene tins. Subtler, yet more moving, were the chimes of the bells in the Post Office tower, once silent, now filling the air with their melodies.

Emma had caught up with Reggie da Costa just before midday.

'You look dapper,' remarked Emma.

'Nice of you to say so. It's the latest from London.'

He was wearing a new suit in honour of the occasion. The woollen fabric was deep tan in colour with a hint of striping, the trousers cuffed at the bottom, and the jacket with wide lapels and three buttons. The white shirt had a round club collar, set off by a fashionably wide polka dot tie. His shoes were two-tone, brown and cream in colour. To complete the look, Reggie wore a new homburg, sitting jauntily on his head.

'You could never have enlisted, Reggie.'

'Why's that?' he asked her.

'Khaki wouldn't have suited you.'

Reggie roared with laughter. Being the ultimate pragmatist, Reggie had long since given up his pursuit of Emma and had become a friend, forged from the day when he and Silas Bacon had rescued her from the hands of Frederick Crabtree.

He looked at Emma admiringly. She was dressed for the cool weather in a long-sleeved Swiss cotton blouse and a navy velvet skirt, cinched in at the waist with a thick leather belt. Her black lace-up boots were high-heeled, so that she just reached Reggie's shoulder.

They had wandered through the crowd enjoying the sight of youths perched on shop verandahs and boys climbing the trees, all eager to see the festivities. Even the tram cars became vantage points, with hundreds of people using them as temporary grandstands.

'It's just as well the pubs are shut,' yelled Reggie above the din, 'or this could be dangerous.'

They pushed their way through the mob until they reached the Town Hall. Inside they found seats. Soon there was standing room only for the thanksgiving service. An hour later, the acting Prime Minister, Mr Watt, passed a motion of loyalty to the King, followed by speeches from the Lord Mayor and the Premier. A highlight was Dame Nellie Melba singing 'God save the King,' and 'Home, sweet home.' That would remain one of Emma's most treasured memories for years to come.

As the crowds started to disperse, Reggie took Emma's hand as they walked back to where he had parked the Dodge Roadster.

'It's been a wonderful day, Reggie.'

'It has indeed. What do you think of my automobile, by the way?'

'It looks brand new,' said Emma, admiring the polished paintwork. 'I never asked you. Did driving through the railway gates cause much damage?'

Reggie laughed. 'Let's just say that I wouldn't recommend it.' He smiled at her. 'But it was worth it. Did I tell you that I saw Clary Blain recently?'

'The policeman?'

'That's right. After the inquiry, Wasp was demoted to Detective Sergeant. Clary's senior to him now.' He laughed.

'Wasp has lost his sting?'

'He deserved it. If he hadn't been so focused on Max, some women may not have died.' He opened the passenger door and helped her into the seat. 'Tell me, are you going to keep your hair short?'

Emma smiled up at him. 'It's the latest in America. They call it a "bob." Aunt Florence is scandalised but I like it. She says that I look wild and unladylike.'

'I think it looks very fashionable. You don't mind upsetting Mrs Darrow?'

'No. It's good for her. She likes to argue.'

'You are funny. What a shame you don't have any money.'

Emma grinned. 'You can't have it all.'

Reggie roared with laughter. 'I better get you home before I reconsider my priorities.'

Chapter Forty-Eight

The day after the Armistice Day holiday was reserved for quiet reflection. On Wednesday, Emma, Aunt Florence, and Sophie attended a thanksgiving service at church and then returned to Seymour Grove for lunch. Afterwards, Mrs Darrow hosted some of her friends for a celebratory afternoon tea in the summer house, while Emma and Sophie relaxed in the library.

'You went back to Donald after Crabtree was caught,' said Sophie. 'How was it at home?'

'At first, I slept a lot. I was totally exhausted. When I was feeling better, I realised that I was better off in Brighton.'

'Why was that?'

'I was famous because of the murders. People would stop me in the street and ask me about the Death Mask Murderer. I found it hard reliving that chapter in my life over and over again. It's not that people were unkind; they were just curious. I didn't want to be seen as a victim anymore so I decided to come back. I tried to explain it to Mum and Dad, but I'm not sure they understood. Donald will always be my home but, for a while, I'm better off here.

'I must admit that Aunt Florence is a big factor in my recovery. "Stop feeling sorry for yourself," she says, if I look like I'm thinking about *that* day again. She's good for me.'

'I'm glad you came back.'

'There's one thing I must tell you. Before I left Donald, I met up with Clive's mother. We had a long talk and made our peace with each other.

That's helped me too.' She held out her hand. On her finger was a signet ring in rose gold. 'She gave me this. It belonged to Clive's father.'

Sophie smiled. 'You've gone through so much and you've survived. That's something to be proud of.'

'You helped me too. When I was at my lowest ebb, I remembered something you said: "When it is dark enough, you can see the stars." I decided that I should look at my experience with Frederick Crabtree differently. The fact is I'm alive. It's my second chance at life and I intend to enjoy it. I'm seeing the stars rather than the darkness.'

'Good for you.' Sophie hugged her. 'I'm going for a walk. It's been an exhausting few days and I could do with a stroll along the beach on my own. Do you mind?'

'Of course not.'

When Sophie had gone, Emma took out her sketchpad and browsed through her most recent drawings. Her newfound maturity was reflected in her art. Her sketches were more thought-provoking, revealing more about her subjects and herself.

Her most recent self-portrait was immensely more satisfying. In May, she had felt that her drawing revealed her lack of direction and her fragile sense of self, but this latest one conveyed something quite different. There was something positive about the set of her jaw and the expression on her face. Emma no longer felt that she was a blank outline, to be filled in at a later date. She was a person who had followed through when others would have given up. Max and Christian Reason were free because she had taken up their cause.

Emma took a deep breath and ran a hand through her short hair. Her thoughts moved to Frederick Crabtree, now back at Ararat. Experts had determined that he was insane, thus circumventing the need for a trial and the necessity for her to testify. She was relieved that she would never have to face him across a courtroom.

She found a blank page in her sketchbook and picked up her pencil. At the top, she wrote: 'November 12, 1918: Armistice Day public holiday.'

For half an hour, she set herself the task of portraying the celebrations that had marked the end of the Great War.

When she had finished, she turned to the next blank page and paused. This would be a test of how far she had come. She wrote: '1918: In Flanders Fields.'

Four years of war were over; four years of sacrifice, heartache, and the death of a generation of young men, who now lay in graves far away in Palestine, Mesopotamia, Gallipoli, the Balkans, Italy, and Belgium.

And in Flanders Fields were rows on rows of crosses, rows on rows of unmarked mounds, nameless, unknown places where the gallant, glorious dead now slept. Of the 400,000 Australian men who had enlisted, 60,000 were dead and 160,000 were wounded. How to convey this sense of loss?

Emma covered the page with the imagined faces of soldiers who had lived, suffered, and died there. And, in the centre of her drawing, she sketched one face that had been dearer to her than any other, that of her former fiancé, Clive Atkins.

She sat back and studied her sketch, her heart swelling with emotion. Clive stared back at her from the page, instantly recognisable with his lively eyes, his lopsided grin, and his mop of curly hair.

She whispered to him, 'Sleep your last long sleep, my dear. In Flanders Field the poppies grow between the crosses row on row.'

* * *

Someone was knocking on the front door. The housekeeper was having a holiday in celebration of the Armistice, so Emma went down the hallway to answer it.

Standing on the front verandah were Max Rushforth and Silas Bacon. They greeted her warmly and came inside. Mrs Darrow had come in from the back garden and smiled broadly when she saw who their visitors were. After exchanging pleasantries, they moved into the parlour.

'You're looking well,' said Mrs Darrow, studying Max's appearance through her pince-nez. The dark circles beneath his eyes were gone and he'd put on some weight.

'It's taken a while to recover from the Jail,' replied Max. 'It seemed ages before they released me.'

'At least you didn't have to share a cell with Frederick Crabtree,' said Emma, laughing.

'Emma! Behave,' said her great-aunt.

Max smiled despite himself. 'Having friends like you changed everything.'

'Make the most of your fresh start,' said Mrs Darrow.

Max nodded. 'I have. I've left the Barracks. I've got an engineering job with a manufacturing firm, starting next week.'

'Any news about Christian Reason?'

'Silas and I visited him this morning.'

'How is he?' asked Emma.

'He's moved in with his aunt. His little boy will live with Agnes's sister until he gets back on his feet again. He asked me to pass on his thanks to both of you.'

Silas addressed Emma. 'You're looking much better since I saw you in hospital.'

'I'm doing well. I'll never be able to thank you enough for saving my life.' Emma kissed him on the cheek.

Max stepped forward. 'I'm grateful too.' He grinned and hugged Mrs Darrow, taking her by surprise.

'I'm a respectable Brighton matron, young man. That is quite enough!' But her smile gave the lie to her words.

'I owe you so much. You paid Upjohn to represent me. You paid my rent. You've supported me throughout this ordeal. Yet you hardly knew me.' He shook his head in wonder.

'I thought that if Emma was prepared to stand by you, then so should I.'

'I'd be sitting in a Pentridge cell right now, if not for you. I will repay you.'

Aunt Florence shook her head. 'There's no rush. I did what had to be done. Nothing more, nothing less.'

Max smiled at Silas. 'And you, my friend. You were incredibly brave to face Crabtree on your own.'

'Speaking of Crabtree,' said Silas. 'I visited him last week.'

'How awful,' said Emma. 'What was he like?'

Silas shook his head. 'Frederick is not coping well. Instead of being sent back to the Lunatic Asylum, he's been sent to the Institute for the Criminally Insane. It's a different world there. He doesn't have the freedom to wander around or talk to the staff.'

'How did he react to you?' asked Aunt Florence.

'He was angry with me. He said that I'd misled him. He asked me to shave him but the doctor in charge refused. I was relieved, to be honest. Then he threw a tantrum.'

'A tantrum?'

Silas took out a cigarette and lit it, his hand shaking. 'It was as if he were seven again. He was ranting and raving, swearing at me. I could calm him once but he's not a child anymore. The attendants came running and put him in restraints. They forced him to take medication. It was terrible to watch.'

'You're not going back?'

Silas shook his head. 'I won't. I can't. There's nothing more I can do for him.'

Aunt Florence looked at Silas through her pince-nez. 'I hope that you no longer blame yourself for his crimes?'

'The doctors assured me that the manifestations of his mental illness in the last year would have occurred with or without my intervention. I'm still not sure that I accept that completely.'

Silas went on to describe how he had visited Garfield Flynn, Alexandra James's uncle, before he left Ararat. They had corresponded after Crabtree's arrest, and Silas had given the owner of *The Ararat Advertiser* information that had not been made public. Being editor of his own newspaper had advantages. Aware now of Dr Stone's role in Crabtree's release, Flynn had started a campaign calling for the superintendent's sacking on the grounds of his deception and negligence, not to mention the fact that women had died because of his actions. He was pleased when the doctors who had opposed Crabtree's bid for freedom joined forces to call for Stone's dismissal. In the week before Silas's visit, the beleaguered Dr Stone had packed his bags and left Ararat.

'Being informed of Stone's departure finished my visit on a positive note,' added Silas. 'Garfield insisted on taking me out to dinner at the local pub. I could hardly refuse.'

He put on his hat. 'Goodbye, ladies. Goodbye, Max. I need to catch my train. I'm having dinner with Harriett Kreitmayer. She wants to hear all about my experiences with Frederick Crabtree.'

'Would you join me for a walk along the beach, Emma?' asked Max. 'We could accompany Silas as far as Brighton Beach station.'

'I'll get my hat and meet you outside.'

The two men went into the hallway, leaving Emma and her great-aunt in the parlour.

Aunt Florence touched her on the arm. 'Max needs an answer. It's time to make a decision.'

Emma nodded. 'I know. I just hope that it's the right one.' She put a book in her bag and kissed her great-aunt goodbye.

* * *

Max smoked a cigarette as he and Emma sat on the wooden steps leading up to the pier. They had left Silas on the station platform, with promises that they would meet again soon. As far as Emma was concerned, she would be forever grateful to the man who had risked his life for her, and she intended to repay his selflessness with a strong and loyal friendship.

Port Phillip Bay glittered beneath a cloudless sky. A gentle breeze ruffled Emma's hair. She took off her jacket and felt the warmth of the sun on her arms. Summer was less than a month away.

'How are you, Max?' she asked, looking at him intently.

'Much better, but this time I think it's true.'

He took a photograph from his wallet and showed it to Emma. It had been taken on the battlefield. Max was sitting in a trench, dressed in his tunic, breeches, leather boots, and puttees. He was wearing a steel helmet and staring straight at the camera. Next to him was another soldier holding a rifle, a cigarette dangling from his mouth. Both were smiling.

'That's my mate, Jackie,' he said, pointing to his colleague in the photograph. 'We went to university together. He was badly wounded in the War. Lost both legs.'

'I'm sorry, Max.'

'I blamed my senior officer at the time. Broke his jaw. Strange, but the whole thing doesn't seem so clear-cut now.' Max cleared his throat. His voice was soft and uncertain. 'You heard about the nurse? I'll never forgive myself for hitting her.'

'Why did you do that?' Emma asked, her gaze holding his. 'I need to know.'

'We were in the field hospital. I'd had one course of electroshock therapy. It was terrible. She and a male nurse were sent to bring me for my second session. I panicked. I lashed out and she was in the way.' He shook his head. 'There's no excuse for that.'

Emma's clear blue eyes searched his face. 'There's one more thing I'd like to know. Do you want to tell me what you were doing in Brighton on the day of the storm?'

Max stood and climbed up onto the pier, Emma following. They walked to the end. Max leaned on the railing, looking out to sea.

'I suppose there's no point in keeping it a secret anymore. You know almost everything about me now.'

'Go on.'

'Before I enlisted, I had a sweetheart. Her name was Katherine. I wanted to marry her but she wasn't keen. When I got home, I visited her and found out that I'd got her pregnant. She'd had a baby. A little girl, Violet. I offered to marry her but she wouldn't have it. She'd met a new man who was prepared to accept the baby as his. They were getting married.

'I asked if I could visit Violet. Katherine's fiancé was apprehensive at first. When he realised that all I wanted was to be a part of my daughter's life, he agreed. I wanted Violet to know who her father was and that she could rely on me. I owe her that much. Katherine lives in New Street, Brighton, not far from the Crabtree house.'

'That's what you were doing on the day of the storm? Why didn't you tell the police? They could have checked and realised that you weren't trying to hide anything.'

'My life has been like an open wound, picked over by buzzards like Wasp. I can cope with that. But this involved other lives apart from mine. My former sweetheart and my daughter. Imagine if the newspapers got word of this? Reggie da Costa, for example. Katherine and Violet would be dragged through the mud just for a story. I decided that this was going to stay private even if it meant I ended up in prison.'

'I don't understand. You were innocent.'

'I'm not innocent. Anyone who served in the War isn't innocent. But my daughter is, and I don't want her labelled as illegitimate.'

Emma nodded slowly. She opened the book that she had brought from the house and turned to the page marked by a thin strand of green ribbon.

'An English friend of Aunt Florence sent this to her. The poet Siegfried Sassoon wrote "Survivors," in 1917. He was like you. He suffered shell shock in the War and was sent to hospital. His poem speaks of emotionally scarred young men who had their youth stolen from them, plagued by nightmares, and the memories of those they killed on the field of battle. I think you might appreciate its sentiments. Let me read it to you.'

When she had finished, Max smiled sadly, tears welling in his eyes. 'You have saved me, my beautiful Emma. I don't want to be a survivor, but someone who can enjoy life again.'

He reached down, lifted her face towards his, and kissed her. 'I love you.'

'I love you too.' She pulled away.

'What's wrong?'

'There's something that I need to say. I'm going away.'

'What are you planning to do?'

'I'm going to France next year, once life returns to normal over there. I'll study art. Aunt Florence offered to pay my tuition fees. It's the opportunity of a lifetime.'

'You're going alone?'

'Not at first. Sophie will stay with me for six months, then come back to the Melba Conservatorium to finish her studies. Aunt Florence has a friend in Paris that we can board with.'

'If you love me, why are you going?'

'It's the best thing for both of us. I want to find out if I have the talent to be an artist. Not just as a hobby. Something I can pursue and excel at.'

'I always thought that you were good.'

Emma shrugged her shoulders. Then she took Max's hands and faced him.

'I'm young and inexperienced. I don't know much about life. But I do know when someone is suffering and is finding life hard. I can see that in you. I love you Max, but I won't marry you until you deal with your problems. Do you understand?'

Max nodded slowly. 'When I was in prison, I had a lot of time to think. I know now that the things I experienced on the battlefield affected me badly. The treatment I had in that first field hospital was traumatic. I brought home a lot of personal issues that haven't been resolved.

'I realised that I wouldn't be in that cell if I'd come to terms with my shell shock. The reason I was suspected of being involved in those murders was because I looked and acted like I was psychologically unstable. I know I have a problem. I need help.'

'I'm pleased you're facing it.'

'How long will you be away?'

'About a year. I must admit that I'm excited at the prospect.'

Max blinked at her through pale lashes. 'I am disappointed, but I do understand. Is there any hope that you might come home to me in time?'

'I believe so. But I also believe that making a rash decision to marry is not the right thing for either of us. We've both been through so much and we need to take the time to mend.'

'Will you write to me?'

'Of course, I will. And I will come home. Who's going to argue with Aunt Florence if I'm not there?'

Max smiled. 'Fate brought us together.'

Emma looked up at him, her golden hair catching the rays of the afternoon sun. 'Fate, a storm, and three death masks.'

A Note from the Author

I have retained Australian spelling, punctuation and word usage, where possible. However, in an effort to avoid confusion, I have opted to use 'jail' rather than 'gaol'. I apologise to my colleagues at the Old Melbourne Gaol!

Acknowledgements

Writers Victoria has been instrumental in my development as a writer. Their workshops and manuscript assessments have proved invaluable to me. Dr Kate Ryan's editing skills helped me polish the manuscript and prepare it for publication.

My work as a volunteer guide at the Old Melbourne Gaol has provided me with a fund of background information on death masks, phrenology and the history of the Gaol, thus giving *The Death Mask Murders* its authenticity. Researching the historical and social background to this book has been aided by the National Library of Australia's research portal, *Trove*, using their digitised newspapers from the past. In particular, reports in *The Argus* and *The Age* provided me with the raw material I needed to convey the ferocity of Melbourne's biggest recorded storm, in February 1918, which I used to bring together my protagonists. I have also drawn on a wide range of resources to portray 'shell shock' and the treatment of the mentally ill around the time of the Great War.

My sincere thanks must go to the Dames of Detection – Harriette Sackler, Verena Rose and Shawn Reilly Simmons – of Level Best Books, for giving me this wonderful opportunity to see my work in print. Their encouragement, good humour and professionalism have made them a pleasure to work with.

I wish to express my love and gratitude to Trevor, Angela, Sam, Ellie and Carol for their belief in me. Thank you to my friends and, in particular, my golfing buddies at the Victoria Golf Club, for their interest in and enthusiastic support of my writing. Finally, I acknowledge the unswerving support and encouragement of my darling husband, Bob, to whom this novel is dedicated.

About the Author

Laraine Stephens lives in the bayside suburbs of Melbourne, Australia. With an Arts degree from the University of Melbourne, a Diploma of Education and a Graduate Diploma in Librarianship, she worked in secondary schools as a Head of Library. On retirement, Laraine decided to turn her hand to the craft of crime writing. Laraine's debut novel, *The Death Mask Murders*, is set in Melbourne in 1918. It is the first in the Reggie da Costa Mysteries series.

Lightning Source UK Ltd.
Milton Keynes UK
UKHW011110151021
392225UK00001B/31